# Acclaim for Mike Maranhas's *Re'enev*

"Great characterizations, lots of action, and a fantastic storyline make *Re'enev* a fantastic reading experience."

—Harriet Klausner, *Amazon's #1 Reviewer* and a former acquisition librarian.

"*Re'enev's* plot pulls you along, and just when you think you have it all figured out, another twist and turn pulls you in a different direction. Mike Maranhas has a talent for pulling in the reader and presenting characters with depth. This is a story for anyone who has ever loved and lost and loved again. It will make you think twice about what lurks behind the beauty of paradise...*Re'enev* is a tale with an important lesson about how we treat ourselves and each other. I especially enjoyed the way [Mike uses] metaphor to pull it all back together."

—Dr. Jose B. Gonzalez, Professor of English at the United States Coast Guard Academy and co-editor of *Latino Boom: An Anthology of U.S. Latino Literature.*

"...*Re'enev* is a passionate and exciting adventure; it's a desperate and violent tale of survival, but also a remarkably intuitive account of a marriage that is slowly unraveling...Tense and edgy, *Re'enev* delves into the human psyche like never before – it's an accomplished and skillful first novel from Mr. Maranhas."

—Michael Leonard, *Amazon Top 500 Reviewer* and a current librarian.

# Mike Maranhas

# RE'ENEV

Mike Maranhas lives with his wife, Bela, on Cape Ann in Massachusetts. *Re'enev* is his first novel.

Chris + Valerie,
I TOLD you ABout THIS Book at BANKY BANX'S JOINT (THATS AN APPROPRIATE TERM, EH?) ON ANGUILLA. Took me a little longer than I HAD HoPeD To get it Published; But, ALAS, it is DONE. Hope you LIKE it.
Sincerely, Mike Maranhas

# RE'ENEV

A Novel By

## Mike Maranhas

Pink Granite Productions, December 2006

Layout and Design by Ari Meil
www.warren-machine.com

Publisher's Cataloging-In-Publication Data
(Prepared by The Donohue Group, Inc.)


Maranhas, Mike.
    Re'enev / Mike Maranhas.

    p. ; cm.

    ISBN: 0-9777809-9-6

1. Abduction—Fiction. 2. Missing persons—Fiction. 3. Islands—Fiction.
4. Self-realization—Fiction. 5. Man-woman relationships—Fiction. 6.
Spouses—Fiction. 7. Adventure stories. I. Title.

PS3613.A73 R46 2006
813/.6    2006900841

"Illusion is the first of all pleasures."

—Voltaire (1694-1778)

"All our knowledge has its origins in our perceptions."

—Leonardo da Vinci (1452-1519)

"Just as you cannot change things beyond your control in life, neither can you hang loose—take the good for granted, an opinion for truth, the veneer of existence for reality--or you will figuratively, if not literally, die."

—Anonymous

"For now we see through a glass, darkly; but then face to face: now I know in part; but then shall I know even as also I am known."

—1 Corinthians 13:12 (King James Version)

# Acknowledgements

I am deeply grateful to Bela—my wife, editor, and most ardent fan—for her love, patience, sacrifice, and support while I pursue this passion. I also owe a special thanks to my agent, Ray Powers, for his endless encouragement and prudent advice.

# RE'ENEV

# Prologue

ad I known the lines were not just scars but omens of imminent wounds, I would not have gone—obviously. I would have stopped right there; or, at least, I would have turned right back around once my sense of direction became murky; but clairvoyant, I am not.

While we paused at the mouth to the path descending into the jungle, dwarfed by a leafy dome of towering Makoa trees, Micheline stood a few feet in front of me and to my left. Squinting, I could see the small, shiny stripes. They scaled ladder-like up her bronze, tanning neck. Flaring through spacious gaps in the silvery-green Makoa canopy, the morning sun caused the healed slices to reflect a barely perceptible white. There were about a dozen white lines in all. Most were short; a few, long; some crisscrossed. If you didn't know they were there, you wouldn't notice them. But even if you did notice them, you would never suspect how they got there. However, I knew how they got there. And Meesha's psychiatrist knew how they got there. And if the razor blade rusting away in our hometown's dump had a brain and, thus, a memory, it would know also.

*If it had a brain.* One might think I were referring to an insecure scarecrow on a surreal pilgrimage, but that's beside the point. The point is the three pounds of gray, furrowed flesh. From my newly acquired seat in the theater of existence with its elevated purview of reality, I trust the human brain as much as I ever have, but with one recently derived condition: *when accessed.* This notion will undoubtedly seem obvious to most, and that is the obvious problem to me.

The veneer of perception has taught me that the inclination to analyze and the possession of an acute eye are critical to survival. Of course, that's what I know now, after I've *done* my tour in Hell; but since there is nothing I can *physically* do at this point, I *must* mentally glance back. It is the only way that my spirit will heal, that I can progress. If I don't acknowledge and comprehend the past, I will be no better off than I was prior; for it is no secret that by studying one's past, a person can acquire vast knowledge; that from understanding history, humankind can prepare better for the future.

So I visualize what occurred. From my mistakes, I cut the keys to survival, though not just for me, but for all people. Marx opined that religion is the opiate of the masses, but I believe oversight, assumption, denial and forgetfulness sedate just as well. I try now to avoid such smoky dens of ignorance. Otherwise, I will undoubtedly step into some other snare belying reality's facade. That would render all of Meesha's suffering in senseless and unforgivable vain. That, I cannot let happen.

However, you haven't heard my story yet, so you might think I'm flinging shit. Well, that's for you to decide. But the truth be told: I'm trying to help you avoid a pit that did me in, so listen a second.

Whatever you see and feel, you've got to remember; and from them, you've got to learn. But to learn from what you see and feel, you must dig beneath the surface. That's where the analysis comes in. That's where the acute eye becomes key. From where I now reside, though, I notice that most people don't bother. They assume, for reality, what they perceive; accept what their senses process, as is. However, the essence lies below. Clams don't just lie on a mud flat waiting to be plucked. You wanna a clam? You gotta scrape through muck, stuffing your fingernails with black, smelly silt. Same thing with the truth: like a nugget of gold, it's gotta be mined. But most people aren't willing. They view life as a temporal lottery ticket, scratching its surface for a solution, but they're not really seeking. If you want the truth—if you want an answer—you have to remain vigilant. You can't just hang loo—.

Ahhh, but enough of my rambling. I could jaw-wag all day. Let's let my prose paint the picture, my story sing the song. The truth is in my tale.

# Part 1

# Chapter 1

W<sup>e</sup> were seven miles above the Pacific when Meesha dozed off, leaving me staring out a plastic window at a vibrating wing and pondering the fragility of life. I didn't want to be in a philosophical mood, but couldn't help it. In some way I couldn't yet comprehend, I suspected that philosophy was really what this vacation was about. *Philosophy and reconciliation,* I thought, correcting myself, as a stewardess handed me a thimble of Coke. I thanked her, then turned back toward the little plastic porthole and sipped from my little plastic cup, but could see only puffy white obscuring the world's largest body of water. I chuckled to myself: *a measly cloud hiding a whole ocean. How apropos.* Then I thought about Dr. Quint and her recommendation that Meesha and I get away for a while, how a vacation could help rejuvenate our relationship after so much trauma and pain. And, now, here we were, with at least our physical wounds healed, airborne to Re'enev.

Cracking an ice cube with my molars, I leaned back in my seat. I thought about the days ahead, the activities we had planned, and how the trip could and might affect us. Naturally, I hoped for the best, but my gut told me to just take things as they come; try to have as much fun as we can, but not force anything; strive for normalcy and just see what happens; let the cards hit where they may and lie where they land. As I thought this, I heard Meesha breathe deeply, so softly and serenely, and it sent my mind sauntering back to simpler days.

I'll never forget seeing Micheline for the first time. It was a Wednesday night, dinner time. We were in the West Campus Cafeteria at Cornell University. We were both freshmen; she from New Jersey, I from Rhode Island, now both in Ithaca, New York. It was fall, a month into our first semester.

Behind the serving counter, spooning out peas to anyone in line who requested some, stood a woman who altered my breathing with her mere presence. The fresh, vibrant blush that radiated from the taut skin canvassing her stunningly high cheeks told me she was around my age—a student working part-time. She stood to the far right of two other cafeteria workers, older women approaching retirement. I don't remember what dishes the others were spooning out. I don't remember what the entree was. I don't even know if I was hungry, for it wouldn't have mattered. I wouldn't have cared. I could only think about peas.

The goddess with the Macintosh complexion wore a maroon smock over a tight red pullover, but that smock didn't have a chance. Some treasures just can't be hidden. I remember watching her out of the right corners of my eyes as I stood in front of her two co-workers. Her straight hair spread silkily upon her shoulders, the color of varnished mahogany, then continued on another foot or so with not only the color, but also the gloss, of such finished wood. She smiled at each person who moved before her. Her teeth, so perfectly pitched, so strikingly white, seemed to reach out and shine the space she occupied. First, they made me think of the way car wax buffs painted steel. Then I likened each tooth to the bulb atop a propane lamp burning at full throttle. She was tall, statuesque, with an extraordinarily thin waist, yet curvaceous hips and, oh, those breasts! When my opportunity came to request peas, I found myself face-to-spirit with the most beautiful soul, visible through the most beautiful eyes, embodied by the most beautiful woman I had ever shared oxygen with in my life. The windows to her being were brown, huge, and oval—two tablespoons of freshly brewed coffee centered with a pupil several shades darker, yet spring water clear with honesty, integrity and character. I instantly fell in love, and the impact of the fall must have injured me badly, for I found myself semi-paralyzed, incapable of coherent speech. Something similar to the babbling of an infant gurgled through my lips and this just widened the smile of the aesthetic marvel holding my dinner. She didn't intend to mock or condescend. She simply found my actions amusing. But I felt stupid as hell. I could feel the temperature of my face rising and envisioned myself standing there: a tomato in Levi's. So when Beautiful-Behind-The-Counter asked me a second time, "Would you like peas?", I cut her off at mid-sentence with a head down, self-conscious "no". Then I retrieved my vegetable-free plate and found a place to sit in the dining area, where I ate my food and attempted to reassemble my fractured ego.

I saw the pea serving siren in the cafeteria a couple times after that, but found ways of avoiding her—actually, not her per se, but rather the humiliation I knew would follow.

Many years have passed since then, but I am still stunned by the impact Meesha's beauty had on my voluntary motor skills; most notably, my ability to communicate. Never before had such a thing happened. I'd always been fairly comfortable with women; smooth, I had liked to think. So meeting Meesha was a slap to my psyche in more ways than one.

And it wasn't that I didn't want to meet Meesha, or had excessive fear of doing so. I just wanted our next encounter to be in a setting where we could talk less superficially and without other people listening. I knew I would feel more comfortable that way and stand a better chance of communicating—that is, of not making a fool of myself.

Such an encounter was inevitable. I instinctively knew it. It was like that phenomenon where once you recognize the existence of something, such as a type of car, you start seeing it all the time. Now that I had noticed Meesha, I had a gut feeling that I would start seeing her around. And I was right.

First, I found her listening, ever so attentively, three rows ahead of me during one of my chemistry lectures. She looked so good. I took so few notes.

Then I saw her in the stands at Schoelkopf field, Cornell's football stadium. She was with a bunch of friends. It was a brisk, sunny Saturday. She sat bundled in a blanket, apple cheeked and laughing. Occasionally, she sipped blackberry brandy and peppermint schnapps from glass bottles passed to her, while the Big Red lost to Princeton.

And, as I was stumbling home from a bar in Ithaca one Friday night, I caught her walking up the front steps of Sigma Chi, the arm of some fraternity goof around her miniscule waist. Seeing this, I instantly developed the urge to single-handedly take on the entire Greek system; but, luckily for me, my inebriated head still contained enough sense to pull me back to my dorm.

It was in the campus Fine Arts Center, though, that I would once again communicate with Meesha—or, at least, attempt to. Freshmen English courses at Cornell were based on a theme. I chose Fine Art, though I can't tell you why. I didn't know Van Gogh from Gaugin. Regardless, every week I had to study some painting or sculpture and critique it for at least five double-spaced pages. It was not my favorite course.

One Saturday afternoon, I was crunching my face at what seemed to be several dozen stainless-steel spools. Welded together in a linear array, they formed a shape so phallic it would have made Sigmund Freud theorize and Mae West blush. I didn't even notice Meesha approaching, so engrossed was I in trying to figure out what the demented artist had intended when creating this thing the museum called contemporary art. But she noticed me, most notably my expression, and laughed that same non-mocking, non-condescending chuckle she had emitted in the cafeteria.

"You like it, huh?"

I looked up into two familiar rows of radiating white, each corner of the mouth stretching the fall foliage complexion. I felt blood leave my brain for my face and pelvis, and I realized that the moment I had been expecting had arrived.

"Oh, absolutely! The lack of reason that permeates this piece is strikingly evident, especially in the continual twisting of the common metal. The surrealism derived symbolizes the pretentious act of creating something ostensibly significant, though actually meaningless, out of an everyday object. The artist's talent is so great, and his insight so profound, that I am overcome with the urge to kneel before his creation and vomit."

And on I went. I like to believe that no dialogue ever spewed by a suitor, in the history of men chasing women, had greater positive impact on the elusive gender than the sarcasm I threw at Meesha that day. From that first statement on, she laughed and bantered with me, displaying the keen wit and loveable authenticity I so desperately yearned for in a woman. I don't know what overcame me while I was in the museum, but I was on. It was one of those moments I have every so often when my intellect is on fire and I can fling sarcasm cloaked in humor with the facility of a kid flicking matches into the wind. And to my fortuitous end, that fire spawned a blaze that would intensify with each year. Call it *Lover's Napalm*. It burned so intensely that it sucked the air from our lungs, leaving us breathless for each other until senselessly shed blood extinguished the flame.

Whenever I glance back upon my life, I can't help but acknowledge that my wife entered it with the impact of a deity, a savior with sensational legs. Her beauty, inside and out, mesmerized me. Never before had anyone seen me—the real me—so accurately, or spoken to me so candidly.

Thinking about Meesha's candor reminds me of a day during the summer preceding our senior year at Cornell. Meesh and I are lying on a beach in Dennisport on Cape Cod. We have come down for the weekend, crashing on a couch in a cottage rented by friends from school—a bunch of guys and girls who bartend or wait on tables at night, party afterwards until the sun rises, then sleep on hot sand until it sets. It is a typical way for my rich college friends to spend their summers. I could never do this. I have to make real money during my summers, and save every penny for the college expenses financial aid won't cover. C'est la vie.

I'm lying on my back, a long towel shielding my skin from sun-broiled sand. Meesha lies close to me, on her stomach to my left, delectably filling an off-orange bikini. Salmon is the color, the hue of cumulous clouds sailing the western sky during a dusk when the sun departs with splendor. It is a beautiful suit with a classy cut, one that does not expose any more of Meesha than would be in good taste, which is so like her: though beautiful and fun loving, she never ventures beyond the boundaries of classy dress or conduct.

This incarnation of class, who is so easy to love, suddenly rises from her towel upon bent arms that eventually lock, exposing the tightest cleavage a set of mammaries has ever formed. I can't help but think: *How many men wouldn't trade their souls for the privilege of being reincarnated into a piece of her suit, a single thread in the fabric?* Then this face, mind, and figure, which so ceaselessly engage me, drags herself forward. She ends up knees-to-chest on my towel, sitting two feet in front of me.

We've been talking about our post-graduation plans. Neither of us knows what we really want to do. I sort of lean toward something in the computer field, but have little idea of what the options are, never mind which one I would enjoy the most.

Meesha has even less of a clue. While lunging her head by stretching her neck from her spot on my towel, she whispers in breathy, sensual syllables that she wants nothing other than to get a job and keep on loving—just keep on loving me, day in and day out. Thinking about this, I realize that we both feel the same way: that there is nothing more important in each of our lives than the other; that we just want to keep on living, so that we can keep on loving.

Then Meesha lifts her pouty mouth up to mine and blesses my sun-dried lips with a long, tender kiss. I taste her usually sweet saliva, slightly seasoned with moist, summer salt. After several long, pleasurable seconds—enough time for my reactive body to involuntarily respond—I slowly lick her lips. When I finish—that is, when her lips are salt free—Meesha places her head on my right shoulder and gently tongue-tips the nape of my neck. The way she places her head in the nook between my head and neck occurs so naturally. It happens the way it can for two people—and only such people—who have performed the movement so many times that it has become smoothly, thus flawlessly, automatic, as if instinctive.

As Meesha's tongue messages my neck, my eyes roll down her arched body, now propped on stiffened arms popping slender triceps. Like drinking-straws, my pupils suck in her tanned back and legs before gulping her behind. So perfectly shaped, so convexly proportionate, no sculptor could have created better, my wife's derriere fills her lower, salmon bikini the way her slender, intelligent hands force conformance from the Italian leather gloves she wears during the winter. And, oh!, the way that sedated orange contrasts and enhances her tan! As well as the blend of sea, sky, and sand around us! And vice-versa! She is just *so* good. How I *love* her. How I *yearn* for her. I can never get *enough* of her. It is like I want to make her part of me, actually suck her entire being into mine. And how often she feels I am trying to do this whenever we are intimate and I focus on her hardened, though sensitive, erect nipples. "Oh Luke, oooohhh Luke!" she purrs.

We often talk about sex, especially after the act, and Meesha tells me that she had never realized how much pleasure she could receive from a man simply sucking on her. She had always thought that only vaginal stimulation, mainly intercourse, the necessity of a man entering her, could produce the sublime pleasure for which her womanhood yearned. But, to her surprise, Meesha found that sex offers other pleasures, more emotional than physical, but no less satisfying; in fact, possibly more so, for the feelings last longer. She tells me that there is something extremely fulfilling, something completely wholesome and limitless, about the way I suckle her. After talking about it, we conclude that it is my intensity, my desire to take her fully in, to make her a component of my being. Of course, logically and physically, this cannot occur; but metaphysics plays a role in our sex life, and my dreams and desires undoubtedly impact the way I make love to my wife. She may be distinct from me in a physical sense, but emotionally and spiritually we are one. And through love making I emotionally try, though I intellectually know it is futile, to move the state of the former to the state of the latter. There is no better way for me to express my feelings, my profound love and attraction, for my magnificent spouse. And for more than fifteen years, I express my feelings this way.

My memory of lying with Meesha on that beach in Dennisport on Cape Cod is significant, for it is just that: a memory. Whenever I think of Meesha dragging her salmon-banded body toward mine, her femininely muscular waist hovering over the faint cavities her breasts had impressed through her towel in the sand, her kissing me tenderly with briny lips, and the optimism with which we discussed our future—her head on my shoulder, when talking; her tongue tip slowly caressing my neck, when not—I remember the beauty our relationship once had. Yes, sadly enough: once had.

# Chapter 2

It all began a few months ago, starting the first summer of the century with sorrow. Just thinking about it gets me down.

Hunter, three years younger than me, had always been kind of crazy. My parents, although divorced, had jointly talked him into joining the military upon his graduation from high school. They thought it would straighten him out, give him structure, a start in life. But it was a mistake. It just made him worse.

Hunter naturally chose the Marines, my father being an ex-jar head, and went infantry. After Parris Island and Advanced Infantry Training, he passed all tests, courses, and requirements for Force Recon, then went nuts. From torching parts of his body in bars with lighter fluid, to beating up squids (what he and my father always called sailors in the navy) all over San Diego, to sneaking hookers out of Tijuana on weekends, to tight rope walking the stay wires between electrical towers, to urinating in parked police cars—all, simply, for the goof—after four years, the Corps had had enough. As good and tough as Hunter was, they were relieved when his hitch was up. My younger brother was simply too wild and crazy, even for the Marines. But surfing his motorcycle down an interstate highway was beyond wild and crazy. Standing sideways, feet on seat, hands on handlebars, Hunter, according to the cops, had been pushing seventy when he hit. A body builder with the vanity of a peacock, Hunter never wore a shirt, or long pants, when he rode during the summer. And that's why he resembled skinless chicken doused with runny tomato sauce when they found him. A swath of viscous red and fleshy white streaked the trail where his sinew inflated body had skid. The hot tar had shredded his pale epidermis the way it would warm cheddar cheese. He was wearing a helmet, but it didn't matter. Hunter was dead before a human finger could scan his chewed up remains in search of a pulse.

Not one cloud bleached the sky on the day Hunter died, while the temperature at noon nicked ninety. This was fitting, for Hunter had a fundamental, primeval love for the sun. (Worthy to note: Yellow was his favorite color; orange, his second; Van Gogh's *Bouquet of Sunflowers*, his favorite painting; F.E. Church's *Twilight in the Wilderness*, the runner-up.) He was always keenly aware of its position in the sky. Every October, when we set the clocks back an hour for daylight savings time, Hunter would sit on the couch in our den and stare at the brick chimney running up our next door neighbor's house. He loved the buttery film that coated each red block for roughly an hour each afternoon as China entered a new day. Hunter introduced me to this phenomenon. I now get a nostalgic feeling whenever the season spawns long shadows in early afternoon, pre-mature sunsets and that beautiful, but almost eerie yellow which tints all things. However, I never could appreciate the sun and all its splendor as much as Hunter did.

Despite being younger than me, Hunter had a sharper understanding of the ethereal aspects of life. Although as savage as a cannibal and wilder than a wombat—he never lost a fistfight in his life and managed at least one every week from first grade through twelfth—Hunter had a very deep and philosophical side to him. He seemed to see things no one else saw and appreciate things everyone else took for granted. This incongruence in his personality never ceased to amaze me.

Hunter began kickboxing when he was seven, won his first contest at nine, and was the local champion throughout his high school years. Whenever he learned a new kick, move, or punch combination, he would go out and practice it on every outlaw biker and drug dealer he could find. He usually ended up being brought home bloody and smiling by the local police, who felt they could do little else given that Hunter was a minor. And what judge is going to put away an honor student for kicking the shit out of slime ball bikers and dope dealing scum? It was this side of Hunter contrasted with the other—the one which read and quoted Kant, Nietzsche, Shakespeare, and Tolstoy—that I found so fascinating and which made him so dangerous. He had the brain of a professor, the body of a linebacker, and the killing skills of a mercenary. So often, when growing up; later, as a sergeant in the Corps; and when, again, a civilian; Hunter would talk about such barbaric acts as hand-to-hand combat, torture tactics, ambush formations, and the techniques and skills used in tracking down another human being, but do it with such philosophy, erudition, tranquil purpose, and intellectual insight that I sometimes found him frightening, sometimes downright chilling.

When Hunter spoke, he did so with the confidence and serenity of someone who knows his subject inside and out, someone who is an expert in his field. Yet, never did Hunter act pompous or wax bombastically; no soapbox ever elevated his feet. Never did he try to impress me, despite my being his older brother, or any of his peers. Although, as a toddler, he sometimes watched and emulated me, as younger brothers will do, Hunter never sought approval, recognition, or acceptance from me, or any other kid. In fact, never at any time during his life did Hunter try to elicit any form of attention, in any way, from anybody—with the notable exception of my father. And although that exception did not endure the duration of Hunter's life—a fact that I believe twisted my father's guts from its inception until my brother's death—the effects of it did and that is what truncated his existence.

Needless to say, Hunter's death rocked me. I'd always had a feeling something weird would happen to him, that his mortality would confront him sooner than it would most and in a uncommon way. But when he did go, I still wasn't ready. Looking back, I don't think I ever could have been. He was my brother, my only sibling and, despite his looniness, I loved him.

When my father called—his voice like hundreds of small rocks being pulled over dozens of bigger rocks by the surging surf of a storm ready to break—I went numb.

My parents split when I was twelve. My mother gained custody of Hunter and me, but we saw our father often enough to maintain a bond. I don't ever remember my parents getting along, always arguing and sniping; but when it came to divvying up the custody rights, no battle ensued. At least they resolved that issue with some civility, and it retained as much normalcy in my childhood as could have been salvaged under the circumstances.

Throughout my youth, there existed an unstated fact that Hunter was tighter with my father than I was. I was always closer to my mother. Why? I'm not really sure. It could have been because I was older and naturally drawn to protect my mother from her turbulent marriage. Or it could have been because Hunter received the name my father wanted to give, while I, the biblical name my mother insisted at least one of her children have. It was their pre-propagation pact: they'd have at least two children; my mother would name the first, and my father the second. If any more followed, those children's names would be mutually agreeable to both of them. But mutual agreement was never needed. My mother had always wanted a child with a biblical name and preferred it to be a boy. Any of the gospels would do. If a girl, there were no options: Notre Dame would be honored for the bezillionth time. My father also preferred a boy and wanted him named Hunter. He'd always loved the name. It reminded him of the Marines, of Ernest Hemingway, and of himself—of his scrappy, gritty ways, of how he lived his life. My father wanted a son in his image and he got one who reflected his image ten-fold, for Hunter was a better man than my father could have ever dreamed of being.

But I think the real reason Hunter was tighter with my old man, while I was tighter with my mother, had something to do with what a shrink told me following Hunter's death. "You're an alpha," he said. "An alpha will fight another alpha, or leave the pack, but he will never follow. He goes his own way, blazes his own path, makes his own rules, but bows to no one." I, being an alpha, according to this shrink, was innately unwilling to satisfy my father's requests, meet his standards and requirements, or crawl in his footsteps. I had no need, nor felt any desire, to please him or gain his approval. Hunter, on the other hand, was the complete opposite and to an extreme with his kickboxing, weightlifting, and Force Recon elitism. It was this loyalty that my father loved in Hunter and the alpha spirit that he resented in me, despite my being his first-born.

Meesha and I had been eating when my father called. When I hung up the phone, I sat back down at our dinner table, then just stared into space, zombie-like. I sat like this for several long seconds before muttering, "Hunter's dead".

While I had spoken—actually, mostly listened—to my father, Meesh had sat in silence, her face ashen, her eyes startled and analyzing my every gesture. She could tell that I was receiving bad news, but nothing I said to my father disclosed what it was. When I finally told her, her face broke, blew open, a water balloon punctured with a pin. Meanwhile, I just continued to sit and stare.

For the following week, I remained the zombie. I buzzed through the closed casket wake and surreal funeral. Everything around me seemed to blur. My curiosity for and attention to detail rivaled that of a long haul trucker blowing through one tavern towns in northern Nebraska. I didn't talk, for I had nothing to say. I didn't listen, for there was nothing worthwhile to hear. And there was little Meesha could do, but watch me and worry.

It killed her, this withdrawal of mine. Ours was a bond that thrived on communication, on the sharing of every pain and every joy. From the beginning, when we first fell in love at Cornell, we understood that a relationship is a living organism, something that constantly evolves and requires work. Daily renegotiation is a requirement to maintaining its quality, for people change; and if the relationship doesn't adjust—or isn't adjusted by its members, the people—it deteriorates.

I recognized and understood these tenets for a solid marriage, but I was paralyzed. Meesha kept asking me if I wanted to talk, and I just kept shaking my head. I wasn't lying; there really was nothing I wanted to say. What could there be? What else could be said? Hunter was dead, and that was that. What else was there? Did she want me to discuss the gory details of the accident? The obvious senselessness of the way in which he went? The terrible waste of such a young and talented life? If she did, I couldn't. There was nothing I could mutter and nothing worth muttering about. I knew exactly what had happened and simply had to deal with it. I had to get through the mourning stage. And being the kind of person I am, I had to do that alone. I'm not one to cry on somebody's shoulder. I'm better off watching—often just staring at, without seeing—finches, chickadees, nuthatches, and titmice eat black oil seed from the feeders in our back yard. Often, resolution comes to me faster and with more clarity when I'm alone, thinking, than when I'm with company, talking.

However, Meesha had a hard time with this. She felt betrayed, abandoned, although she wouldn't have been able to diagnose her feelings as such at the time. She just knew that I wasn't talking to her, confiding in her, and this hurt her deeply.

In response, she struck back; her weapon: her tongue, the same one that had once so lovingly caressed my neck and French kissed my own. She didn't know she was striking; it was a reflexive action, a defense mechanism, nothing premeditated. The incoming ranged from snipes—the kind I'd heard my parents constantly fire at each other—to the verbal equivalent of nuclear missiles. Rare was the word that escaped her face free of sarcasm. Husband hurting venom seemed to flow through her veins. The pleasant and serene woman I loved had somehow turned into Frankenstein's monster sans the electrodes. I did not understand. When not yelling, she remained quiet and depressed, yet never took off her gloves should she need to hop right back into the ring. And to the same extent that Meesha was oblivious to the friction igniting her reaction, I was unprepared for the assault. I knew of no reason to expect it. Today, however, when I ponder the past and contemplate the circumstances, the cause appears so bloody obvious.

Meesha had arrived in the States speaking fluent English when she was eight, her father emigrating from Paris at the behest of his company. He worked for some chic suit manufacturer and they wanted him to run their New York City office.

Meesha's father, Francois, had a college degree and, like Meesha, an excellent command of the English language; Meesha's mother, Monique, had neither. While Francois was reared in a luxuriant apartment in Paris, Monique grew up in a shack on its outskirts. At the age Francois attended boarding school, Monique grew terribly bored with school. While Francois excelled academically in college, Monique excelled in embroidering collages. The two seemed like caricatures, hero and heroine plucked right out of the prosaic tale of rich boy falls for poor girl.

Francois met Monique by chance when visiting—as a suave, young buyer for his suit company—one of the stitching mills with which his firm subcontracted labor. They met in a freight elevator, which Francois was taking as a short cut through the building on his way to meet with the mill president. So overcome was Francois by Monique's delicate features, and slim but almost disproportionately robust figure, that he asked her out on the spot—in the elevator—before even introducing himself. Didn't matter. Monique, barely eighteen at the time, instantly saw a different, brighter future in the dark, chiseled, high-cheekboned aspect of the man who made no attempt to cloak his impassioned interest. Interest, Monique knew, in the tantalizing combination of her freshness, innocence, and raw sexuality. Though uneducated in the scholarly sense, Monique had a clue. Ever since her breasts had begun to blossom and complement her pretty face—which spouted thick lips and a pouty, seductive mouth—creating a consummately beautiful woman, Monique had been aware of the primal attraction she held for men. Age rarely mattered. Monique could remember being twelve and turning the heads of men two and three times older.

Francois made Monique a Levesque within a year following the freight elevator encounter. Meesha Levesque arrived a year later; Pierre Levesque, a couple after Meesha.

While living in Paris, Monique raised Meesha and Pierre relying on that most accurate compass: maternal instinct. This was a good thing. It meant that Meesha at age eight and Pierre at age six had received sound parenting during their most formative years. It was a good thing, for it ended as soon as the Levesques reached the States.

What happened to Monique upon emigrating remains vague. "She crashed," is the way Meesha put it. According to stories Meesha has told, Monique seems to have become overwhelmed by the move to New York—the difficulties of adjusting, the language barrier, and the distance placed between her parents, siblings, extended family and her. She appears to have fallen into a deep depression, leaving every aspect of her life, beyond her tormented mind, forsaken at the surface.

Monique remained in this psychological ditch for the remainder of Meesha's grade school years. It wasn't until Meesha had entered Cornell and taken a couple of psychology courses that she realized, with both alarm and post-trauma regret, that her mother suffered from major depression. The discovery prompted two events: first, Meesha decided to major in psychology; second, she approached her father. Francois, who had been too busy with his job from the moment he arrived in the States to monitor his family's life—usually working seventy-hour weeks, not including his frequent trips to the west coast—immediately took Monique to a good Manhattan shrink. The doctor promptly placed Monique on medication and in therapy.

Monique began climbing out of her hole within a couple of months and made continual progress over the years. However, for Meesha and Pierre, the damage had been done. From the minute they arrived in the States, the two tots had been on their own. Their father was too busy to take care of them, while their mother couldn't even take care of herself. As a result, Meesha entered a new and often hostile world, completely alone. To make things worse, she also became a surrogate mother. While his biological one lay home in bed, unable to rise and face each day, Pierre had to rely on the precocious wisdom of his eight-year-old sister. Meesha's young, untested intelligence suddenly found itself responsible for a litany of tasks: determining what Pierre and she were to eat for breakfast, lunch, and dinner, and do after school; assisting in and enforcing the completion of Pierre's homework, while concentrating on her own; ensuring that scholastic requirements, such as the proper dress code and course load, were met for them both; as well as resolving the problems that arose much too frequently at school. The latter caused Meesha the most anxiety, for Pierre was a born trouble maker and class clown and was constantly being sent to the principal's office. Since phone calls to Mrs. Levesque did no good for they were rarely answered and, when they were, Mrs. Levesque was too incapacitated to deal with the problem, school officials brought the problems to Meesha.

The apparent disappearance of her father, "crashing" of her mother, and consequent responsibilities placed on her, left their mark on Meesha. She metamorphosed into a woman/child, one who would play with dolls one moment and make grown-up decisions the next. This role triggered in her the premature development of adult-like cognitive reasoning, but at a stiff cost. While Meesha acquired the confidence and wisdom of an adult, she also incurred the fear of being abandoned. It is very possible that this fear was, like the shape of her body and mouth, inherited. But unlike her mother, Meesha was never incapacitated by her phobia. It did, however, significantly impact her life and, notably, our marriage.

When Hunter died and I withdrew, Meesha flipped. Her panic, immediate and intense, chose fight over flight. She snapped and tore—at my occasional word—at my mere silence. No matter what I did—speak or play the mute—she riddled me. Verbal rounds, subtle but scathing, they usually began as jabs, so I tried to ignore them. But jabs are just a precursor to Tyson upper cuts and Marciano Susie-Q's, to the punches that knock you into next week. And before I could even determine what was happening, Meesha released. Rhetorical carpet bombing, her deluge hit me like an avalanche. Then I freaked.

I remember times when we were driving to work and something insignificant would happen—such as my pointing out a hawk in the sky, while Meesha was listening to the radio—that blew her temper like the entrails from a volcano:

"Ohhh! You're so inconsiderate! You *know* I'm listening to the news! Now I *missed* that!"

"Sorry." I'd mutter, then simultaneously purse my lips and raise my eyebrows. I wasn't, really. I was hurt and confused.

Or times when an old friend would call and Meesha would start moving furniture, or crinkling a newspaper, in the same room where I was talking. On these occasions, it was *my* turn to blow and blow I did. When I got off the phone, I'd roar that *she* was the most inconsiderate jerk *I'd* ever met, among other things I would later regret, and we'd go at it until she cried. Meesha's crying always made me stop.

The more frequent and intense our arguments became, the more frequent and intense *DIVORCE!* rang in my mind. It became the rattling bell that ends my short recess from school, the break-truncating wail that throws me back to the grind, the howling alarm that a known crisis is resurfacing—specifically, one that will require me to re-suffer.

At the same time, the word itself flashed inflammatory red, and in capital letters, against the black back of my injured, aching mind. And it wasn't long before my unspoken thought became a vehement threat, a constant in my offensive; one which, to be expected, was immediately reciprocated by Meesha. *Ah yes,* I'd often think: *"For better or for worse"—such sacred words, so honorable, memorable and sweet.*

During the midst of this storm came Sandy. A new administrative assistant to my boss, Sandy was nice looking in a wholesome, healthy way and more cerebral than her position suggested. There seemed no subject about which she couldn't talk, and talking with her was very enjoyable.

Sandy had been a country girl, brought up on a Vermont dairy farm, and her tomboyish manner spoke for her background, but in no way detrimental to her femininity. She could break in a quarter horse and seduce a cow hand with equal dexterity, and carried these traits with her into the Boston office in which I worked. When not hiding behind hair, her eyes burned so electrically blue they could have been swirls from Van Gogh's palette. She habitually brushed aside parted bangs colored several shades lighter than her name and smiled often, flaring inner embers which tinted fleshy cheeks, exposing just a hint of her internal flame. Hers were cute cheeks that uniquely glowed, not just during skin-searing winter but through every season of the year, the incandescence of her spirit beaming through. But improbable as it may seem, it was Sandy's nose that I noticed first, and remember most, from the first time we met. This was a brief introduction at the reception desk, where she would often sit during her initial three weeks on the job. The fact that I noticed Sandy's nose first would probably surprise people who have not met her, but have only heard her described, for Sandy's nose is small and pointy, hardly the kind that draws attention. But those who have met Sandy know that her nose also sports a band of freckles across its bridge—freckles that look, due to their incongruity with her otherwise unblemished skin, as if they had been sprinkled on, by her creator, as an after thought. No one ever remembers to mention this trait when describing Sandy, but after meeting her, it is the thing that one remembers most. As consistent and conspicuous as Orion's belt in a clear, evening sky, those freckles are just too damn cute.

It wasn't long after Sandy started that my boss realized her capabilities ranged far beyond answering phone calls, greeting guests, making photocopies, and typing an occasional memo. Graduating from some small college in upper Vermont with an Economics major and English minor, she had embarked toward Boston the following week. The job market was tight, so she took the first one she could get, hoping she could swiftly scale the corporate ladder. Her aspirations materialized even sooner than she had hoped. Within three weeks, she found herself editing the documents other analysts and I produced, an indispensable task during the early stages of the project life cycle. She also participated, as a scribe, in Joint Application Development sessions. In the process, she gained exposure to detailed requirements for the relational database my systems department was preparing to build.

During the months that followed Hunter's death, my time spent with Sandy increased exponentially. Some kid with over-teased, spray-stiffened hair, as black as the leather skirt she wore too often to cover too little, took over as my boss' assistant. As a result, Sandy could move into the systems group to which I belonged. Now, an entry-level analyst, she dove thirstily into the fresh waters of her new career. Time barely passed before my colleagues and I discovered that Sandy was creative, analytical, and retentive, remembering almost everything she learned while sucking up new material like a nuclear-powered Electrolux sweeping a coral covered beach.

Entry-level analysts in the Systems Department of my company are initially assigned to a specific project as well as to an analyst with experience. This way, they'll develop skills and acquire knowledge while occupying a position where they can apply them, thus contributing immediately.

Sandy was assigned to me. We hit it off from the start. Our chemistries couldn't have been more compatible. She, the combustive hydrogen; I, the two parts of oxygenating guidance; our synergy flowed—no, make that rushed!—like Alaskan white water. I taught her the mechanics of business analysis: eliciting information from clients, writing business requirements and system design specifications, producing process and data flow diagrams, and a variety of other tasks.

In turn, Sandy corrected some of my grammatical misconceptions and helped me to tighten my style, making me a better writer. The final product was that we, as a pair, generated more as well as better results than any other team of analysts within my department. But those results spoke only for the professional realm.

On a personal level, intangible, less visible developments were spawning, though I wouldn't have been surprised if some of my co-workers had noticed their generation also. While getting lacerated at home, I was healing at work. While my wife berated me, whipping daggers with every flip of her tongue, my job comforted me, an unexpected port during the storm. And Sandy, my figurative harbor master, played no small part. She bore no anecdotal knowledge of my tribulations, but with her uncanny intuition, she knew something was amiss. And she knew it wasn't car troubles, a leaky roof, or crooked-toothed kids running up an orthodontist's bill. Some things a woman just knows, and I could tell that she knew. It wasn't anything she said or overtly did. It was just a certain flick of the eye, or pause in her movements or speech, where she seemed to reflect on something other than the work at hand. It would last only a moment—but I would catch it. And it usually occurred whenever she asked me something quasi-personal, such as how my weekend went, or, on days when I wasn't feeling so perky, if anything was wrong.

"Naw," I would answer, "I'm alright." But she knew I was lying as well as the nature of my problem.

During the months that I worked with Sandy, I also toiled closely with some male colleagues; but none of them ever indicated, in any way, that they felt or saw something different about me. I found this interesting in light of all the talk about male bonding circulating society and, most notably, the artificially impersonal office environment.

Impersonal or not, however, the ambiance of my office did not prevent Sandy from detecting my pain, or sympathizing with my anguish. I've always tried to be stoical about my feelings, especially at work, but Sandy saw right through the iron countenance I donned each morning. Meanwhile, my male colleagues saw only my mask, the face of the "regular guy".

As time dragged, my home life coarsened, for my marriage worsened, for my wife became intolerable. Weeknights were nasty, but weekends were emotional torture. It became so bad that I looked forward to going to work more and more each day.

I felt guilty at the time and still do, but I couldn't help myself from glimpsing the firm, caramel thighs I constantly found in my field of view. Often beside me while we reviewed and modified documentation, Sandy would sit to my left, her svelte lower appendages protruding from the narrow hem of a short skirt. Wrapped in darkening, smoothening silk, they drew my eyes against my will and through my shame with such facility, the utmost of ease. Though sometimes they crossed or stretched, they usually just hung there, angled, beautiful extensions to a beautiful body, beneath my arms and beside my own. At a time when I was seriously considering divorce, battling a heavy dose of daily anxiety and depression, basically watching my life decay before me, I worked closely with this cute and comforting creature, ten hours at a pop, five pops each week. When I appeared down to her, she wouldn't insult me with meaningless rhetoric. Instead, she'd massage my wounds with warm eye contact, the electric current of her Van Gogh blues flowing through mine, to gently stroke my psyche and soul. She did this so deftly, and it felt so good, that I couldn't resist. How often I saw her say with lips that didn't move: "It'll be okay. Things'll get better." And when her luscious lips did part, how often I detected genuine care in her tone of speech. But most impacting of all, how frequently I felt the firm pull of her primal urge, a tug with tenacity disguised as passivity—passivity in the way she did not reject, did not mind, seemed to even like, seemed to even encourage my desire for her— conveyed through expressions and gestures as well as actions free of movement, the most common and enjoyable being her willingness to let me fondle with my eyes.

The acrimony between Meesha and me climaxed one day that began with an exceptionally turbulent ride to work. Meesha was having her period, a time that always made her touchy, regardless of our tribulations. Striving to be a good husband, I would try to have compassion for Meesha when she was menstruating. I can't say I empathized with the pain—I'm a guy—but I'd seen her endure enough suffering in the past that I could sympathize; thus, I tried not to make things tougher for her.

But on this particular morning, Meesha was an absolute beast: Godzilla in pumps. You might have thought I had murdered her whole family, the cat and dog included, by the way she went off. She was unbelievable. Listening to her wail, I half expected to see Rod Serling pop into the back seat and start narrating my circumstances with one of his punctuating monologues: "LUKE FERless—your averAGE HUSband—undergoING, what MAY seem, TYPICAL TRIals with HIS wife. But on THIS day—his triALS WON'T BE THAT TYPical...."

Well, Rod would have been right. They weren't. And they happened so fast that I felt carried, as if riding a fatalistic piggy back through the barbed wire gauntlet of my existence.

The company for which I work is constantly shuffling its employees around. Space constraints continuously appear, so departmental moves continuously occur. It's not uncommon for me to move two or three times a year; so, luckily, it's easy. All I have to do is pack my stuff in foldable cardboard boxes, and some moving company will haul it to my new location overnight. The next morning, when I go to that location, all my stuff will be sitting in a numbered cube within the boxes I had placed them. Pretty efficient, but pretty impersonal. I'm a human being with a thumping pulse, wiggling toes, and thoughts that make me intrinsically unique; but, to the company, I'm simply number 452, or 167, or any other of the thousand or so that moved on that day. It's no wonder that one of the first things many people do at their new sites is hang their name tags on the outside wall of their cubes.

At the end of that infamous day of Meesha's record breaking wrath—one on which she maxed out the bitch meter, pulling sparks from its size-measuring console—my department was scheduled to move. We were to stay in the same building, but relocate to a different floor. At that time, the building was incurring a lot of alterations, including some structural changes to the floor below which we would move.

The move began promptly at five o'clock. My current floor—the one from which we were moving—was invaded by a slew of burly guys in blue shirts bearing a breast patch: *McConnell and Davis*. They stomped in and around our cubicles, loading dollies with our cardboard-boxed belongings, then pulled their steel and wooden carts toward our floor's elevators. There, another team of McConnell and Davis employees grabbed the dollies and hauled them to their destination, where they unloaded the numbered boxes into the correspondingly numbered cube.

I usually worked past five o'clock, as did Meesha, creating a routine where we did not leave our offices until six or later. Both our jobs required that we work long days. In addition, working until the peak of rush hour had passed made exiting the city a bit easier. Boston traffic is always bad. At the peak of rush hour, it is insane.

However, because McConnell and Davis were stomping around in the cube I currently occupied, as well as the one to which I was moving, there was no way I could work. My stuff was packed away in boxes and my PC had been disconnected. As a result, I simply took a seat against a window, plopping my butt on top of the base board heater, and watched the movers move. After a few minutes, Sandy joined me.

"These guys are pretty efficient," she said.

"Yeah," I murmured, nodding, while watching them whip around dollies and yank PC's out of the local area network. I felt a bit uncomfortable sitting next to Sandy for we weren't doing any work, making this a more personal encounter than any we'd previously had. But I also felt good, for sitting next to Sandy without having to work meant that I could talk to her, thus enjoy her company, without having to use some job-related task as a ruse for doing so.

"What are they doing to the floor downstairs?" she asked, and I could tell by the way she was forcing conversation that Sandy also felt uncomfortable. *But she could just go home,* I thought; *instead, she's choosing to stay and talk.* As a result, I knew she wanted to be with me.

"Looks like they're gutting it and moving walls. A total renovation." I had taken a walk around the floor a couple days earlier, just to observe the changes.

Suddenly, Sandy said, "You wanna go down there and have a look?"

This surprised me. I hesitated. I did not want to do anything that would appear inappropriate. After several contemplative moments, I said through quiet exhales: "Yeah. Sure."

We took the stairway. No sense using the elevators for one flight. Plus, they were all being used by the movers.

Reaching the entrance door, I peeked through a small window reinforced with crisscrossing wire. The sheet rockers, painters and other tradesmen had already left. *They don't care about rush hour traffic,* I thought. *Probably in a bar, anyhow.*

I removed the plastic card clipped to my belt, then slid it through the slot along the top of the reader attached to the wall, to the right of the door. In the reader's upper right corner, small round red turned small round green as the door's lock disengaged with a metallic *click!* I grabbed the door's handle, yanked down and out, then let Sandy and myself in.

We entered a long, wide, dusty chamber. The *clunk!* of the door shutting behind us echoed against walls and windows literally a city block away. I felt the hollowness immediately, for it was so unlike the dense, sound absorbing congestion in which we worked. *What a difference a few desks and chairs make,* I thought, followed by: *I've got an entire floor in a Boston high-rise ALL to myself!*

Before Sandy and me, a layer of white spread across the broad, deep expanse almost completely hiding what appeared to be a brownish rug beneath. Pieces of copper wire sheathed in colored rubber lay sporadically upon the white along with screws, nails, candy wrappers, soda cans, putty knives, fractured plaster and a myriad of other debris. Similarly, a few gray aluminum filing cabinets stood here and there, temporarily placed, waiting for a home.

Without furnishings between them, the four walls enclosing the floor appeared even longer than they did when occupied—which was very long indeed. Penetrating the outer walls, large rectangular windows sucked in the pretty city from the direction each faced. Along the West side, I found myself practically kissing the Hancock and Prudential towers. To the North, overlooking the harbor, I witnessed jumbo jets take off from, and land at, Logan Airport. To the East, I could see human dots bustle about Quincy Market and Faneuil Hall. And to the South, I tracked lines of cars, linked by lights along the expressway, crawling like fluorescent ants toward Ho Chi Minh, Fred Flintstone, and whomever else resides in the rainbow colors streaking the Dorchester gas tank.

I felt kind of strange enjoying these views of the city in which I worked, from the building in which I worked, and told Sandy so.

"Why is that?" she asked.

We were both still watching the long, serpentine lines of break-light-red undulating to the South. At the same time, I could feel myself sinking deeper into contemplative tranquility as the sun sank deeper below the horizon to my right. This cerebral descent impacted all parts of me. My breathing slowed to a relaxing rhythm. My hands warmed; my fingertips tingled; my stomach lightened. Even my voice softened to a more tender tone.

"I think it's because I've never taken the opportunity before."

"What do you mean?"

Now *her* voice had changed; obviously, in conjunction with mine. Not only had her tone softened, but her words—like linguistic salves, like verbal balms—now floated with the utmost of femininity. Naked nurses couldn't have soothed me as much.

"Just that. I've probably looked out these windows, and down at this city, a thousand times, maybe ten thousand. Y'know, just walking around and taking a glance below. But I've never really *looked* at the city. I've never really studied the city, appreciated all that it has. This is the first time."

The voice didn't change again, but the countenance darkened—intellectual interest drawing emotion, hormones, and blood—followed by, "And what do you see?" So soft, so gentle, the question was a butterfly fluttering off her tongue.

"I see buildings. I see architecture. I see engineering marvels. But even more interesting, I see people—lives—hundreds of hustling points in a picture, yet, within each, an entire existence unto itself; lives full of the same loves, desires, hurts, and fears that comprise my own, yet lives that I will never get to know. There are just *so* many people, *so* many people—so many thinking, breathing, laughing, feeling, loving, bleeding people."

The countenance didn't change, remained dark; but the jaw dropped lower, her mouth now a letter O with pointed corners, the shape of hard candy twisted in cellophane.

"Don't you see what I mean? Doesn't it confound you to know that billions of other minds, just like yours, exist on this planet; and that they think and dream, just like yours, but with thoughts and visions you'll never know or see? Like right now, there's a guy walking on the street down there." Extending my right arm, I pointed with my index finger. "The one with the tan trenchcoat."

"I see him."

"Right now, that guy's probably thinking about what he's going to do tonight, or what he did during the day; or, maybe, if the persistent pain in his side is cancer, or some other disease; or maybe, even, if God exists. You don't know. You'll never know. But, then, right now, at the same time, leaning out of some third floor apartment in Bogotá, Colombia, some woman is thinking too. She's scanning the city, maybe wondering what kind of bird she hears singing, or if her daughter will ever find a good man, or what causes shooting stars like the one she witnessed the night before, when leaning out of the same window to shake dust from her mop. Every time I acknowledge how extensive, how pervasive the masses truly are, how populated this planet really is, I realize how miniscule my percentage of experience is to the whole and, as a result, how little I must see and how little I must know."

Silence ensued for a moment, followed by: "Is that necessarily true?" For it was cloaked in sincerity, the question enhanced my serenity.

"Yeah, I think so. I mean, if this planet has twelve billion eyes and twelve billion ears scoping out things, what percentage of those things do my two perceive? It's gotta be tiny. I can't see and hear everything. And don't tell me that we all get to pretty much hear and see the same things."

"No, I don't think that. But what makes you think of these things in the first place?"

"What do you mean?"

"These thoughts, these feelings—they're pretty deep and rare, far from the superficial 'here and now' plane on which most people function. What makes you think of them?"

"I don't know. I just do. Don't you?"

"I do, though not to the extent you do. But most people don't."

"Does it bother you, my thinking like this?"

Slight hesitation followed, as well a deeper rush of red to the already sanguine cheeks, and a partial lowering of the head.

"No, in fact, I find it—I find it rather—rather attractive." Now, the blood poured while the head bent further. In addition, the head tilted—almost away from me—almost to avoid me—to avoid my assessment—to avoid my reaction.

"What do you mean?" I said it softly, slowly, as if to preserve the sound of each word.

"I mean it's—it's nice to meet someone who thinks beyond the, y'know, ordinary realm of things—who sees more than just what is in front of him."

I studied Sandy's sharp profile; her lean, pronounced features; her cute, ruddy cheeks. Then my eyes dropped to her perky breasts; to her curvy, skirted hips; to her silky, slender, sinewy legs. Despite my guilt, I could not stop. I was enjoying her too much. And while I looked at Sandy long and freely, she would not look at me; she could not look at me; yet, I could tell that she wanted to desperately. For now, though, it seemed that she would just enjoy being ogled, that her barely suppressed grin practically blurted how much she liked it, that my appreciation of her physical being was more than merely welcome.

But beyond all that, I could tell that Sandy was anxious for something. Her left foot tapped beyond her awareness. Her delicate fingers dug into pockets devoid of objects. Her eyelids flapped frequently. Her rapid breathing sounded shallow. And her shoulders shrugged, as if cold, in a room heated far more than a healthy human required.

"Do you mean, Sandy," I continued with deliberate, prosecuting-attorney articulation, "that you appreciate a guy who thinks about the world around him?" She reacted with only a nod, and not much of one at that, but took a small step toward me.

"Do you mean, Sandy, that you appreciate a guy who can look past the ambience of stuffed cubicles, grinding hard drives, flashing monitors, buzzing printers, looming dead lines, and neurotic managers who can practically smell workers not working?"

This time, the nod came with a smile and another small step. Her pupils rotated toward my feet. The top of her head wavered slightly below my chin. Grabbing her shoulders firmly, gently pulling, I could feel her breasts press against my ribcage. I kept my head straight, gazed down at the crown of her skull, and noticed that her dark vanilla mane grew clockwise from her scalp. I also noticed that its color remained constant at any length. *No dying for this kid; she's a natural.*

I pushed my nose through her soft, silky hair, inhaling her clean, wholesome beauty. I immediately detected that she used a coconut scented shampoo and thought how incongruous a tropical fruit seemed to jive with her Vermont freshness. I squeezed her firm, tubular arms a bit harder and felt a small circle of momentary pressure on my left breast as she kissed me. I did not expect this, and the sudden manifestation of her desire sent hot blood to my groin and cold truth to my brain. While my penis told me I was horny, my brain told me I was about to hurt Meesha and fuck up my life.

I lifted my hands to Sandy's neck and lowered my mouth to her right ear. While I spoke, I could smell the sweet but subtle perfume with which she had dabbed herself that morning.

"Sandy, you're a very attractive woman, and you've been very kind to me. I appreciate that—very much. But—but I'm a married man. And my wife and I, well, we're going through a tough time right now. I don't know what's gonna happen. I just gotta wait. See how the pieces fall. Let things sort out a bit. Ya understand?"

My hands fell back to Sandy's shoulders, gently pushed, then held her again at arm's length. She nodded while pursing her lips, pressing their inner tissue together and outwards, making them fuller. Her Van Gogh blues no longer appeared electric, but rather sultry, big, and heavy, as they gazed up at me like those of a puppy wishing to be petted. All I could think to do was return her gaze with kindness and warmth.

When I picked Meesha up, she was just as irritable as she had been that morning. Driving home, I tried hard to soothe her, to somehow make her feel better, to snap her out of her funk—but I failed. She refused to give, to bend even a little. It was like she *wanted* to stay depressed, to stay hunkered down and sour. I didn't get it. She was my wife, but I didn't know her—didn't know her now, hadn't known her for a while. She seemed stuck—rigid—immobile—not willing, or not wanting, to rise out of the muck. It didn't make sense. Nothing made sense. I felt frustrated as Hell, like putting my fist through the windshield. My world was unraveling, my marriage the unbound fabric at the core, and I just didn't get it, just didn't know what to do. And to make things worse, a cute little blonde with a constellation of freckles across her nose kept slipping into my head.

Stopped at a red light, thinking it was excessively long, I glanced over at Meesha. She sat sullen, gazing out the passenger door window past the Bronco's right fender, where water was collecting within a recession in the tar. Rain drops were poking momentary pockets in the puddle the way arguments had been poking holes in our relationship.

The light turned. I punched the pedal. Four tires grabbed wet tar. The Bronco burst forward. When I realized that I had hit the gas faster than usual, I thought: *you can't DRIVE yourself out of marital problems, you know!* Meesha followed: "Are we racing somebody?" Her words were sandpaper against an emotional boil, but I did not respond in kind. Instead, I reached for the stereo, finger-punched in an FM rock station, then raised the volume to a level that audibly displaced her. Auditory solitude enabled neither of us to speak for about a minute. Then I just as abruptly flipped the radio off. I could feel myself swiftly losing control, my vocal governor dissolving, my face filling with heat. I had had it—couldn't take it anymore—enough was enough. Steam hissed through my brain's synapses. The taste of bile burned my throat. My tongue felt more like fire than flesh.

"Meesha," I said, pausing to gain command over my raging mind, strained voice, and accelerated breath, "I never thought I'd ever feel this way. But I'm really starting to resent you. Maybe even despise you."

I kept my eyes on the road, but could feel the intensity of her incredulous stare drilling into the right side of my skull. Something told me her jaw was hanging also, her mouth partially open. I didn't care. My heart was empty, my compassion gauge on LOW, my soul temporarily misplaced. I continued, my tone like sharp steel scraping ice.

"I don't know what's goin' on with you, but you've been misery to live with. I'm not sure I even want it anymore. I used to think you were the most beautiful thing on this planet; but, lately, I sometimes find you downright ugly. Sometimes, I actually find myself hating you. If there's one thing I'm happy about, it's that we don't have kids. I'm just glad nobody else is screwed up from this relationship. I'm not even sure I'd *want* you to have my kids. I'm sick of you. I'm sick of your attitude. I'm sick of living like this. It really, truly sucks."

I knew I had gone too far before I even finished. I could feel it in my gut, but I was out of control. I couldn't stop. About the same time that I felt my conscience cringe is when Meesha started crying. She wept quietly the rest of the way home. When she stopped, I do not know.

Dinner was a bowl of cereal; dinner conversation, something we did in the past: I ate alone, yearning for bed. When finished, I brushed my teeth, but did not floss or wash up as usual. That would require too much time and effort. I was too depressed. All I wanted was to slip beneath the sheet and down comforter.

I usually read myself sleepy. This night, though, I chose to think before I slumbered. I felt the need to sort things out.

I did not think long. In fact, I don't remember thinking much at all. I must have fallen asleep almost immediately, because what

I remember most is suddenly waking when Meesha came to bed. We usually turn in at the same time, but on the infrequent occasions when we don't—such as when Meesha has to prepare for a meeting early the following morning—she doesn't wake me. She enters the bed quietly. However, on this night, such treatment I did not get.

I lifted my head a couple of inches off my pillow and gazed blurrily through darkness in Meesha's direction. Below half drawn lids, my eyes tried to focus the white cottoned silhouette into a clear outline; but they failed. Nonetheless, I, of course, knew it was Meesha and, following the nocturnal routine of my married years, reached my right arm across the bed and pulled her toward me. I did so out of sleepy forgetfulness and habit, the latter embedded in my long term memory, which remained unimpacted by the recent turbulence in my marriage. It seemed that my subconscious lived a different life, in a different world, than my conscious, daytime mind. Had I been fully awake, I would have been surprised when she did so, but it wasn't until I was downstairs with a clear head, wide eyes, and a pounding pulse that I realized how willingly Meesha had slid toward me. She moved as if there hadn't been any friction between us. What pulled me downstairs, though, was what I did next.

Facing me, Meesha had tucked her head beneath my chin and pressed her body against mine. Then she had lowered her chin against her chest, so that she could sleep-cuddle while breathing comfortably. My chin rested on her head, the silky ends of her hair tickling my neck. I slowly scratched the soft, pliable muscle running along each side of her spine. Then I decided that I would rather hold Meesha, while I slept, with her back against my chest, each of us facing the same way. I had always found this position—the back of Meesha's head tucked beneath my neck, her upper body arched in the same pattern as mine—more comfortable for sleeping. So, I dropped my right hand lower, down Meesha's back, and grabbed the fleshiness of her upper right arm. Then I pulled Meesha's arm upwards, spinning her a hundred and eighty degrees. It took Meesha a fraction of a second to realize what I was doing, but once she did, she moved along with my motion, making the spin almost effortless for me. I moved my hand to Meesha's stomach, pulled her tight against my body, then moved my hand up to her neck, where I pulled her against my body again. I scratched her head and stroked her right cheek and nose bridge until sleep dragged me unconsciously back into its warm, safe cocoon.

The back of her hand and squeal in her voice are what woke me. Incandescent glare pierced my pupils a moment later. I rose quickly upon my left elbow and threw my right hand in front of my face, just in case she swung again.

"What the hell are you doin'?" I yelled, trying to bring her into focus through the blur of my eyes acclimating, "Whadja smack me for!"

"What's on your *hand*?" she screamed, her pitch on the edge of hysteria, her emerging countenance rippled with anger and fear.

"*What?*" I looked down at my right hand.

"What's on your *fucking hand*! What the hell do I *smell*!"

A siren screamed in my skull: *Meesha just swore.* I had never heard my wife use such language before. Raising my hand to my nose, my mind skipped back to dinner. *I had cereal—Raisin Bran. I put sugar on top. Did I dip my hand in the bowl? Did I get milk and sugar on my hand? Does milk and sugar smell?* I didn't think so. *Or is it toothpaste? Does she smell toothpaste? Or underarm deodorant?*

I inhaled gently, index finger to nostrils. Faintly sweet, but detectable. Mind blank for a moment, then I remembered. *Sandy. Shit! Sandy's perfume. When I held her neck. Fuck! How am I gonna explain this?*

"Huh? What the *fuck* do I smell!"

"Perfume." I looked straight into Meesha's eyes as I said it. I had no choice. I couldn't look away. That would convey guilt. Besides, there was no other answer.

"*Perfume*? *Who's* perfume! *Sandy*, I suppose?"

Still looking into her eyes, wishing I had never talked about people at work, trying to keep my voice even keeled: "Yes, it was Sandy."

"And *how*, may I ask, did you get this *slut's* perfume on your *hand*!" Her tone no longer just bordered on hysteria, but rode her emotions like a surfboard. I sensed imminent tears. I could also feel my throat tightening. Staying even-keeled was going to be difficult. I licked my lips, then said: "She's—not—a slut," punctuating the consonants, the pauses in between slightly extended.

"Oh! Then what *is* she! Your *girl friend*! Your *mistress*! Is that what this is, you fucking bastard!" Her right fist flew, followed by the tears. I caught the right with my free hand, but she followed maniacally with her left, punching and slapping my flesh with full-throttled rage. She held nothing back. My eyes had fully adjusted now, and I could see the venom in hers magnified by the tears. I sat up on the bed to free my hands and tried to grab her wrists, but she scratched me deeply before I could.

"Stop it, Meesha!" I yelled, "Stop it!"

When I finally clasped both my hands around her wrists, she screamed, "You cheating *bastard*! You cheating *BAStard*!" then sunk her teeth into my forearms, biting with fury. Her teeth hurt, tearing away skin, so I swung her entire body from side to side by her wrists, yelling "Stop it!", trying to break her bite, but not cause her any physical harm. I could feel that fine line between physically controlling her and physically hurting her, and didn't want to cross it. But as soon as her teeth released my forearm, they clenched onto my upper arm, then my shoulder, then my biceps, then the fleshiness of my right pectoral. I finally got her pinned to the bed, on her back, holding her down by her wrists. She tried to kick me every which way she could, but I kept my body out of range. I noticed my chest and right biceps were punctured and oozing thin red streams. Meesha continued trying to kick me and started calling me a "scumbag!" in addition to a "cheating bastard!" She thrashed, screamed and cried as my tolerance waned. And though I knew it would be impossible for her, in her current emotional state, to comprehend and accept what had happened between Sandy and me earlier in the evening, I knew I had to try. I had to explain the source of the perfume. There was no other way out. *God, why didn't I WASH MY HANDS! Fuck!*

"Meesha!" I yelled, grasping her wrists tightly. This made her squirm, thrash, yell, and gnash further. I didn't know what to do, but I had to do something. I needed her attention, but in a calmer state. I needed to tranquilize her somehow. Pain was the only mechanism, by which I could reach this end, that my mind could think of at the moment. Thus, I dug my thumbs into Meesha's inner wrists. She screamed even louder, so I dug even deeper and told her I wouldn't stop until she quieted down. She finally did, after a few moments, so that I could simply hold her down by her wrists. Her crying abated to a whimper and I said, "Listen, Meesh, you're out of your mind. You're out of control. You're also out of line. You've wounded me. I'm bleeding."

"Oh?" she screamed, "you don't think *you've* wounded *me* with your *slut*? What did you do with her, Luke? Did you *fuck* her! Did you take her to a hotel for *lunch*! Huh, Luke, you *stinking bastard*!" Then she started thrashing and kicking and trying to bite me again, so I dug my thumbs into her wrists once more. She screamed when I pressed hard.

"Stop yelling and moving!" I said. She did. For several moments, silence ruled. I felt her limbs gradually slacken, then I watched her anger fade. Tears continued down her temples. She bared beautiful white teeth by pulling back lips that trembled. I felt sorry for her, pity for her, anger for her. But I could not tell if I felt anything else for her. *I'll deal with that later*, I told myself.

"Are you in love with this woman, Luke?" It wasn't a slap, but a plea. I should have expected it—a cannon shot from hidden headlands—but I didn't. Neither did I answer. In truth, I did not know; not if I did, not if I didn't. It suddenly occurred to me that, at this moment, I did not know much, if anything. Everything inside me felt numb, while everything outside me seemed in transition. Everything important in my life was either dying or flipping out. Nothing seemed real anymore. I couldn't nail anything down, I couldn't be definite, so I couldn't answer. I just stared back.

"You are! Aren't you, Luke!" Meesha raised her head, pushed herself backwards on the bed, onto her elbows. "That's it! Isn't it, Luke! You're in love with another woman! That's the issue here—with us—isn't it!"

"I didn't say that, Meesha." She ignored me.

"I can't believe I've played the fool! Right in front of my eyes, it happened right in front of my eyes! How long, Luke! How long's this been going on!"

"How long's *what* been goin' on?" I was getting nowhere, and I was getting weary. My words came out edged with irritation.

Meesha burst insanely, grabbing both sides of her head above her ears as if her rage could dismantle the sections of her skull. "This *affair*, you bastard! How long has this fucking *affair* been going *on*! Will you please fucking *tell* me? I can't *take* it anymore! Will you please *tell* me, you *bastard*! I can't *take* it! Telllll meeeeeee!"

She didn't cry—she trembled while exuding fluid from every orifice North of her neck. It was torture to watch, but I didn't know what to say. Her hands shook. Her lips quivered. My gut kept telling me: *Just tell her the truth. Whatever she asks, just be honest. You'll be better off in the end. So will she.* What shit that was.

"Meesha, I am not having an affair, nor have I been."

"Then—then how—how did you get perfume on your hands! You can't get perfume on your hands unless you touch a woman!"

I sighed deeply. There was no easy way out of this. "Meesha, I did touch a woman. I put my hands on Sandy's neck."

"What—what the hell are you doing touching this woman's *neck!*"

The tightness in my chest made it difficult to talk. I coughed. "Meesha, this woman's been very kind to me since Hunter's death, and we had a discussion about things today—the way things are going in my life. As we were talking, there came a point where she wanted to hug me. So I hugged her. It was then, I assume, that I got her perfume on my hand."

"You hugged some woman in the middle of your *office!*" Anger had crept back into her tone with a strain of contempt.

I caught myself licking my lips. I just knew this wasn't going to be easy. "No. We had gone down to an empty floor—a floor where they were doing construction, putting up offices and stuff. No one was around."

"Luke, you *purposely* went down to some *vacant* floor to be with this slut you hugged? Is *that* what you're telling me!"

"Meesh, it's not what you think. Nothin'—nothin' happened. Nothing's ever happened. You're jumping to conclusions."

"Bullshit! You've obviously had discussions with this woman—discussions about our lives."

"Ah, yes," I said, nodding my head slightly left, then slightly right, "yes I have. Sometimes—sometimes we talk."

"Damn you, Luke! What does this bitch know about me!"

It was at this point that I felt myself starting to slide. It was a reaction; it wasn't deliberate. I could just tell that Meesha wasn't emotionally capable at this moment of seeing the situation in its true light, that she would have to make more out of it than reality presented. She had her hooks into me, and I could feel their permanence regardless of what I said. I could sense the incoming, her verbal shells, our impending clash, and the imminent doom.

As a result, I found myself becoming defensive, more irritable, actually angry. I had tried to share the truth with Meesha and settle the issue, strive for peace, move on with our lives, but she would have none of it. She was really starting to get to me.

"She doesn't know anything about you, Meesh, other than you're my wife."

"Then what do you talk to her about! What's so important that you have to have a confidant at work!"

I sighed again. "Nothing, Meesha; nothing's that important. I'll stop talking to her. Okay?"

"No, Luke, that's not the answer. The question is whether you want another woman. You've been indulging in personal discussions with this *Sandy* at work, while pretty much ignoring me at home. Would you rather have her than me, Luke? Huh, Luke? Would you rather have her than me?"

"Sometimes I would." My own words stunned me as they left my mouth. I felt as though I had gone too far, as if I had run off a cliff. Meesha erupted, face in waves, tears like rain. But I wasn't done. This was a discharge, cathartic, an expectoration of muck, an orgasm of shit, and I couldn't just stop in the middle. I had to finish. It had been in me too long.

"Yeah, Meesh, to tell you the truth, sometimes I would. Sometimes, I get damn sick of your nastiness. I'm tired of living with such a bitch. I can't remember the last time you said something nice, or smiled, or were simply content to be alive. Everyday around here is torture. It's like living in fucking Hell—like it was living with my parents. Just constant, fucking bickering. So, yeah, sometimes I would rather be with someone else. Sometimes I would rather be with Sandy. Sometimes I do prefer to be with Sandy. She makes me feel good and warm. She doesn't hurt me like you. Sometimes, I do wonder what it would be like to make love to her, to have her cuddle against my naked body, to have her wake up in my arms, to share my life with her. Yeah, Meesha, I have to tell you the truth: sometimes I do."

Then I turned. I shut my light off and dropped my head. I was tense, but the whole day had been so emotional that I felt completely drained. Falling asleep, I knew, would not be a problem, despite my emotions. Meesha still wept beside me, her light still on, but I had nothing left to say. My mind, at this point, was blank. *If I have anything more to add*, I thought, *I'll tell her in the morning.* There was no doubt in my mind that we would discuss the issue again. It had to be resolved. Many things had to be resolved. Otherwise, our marriage wouldn't last. But, right now, I'd had enough.

It was the chill of the night that woke me up. October can summons cold weather to New England. The rain I had watched popping puddles earlier in Boston, while waiting at a traffic light, had turned to sleet during our drive home. And now, barely covered at two in the morning, I found myself goosebumped from head to heel while ice *pinged* the window panes around the room. More importantly, though, I also found my wife missing from our bed.

I shot my eyes toward the bathroom, a master bath enterable only through our bedroom. But the door was open and no light was on. *What the hell?* I ran my hand over the spot in the bed where Meesha always lay. The sheet felt as cold as the other side of my pillow whenever I flipped to it during the night. *She's been gone a while*, murmured my mind.

I got up, wrapped a thick bathrobe around me and pulled ankle covering, booty slippers onto my feet. Then, rubbing crusty sleep-gook from my eyes, I shuffled across the bedroom floor. My slipper's leather bottoms *swooshed* with each stride along the varnished hardwood. My body walked, but my mind ran. *This is unlike Meesha*, I thought. *She never leaves bed during the night, except to use the bathroom. Is she sick? Is she still really upset by our argument and wanted to be alone? Maybe she's still crying. Or maybe she's just hungry. Maybe I'll find her in the kitchen chomping on a banana, or licking spoonfuls of Haagen Daz rum raisin.*

I descended the stairs, holding onto the banister with my right hand. Still groggy, I was afraid of slipping or tripping.

When I reached the bottom, I saw no lights on in the kitchen at the end of the hall. *Is she eating in the dark? Maybe—if she doesn't want me to know she's up. But that would be weird. She coulda just turned on the tiny counter ones. They don't give much light—very little, in fact—would never've caught my attention had I woken for a second while she was gone. But, then again, neither would the ceiling ones. Kitchen's a floor below the bedroom and on the other side of the house. There's no way I would have detected that she was up simply by the lights being on. So what's going on?*

I moved into the kitchen, closed my eyes, and flipped the wall switch. The back of my eyelids, at first black, flashed bright orange as the chandelier above burst with life. I opened my eyes slowly toward a spot below the circular array of soft yellow points. As subdued as it was, the soft yellow still stung my night adjusted pupils. I closed my lids several times in quick succession as my eyes swept the kitchen. I found nothing.

I shuffled into the den and flicked on the lights, my eyes now better adjusted. But again: nothing. Then I checked the living room—the dining room—the pantry. But again and again and again: nothing. *What the fuck?* howled my innards, a bit shrilly with alarm.

I opened the door to the garage. The Bronco sat there, second bay over, exactly where I had parked it, its vibrant red a dour crimson in the dark. My lips moved, but the words resounded only in my head: *C'mon Luke, stop freaking! You woulda heard her. She never would've gotten out of the driveway without waking you up. The gravel's too loud.*

*Yeah, so, then what's up? Where is she? Humans don't just vaporize.*

Abruptly, another possibility planted roots in my increasingly fertile fear: *maybe she just WALKED out. Left me. For the night—or maybe PERMANENTLY.*

*But where would she go at this hour? A hotel? She woulda had to have taken the car.*

*Not if she took a cab.*

*I woulda heard it on the gravel—just like I woulda heard our car.*

*Well, maybe she's just sleepwalking.*

*Maybe—but c'mon Luke! Meesha's never done that. Why would she do it now?*

I couldn't figure it out. I had checked the whole house, but she was nowhere to be found. *Maybe she's just outside in the yard.*

*But it's freezing out there! What would she be doing?*

*I don't know, but she could be there. She's certainly not here. And like I said: "Humans don't just vaporize."*

Then I remembered: *the cellar.* I had completely forgotten about the cellar.

*But Meesha hates the cellar. She never wants to go down there. She's always complaining about the spiders.*

*True, but you never know. You still have to check it out. You'd hate to call the police and have them just find her on the cellar stairs drinking a cup of tea. What an asshole you'd look like. Think about it.*

So I shuffled toward the cellar door.

On several occasions in the past, I'd realized that I had left the cellar lights on earlier in the day by passing the cellar door at night and finding an illuminated sheet shooting below it, across the hallway. However, no light currently emanated from this crack between the door and the floor, indicating that none were on behind it. Regardless, I decided to check things out, just to be sure.

I opened the door, threw on the lights, descended the stairs and found, across the cellar slumped on dusty concrete, the most horrible sight a married man can ever find.

She still wore her cotton nightgown. With the temperature so low and Meesha hating the cold, I knew she must have intended to take little time. Petrified, I ran toward her yelling, "Meesha! Meesha!"

Her undulated body lay on its right side, an inverted S curled along the concrete, her head upon her right arm. Her eyes were closed, the lids peacefully tight. She wore an expression of bliss, which my thundering mind found so incongruous with the streams of red oozing from her neck. There were many gashes and I was only looking at her left side. *How many more are there!*

Falling to my knees, I gently lifted, then turned, Meesha's head. Her right side was slashed even more, even deeper. I lowered my face to Meesha's mouth and held it there for a few seconds. When positive that faint puffs were warming my cold cheek, I grabbed Meesha's right wrist and shook the paper cutter from her hand. She did not wake and, therefore, did not resist.

Picking up the sticky, coagulated-blood-stained, aluminum handle, I flicked the razor blade back in with my thumb. Then, tossing the fucking thing over my shoulder without concern for where the fucking thing landed, I jumped up and ripped a roll of paper towels from a dispenser nailed to a beam in the ceiling. I knew what I had to do. I knew what I had to use. And the paper towels were the best thing I could find at the moment—this being a time when every moment mattered. The blood didn't just trickle from each side of Meesha's neck: it gushed with each pump of her pulse, each contraction of her heavy heart, as if the sanguineous spurts were batches of shrill incoherence blurting from the oscillating mouth of an hysterical rape victim. The puddle beneath her right arm, upon which her head lay, was spreading rapidly. In addition, I thought: *This is cement, which is very porous. A lot of her blood has already sunk into the floor. She's lost even more than I'm seeing here.*

I had to work fast. I had to move fast. I had to think fast. I wrapped Meesha's neck so thickly in paper towels that she looked as if she were wearing a long, white scarf twirled around her multiple times. Then I pulled a brown electrical extension cord down from one of many nails in a ceiling beam behind me. The cord provided me with a means of gently tightening, therefore applying pressure to, the makeshift bandage.

The closest phone was upstairs in the kitchen. I didn't know how much time I had before Meesha would bleed to death, but I knew it wasn't much. So I ran as fast as I could, pounding the wooden planks up my cellar stairs. Reaching the phone, I yanked it off its vertical, wall cradle and lost my grip. The phone flew from my hands, crashed into cabinets behind me, then hit the floor. Picking the phone back up, I thought, *She's gonna need blood, but I don't even know her fuck'n type. Is that something a husband should know? When would I have asked her that? I don't even know my own.*

I punched 9-1-1 into the glowing numeric display with my mind still racing: *How am I gonna find out her blood type!*

A guy picked up on the other end: "Tranquil Valley 9-1-1. This call is being recorded. What's your emergency?"

I had never called 9-1-1 before. For a nanosecond, I contemplated what to say. What came out was: "My wife is bleeding badly! She tried to kill herself! I live at…."

I slammed the phone back onto its cradle and rushed down cellar. A police cruiser and an ambulance arrived minutes later. One cop, and three EMTs with a stretcher, tore into my house through the front door. I had told the emergency line dispatcher that I would be in the cellar. The cop and EMTs found me there pressing white, dish towels against Meesha's neck. I'd grabbed the towels from a kitchen drawer upon hanging up the phone.

Meesha, still unconscious, now sat upright, her back against the cellar wall, her body an island in a pond of its own life sustaining fluid. Pads of paper towel, saturated with ink-like red, lay scattered around us. It wasn't until later that I learned she had gulped over two dozen milligrams of Clonazepam, a sedative her doctor had prescribed to treat her occasional anxiety. The drug itself would have kept her cold for over twenty-four hours, never mind the fact that she had lost a massive amount of blood. Each side of her neck bore parallel lines as numerous as the tracks in a train depot. The emergency line dispatcher had told me to sit her up against a wall, like I had. But it had been my idea to grab the dish towels—I had noticed a dirty one lying on the counter while I was barking into the phone. I figured the thicker, cotton fabric would impede the flow of blood better than paper.

The EMTs untied the brown extension cord, peeled off the dish towels, and wrapped Meesha in their own first aid stuff. Then they whisked her away on the stretcher as I, silent and numb, followed in my bathrobe and goofy slippers, watching the surreal event as if it were a scene from a horror flick I'd rented rather than an horrendous occurrence within my own life.

# Chapter 3

**M**eesha was in the emergency room for several hours, but in the hospital for two weeks. Not the same hospital, though; they moved her to one on the other side of town. This one contained a trauma ward for the suicidal, the severely distraught. Thick metal doors barricaded each room. Each exit, locked and alarmed, required anyone leaving the ward to call the enclosed nurse's station from a phone beside the double doors, to request that they be buzzed open. Prohibited on the ward was anything sharp, or long and ropy. This included such seemingly benign stuff as dental floss. Every five minutes, a member of the staff would circle the ward to make sure nobody had found some ingenious way to biologically check out.

Despite the fact that I was infinitely grateful for Meesha's survival and well being, I reacted negatively to the trauma ward and her mandatory stay on it. This was due, in part, to the ward's overly restrictive ambiance. I logically knew that each rule in effect existed for the benefit of the patients. However, I reacted to the rules as though they were punitive; and did so, I believe, for that was the aura with which they were enforced. I felt as though the hospital, which came to represent society in my eyes, was treating Meesha—and sometimes, by association, me—as a delinquent and I resented it.

When I visited Meesha for the first time, I analyzed the articles in her room. It became obvious to me that the measures the hospital took to prevent suicide were simply procedural: a meaningful step, but not effective. It seemed to me that there was no way they could stop somebody who really wanted to go. I didn't mention it to Meesha—obviously—but if a patient desperately wanted out, he could simply place his head in between the mattress and metal frame at the foot of his bed, push his feet up into the air, then let them drop sideways. His body would fall, but his head would catch, securely lodged between the mattress and frame. *Guaranteed to break his neck*, I thought.

During Meesha's stay, I visited her everyday that her primary psychiatrist would allow me. Sometimes, this required that I leave my job during working hours, so that I could attend some session or another where Meesha and I would discuss things with one of the counselors. "Mental therapists," I called them. They all had master degrees, some a Ph.D., but to me they imparted nothing more than common sense: you get down, you gotta find some way to pull yourself back up. Yeah, well, no shit.

Meesha's psychiatrist was different. She was a real classy, no-nonsense woman with a keen, perceptive mind. This lady could pick off an unhealthy thought at fifty yards through a cloud of doubt. She was director of the trauma ward and didn't coddle the "residents"—which is what she required the patients to be called by both themselves and her staff (Forget "residents" or even "patients"; I called them "inmates".), to minimize the feeling that they were in a hospital—or harass them as some of the nurses sometimes did. She treated every "resident" with both respect and authoritarian firmness to effect a successful rehabilitation. This approach combined with the anti-depressants, sedatives, and mind-easing rest Meesha received helped her make substantial progress. She was only in the place for fourteen days; but from the difference in her demeanor, one might have thought she'd been hospitalized with therapy for fourteen weeks.

During my first visit to the ward, I felt very awkward. I tried to act as cool, calm, and normal as I could—but how cool, calm, and normal can a guy be when visiting his wife for the first time after she's attempted suicide because of him?: *not too,* I discovered. In truth, I felt very much like shit and sensed that everybody on the ward viewed me as such. I felt that in their eyes, I was the reason my sweet wife was hospitalized, and I reasoned that they all resented me for it. It could be that I was paranoid, imagining it all; but to me, that didn't matter: it was still the way I felt. *Whatever the case,* I eventually concluded, *I have to ignore my feelings.* The sides of *my* neck were not symmetrically laddered with the coagulated remnants of razor slices; *my* emotions were not suffering from acute desperation and trauma; *Meesha's* were. So as far as I was concerned, it was time to forget about me and concentrate on her, and I found this easy—actually, natural—to do. Despite all the rotten things I had felt about and said to her, the instant I had found Meesha on our cold cellar floor, all my ill feelings had dissipated. All of a sudden, little else mattered to me but her health, her welfare—her life. I *did* feel guilty about what I had put her through, but I immediately flagged that emotion as self-centered and tried to ignore it, the way I was trying to ignore how I perceived what other people were thinking about me. I felt it was not the time for me to be egocentric. It was time for me to concentrate on my wife and her rehabilitation.

Entering the trauma ward that first time—through the buzzer-controlled doors; past the locked, fully-enclosed, plastic-barricaded nurse's station; then down the long hall of glossy, antiseptic tiles—felt strange and ominous. When I found Meesha inclined on her bed wearing robe-like, tie-in-the-back, hospital garb, a jolt ripped through my entrails. I tried to remain stoical—

didn't want to let her see that I was shocked, needed to make her feel everything was okay—but I don't think I succeeded. She picked her head up, turned to the right; then, seeing my face, immediately glanced back down, emitting a feeble "hi" during her descent. I returned it, then slowly approached her bed. The nurse who had escorted me down the hall began walking back to her plastic barricaded fortress. I approached Meesha's bed wordlessly. As she lifted her head, my eyes took in the white bandages protecting stitched flesh up each side of her neck. She tried to smile, got as far as a grimace, then started to cry. In all my life, I cannot remember feeling someone else's pain as acutely as I felt Meesha's there and then. It pierced my insides like the prongs of a fork, virtually twirling my intestines as if they were sausage-sized strands of spaghetti. I bit my lower lip and frowned, remotely aware that my chin percolated with dimples of anguish.

"How are ya, hon?" My emission barely ranked higher than a whisper.

"I'm still alive," she whispered back, trying again to smile, the syllables of her response ascending with her eyebrows. The white dressing that patched her wounds wrinkled with every bend of her neck.

Our eyes danced, hesitant to meet. I wanted to reach my hand out and comb her hair through my fingers, but decided against it: *too early*. I chose, instead, to talk.

"So, how are they treatin' ya?" I glanced down at her wrist, around which a transparent blue band identified her with administrative data, then back up at her face. This time, my eyes held hers for a solid moment before hers broke for solitude. I saw the fragility of her psyche, beyond her tears, through the coffee brown lenses she briefly lent me. The glimpse clearly showed the work that lay ahead. My gut told me there was no better time to start than now.

"I've been thinking."

Head up, eyes toward me. "About what?"

"What happened."

Head down, eyes toward lap, silent for a moment—hesitant—diffident. "What thoughts—have you had?" Eyes and head remain down.

"That we let the thing most important to us slip away"—head abruptly up; eyes up and down, up and down—"and the result was disaster."

"What—what was that thing? What—did we let—slip away?" Opening up now, slowly, a fresh clam in steam, a day lily in morning sun.

"Our bond, hon. Our alliance. Our pod."

Eyes and head still up, eyebrows arched down, forehead creased.

I smiled, lips together, punctuating a brief exhale through my nose. "Yeah, our pod. You know, like two-peas-in- a…."

Now a tiny smile. Some teeth even. This told me something: any doubt I had about progression, about going forward, was erased, eradicated, yanked out by the roots. *It is time*, I thought, *for us to get to work, to get back to where we were. No, beyond where we were. A new relationship. Stronger, closer, tighter than before, as a result of our experience, due to how we have grown and will grow.*

Although most of the work would be accomplished between us, some of the progress Meesha and I made with our relationship occurred, or at least began, during sessions with counselors. First and foremost, we had to reestablish strong, clear, open lines of communication. This process started during my first visit to the ward and gathered momentum throughout Meesha's stay. The pinnacle of progress, I believe, was reached during a session we had with Meesha's psychiatrist. The reason for the progress was the depth of the subjects our discussion reached. We sat in a small office, just the three of us. Dr. Quint started the meeting.

"Luke, thank you for taking time away from work to meet with us. As you know, these sessions are key to Meesha's rehabilitation."

I nodded.

"I'd like to start by asking you what you believe may have been the catalyst, or root cause, for Meesha's drastic actions. It's important that we gain your perspective."

I nodded again. "Sure. Well, uh, I've actually thought about this quite a bit, as I'm sure you can imagine. I've been able to think of little else during the last week or so. And every time I drill down to what seems, to me, to be the specifics—the important details?"—Glancing at Doctor Quint, I inflected my tone as if saying: 'You know what I mean?' The doctor nodded.—"I keep coming up with the same answer, and that is this lack of communication we keep referring to; or, not necessarily lack of communication, or even simply ineffectual communication, but lack of useful communication. Y'know, people can communicate a lot but convey little, when honesty and integrity are lacking. And I think after Hunter's death, I somehow, for some reason, lost my ability or desire to divulge, to share my hurt with Meesha. Now, why that occurred, your guess is as good as mine, but I know that I shut down. Not intentionally, but I do remember doing it, sort of like just pulling a verbal hood over my head. Somewhere inside me, there seemed to be an answer, and I thought if I just stayed hunkered down long enough, the answer would come. But, of course, this action of mine excluded Meesha from my life and that's when she—she—reacted."

"'There seemed to be an answer,' you said. An answer to what?"

"The madness. The insanity of it all."

Dr. Quint nodded, her graying blonde bun pulled tightly from her scalp. There was much more going on behind the green eyes and dainty wire glasses than her appearance led one to think, but I knew better. I've met shrewd people before and this lady was damn shrewd. She seemed to have answers before the questions were even asked. So I really wasn't surprised when she bluntly brought up Sandy.

"Now, Luke, you say that you felt you couldn't open up to Meesha while you were grieving over your brother's death. But you were able, according to your own admission, to open up to others; specifically, this Sandy. Why do you suppose that is?"

I felt a tug of anger. I could tell that the doctor, not unlike a lawyer, was using interrogation techniques to drill into my psyche. Were it a different occasion, I might have expressed irritation at such a subtle attempt to manipulate me. But I knew where she was headed and why, as well as how the discussion could help Meesha and our relationship. Thus, I responded without complaint.

"I'm not really sure, Doc. I haven't thought that much about *my* thinking as I have about Meesha's during the last few days. But my gut tells me it has something to do with rejection, pain, and some kind of reciprocal effect."

"What do you mean?"

I looked over at Meesha, who sat to my left, her right hand nervously tugging at the bandage down that side of her neck. She didn't let our eyes meet, choosing instead to study her lap. I wondered what was going through her mind, but the possibilities were endless. However, I knew it invoked pain. Her expression told me so. It hurt me just to look at her.

"Well, I'm no trained analyst, so I might not use the right words. Please bear with me."

Dr. Quint nodded.

"It just seems to me that people—individuals—are tremendously complex. They—we—have so many layers, or dimensions, to our personalities. And it takes time to see, experience, and understand all these layers. For most people we know, we only get to see the most superficial layers, the top ones, which often aren't even real; just facades, so to speak; roles people play in the world. But for those whom we're close to, we get to peel down further; y'know, like an onion; and so ya know those people better. The problem comes when there is conflict, or a deficiency, between the depth to which life's circumstances take a relationship and the depth to which that relationship has matured."

"Okay, Luke, hold on a second," Dr. Quint said, "I need to break in here. What you're saying is interesting. You've obviously thought about this issue quite a bit. But if we're going to crack this nut, we need you to bring it closer to home. We need you to talk from your heart. You're giving us theoretical reasons for what occurred. I need to know the personal, emotional reasons why things happened. Talk about yourself, Luke. Try to recall what you were feeling. Do you understand what I mean?"

"Yeah, I think so. Just stop me again if I go off."

The doctor nodded. She seemed no longer to be conducting a meeting but, rather, an interview. For a moment, I felt as if she had forgotten Meesha was also in the room, though I knew she hadn't. Dr. Quint was too good, too conscientious, too conscious of her objective. But for that moment, I did feel that she was honing in on me and, since my objective was to help Meesha and our marriage, I gave her all I could.

"Well, I see Meesha and I—our marriage—as an entity that has evolved over time. It's grown, *we've* grown, adapted, in response to the things we've experienced: adversity, success; y'know, typical life events."

Dr. Quint nodded. I glanced at Meesha. She dropped her head, focusing again on her lap.

"The longer we've been together—that is, the more we've evolved as a couple—the better we've been able to handle life's curveballs. And although I think we have grown a lot, we could only grow so much during the time we've had. Like

I said, Meesha and I—*any* couple—is an entity, governed by its own life cycle, which is a reflection of its two members. Thus, every couple matures at its own rate. Unfortunately, what I think happened to Meesha and me is that we hadn't matured enough in our relationship to handle the adversity that was thrown our way. We had a pretty strong bond; had peeled away many layers of the onion over the years; had gotten to know, as well as how to handle, each other's strengths and weaknesses; but not enough to handle Hunter's death and our subsequent reactions to it. I think this situation brought out things in the both of us that we hadn't dealt with before, and it was reciprocal: I reacted, and she responded to my reaction, then I responded to hers, and so on…. And since this all occurred in a sequence, seemingly at once, a domino effect without pause, it was too much for us to handle. Had it happened ten years from now, when we knew each other better, had gone through further trials, maybe it wouldn't have invoked such disastrous results. But it happened now, and we got what we got."

I inhaled deeply through my nose while Dr. Quint sat patiently, motionless, then I continued: "Your question was 'Why could I talk to Sandy and not my wife?', and I think the answer to that lies imbedded within my previous response. I think that, in time, I would have wanted to talk to Meesha. I *know* I would have wanted to; I would have *needed* to. She's my wife, my kindred spirit. But, at first, right after Hunter died, I couldn't. I was stunned, vocally paralyzed. I couldn't say anything. There was nothing *to* say. And Meesha reacted to this, attacking me for withdrawing, which in turn prompted me to turn on her instead of opening up."

"So Luke," Dr. Quint interjected, "correct me if I'm wrong, but what I think I hear you saying is that Meesha hurt you when you withdrew, by 'attacking you' as you've put it. Then, in turn, you attacked her. In short, she hurt you, so you hurt her back, also by attacking. Is that right?"

"Unfortunately, juvenile as it may sound: yes. And that is where our actions reciprocated, the domino effect. I was in pain, and when the desire to talk came, I turned to someone who seemed interested in listening. Someone, I guess, who offered me warmth and comfort, a port during the storm."

"And someone, is it possible," Dr. Quint added, "that you found physically attractive?"

This one hurt—came from underneath—yanked my anger loose again. But I had to stay calm, had to answer, had to be truthful. "Yes, that is possible."

Dr. Quint nodded her head several times in contemplation, then said, "So, Luke, where do you think we should go from here? What's your assessment of the situation?"

I hesitated. I knew conceptually what I wanted to say, but I wasn't sure how to say it. I prayed silently that my words would not come out wrong. "As I mentioned, when I was down and needed someone, I didn't turn to Meesha. That was a mistake. I know. But it's what happened. It's what I did. I can't turn back the clock. What I *can* do, and what I think our *objective* should be, is to fix things; to mend this marriage, the bond between Meesha and me; to make it stronger, so strong that nothing can ever break it again; and to make use of this experience, so that we can handle whatever fate throws our way in the future."

To my left, I saw Meesha nodding, and this sent a warm current through me, along the same visceral path that had been jolted earlier when I first saw her in bed. I knew the days and weeks ahead were not going to be easy, that she and I had a lot of work to do, but Meesha's nodding infused me with peace and optimism—made me feel good—told me that I hadn't lost her, despite what I had done and all the awful things I had said. In my mind, that spoke volumes for both my wife and our future relationship, the one we could—and *would*—resurrect and build upon. From my eyes, the future looked promising.

"Meesha," Dr. Quint said, turning away from me, to her right, "how do you feel about everything Luke has said? Did his words invoke any emotion in you? Any reaction?"

I couldn't help but notice how differently the doctor spoke to Meesha than she spoke to me. Her tone was softer, gentler, so obviously out of regard for Meesha's fragile state. It wasn't that she was harsh to me; she wasn't. It was simply that she was so concerned about Meesha that the difference with which she treated the two of us was distinctly noticeable, practically palpable. You could feel the sensitivity of the doctor's words slide off her tongue and land on your skin, warming your exterior, then your whole being. The fact that I reacted this way to the doctor's verbal delivery indicated to me what she had been, and was still, trying to accomplish with Meesha. It was also a reminder of how tender Meesha's psyche was, thus a reminder of how to treat her. My wife had been through so much. I needed to keep that in mind. I had to help her along, not rush her or force her.

"I think," Meesha said, "tha—that Luke has done suh—some constructive and insightful thinking about what has ha-ha-happened, and I agree with what he has said, but he has not ta-touched upon everything of importance—actually, the thing that is most important."

I had never known Meesha to stutter before. Her nervousness and hesitancy caught me off guard—further off, even, than my initial reaction to her had thrown me.

"And what's that, Meesha?" Doctor Quint asked, scraping the question off my tongue.

"I—I just don't feel Luke understands how damaging, ha-ha-how hurtful, it was to me to find out my husband found solace in another wo-woman. Men think that sexual infidelity is the worst marital crime. Bu-but to a woman who is in an extremely emotional relationship; one that is profoundly intimate, as ours was; this is not true. To a woman like me, emotional infidelity is even worse—more destructive, more painful, more damaging. Our marriage—our relationship—has gone through he-hell in the last few ma-months. A lot of things have happened. But none, to me, is as difficult to face as the fa-fact that my husband went to another woman for consolation and comfort, rather than to me. His sleeping with a whole squad of NFL cheerleaders would have been easier to accept."

As Meesha started to cry, a lead ball fell from my throat to my groin. My brain felt vacuous, my jaw like rubber. If I hadn't heard it, I never would have known it. Though just words, they hit me in the heart like a straight right from Hell.

"God," I said, "I'm sorry, Meesh." Then I unconsciously shifted my eyes into an unfocused gaze upon the floor between them. My voice lowered, my speech slowed: "There seems to be a lot more to marriage than I know. I'm going to have to listen more—to you"—I lifted my head and nodded gently toward Meesha—"to others"—then toward Doctor Quint—"and not just with my ears."

A silent second passed during which Doctor Quint sat still, I raised my head and Meesha lowered hers, wrinkling the white bandages pasted to her neck. Her head stopped, her eyes fixed upon her thighs; she seemed to be thinking. I let her ponder a moment, then said, "Meesh?"

She looked up, her big brown eyes so sad.

"Meesh, I'm really sorry. I love you—and only you. I want you to know that. I'm not interested in sharing myself or my life with anyone else. Can we please work this out?"

Lowering her head once more, Meesha nodded several times, gently, slowly, pensively, eyes fixed upon her thighs again, neck rippling the bandages again.

We would meet several more times over the next week or so, either with Dr. Quint or one of her subordinate counselors. Each session went well with progress made each time, yet

Meesha and I still had a difficult time communicating. There remained a discomfort between us, an uneasy barrier. I wondered if this obstruction existed because Meesh was still in the hospital, or because an intermediary was always present during our sessions, our heavier discussions.

My question was answered one day near the end of Meesha's stay, when she was allowed temporary leave. Her doctor felt that she was past the "critical" point—in other words, she wasn't likely to jump in front of a truck, or hang herself from a flag pole—so they let her go out. This permission for leave made me feel like my wife was in the army or, worse yet, prison.

It was a Saturday, and I was told to have her back by eight o'clock that night. This just enhanced my feeling that Meesha was on parole, but I followed the rules nonetheless.

We drove down to Boston to walk around for the day. Meesha had a desire to stroll down Newbury Street and enjoy the city during the cool of autumn. It turned out to be a colder than usual October day and trees everywhere were either undressing or blushing. I started out feeling strange, a combination of awkward and guilty—how could I not after picking up my suicidal wife from the loony bin?—but the fall colors and brisk, dry air soon eased my mind. Walking past the chic clothing stores, pretentious art galleries, and beatniky coffee shops, I felt *strange* turn to nostalgic. Watching Meesha saunter down the sidewalk in her blue, scab-hiding, turtleneck sweater, I yearned for reconciliation, peace, and the restoration of our former love. I longed for the way things once were, when I could just walk up to my sparkling spouse and engulf her in my arms; when I cared for nothing more in this world than simply sharing space and spending time with the luscious creature who had told me: "I do."

A diversity of characters—girls with pierced faces and hair dyed colors of the rainbow, foreign tourists, well dressed shoppers, and guys holding hands with guys—passed us as I sucked in the city with deep even gulps. I had gone for a run that morning and now felt the raw elasticity that I experience in my lungs whenever I expand them beyond their normal operating capacity. For the rest of the day, I would feel as if I had taken a fine brush and gently scrubbed my inner chest.

Meesha had not eaten her breakfast and I, thus far, had had only a bagel; so, by the time we were strolling down Newbury Street, we were both hungry. We decided on a restaurant that took us past a bunch of antique shops. Their window displays contained both wooden and metallic relics, the latter mostly brass. The sun above burned bright, despite the air being chilly, and every reflective surface—antique metal displays, shiny automobile hoods, sheeny street signs, store-front glass panes—did so with a luster so brilliant it blinded me. I found myself frequently looking down at the sidewalk to kill the glare that temporarily burned my eyes, stealing my vision.

Despite the discomforting, depressing alienation I felt between Meesha and me, I couldn't help but acknowledge the weather. I've always loved days like this, with the temperature not so low to give you chicken skin, nor so high to make you sweat. It was the type of day on which you could do anything—even tan your face, given you lay between wind breaking barriers to minimize the chill. The light embellished everything in sight: girls looked prettier, cars appeared newer, sidewalks seemed cleaner, the whole world focused better. The light, it seemed, sharpened reality for me. Each item I looked at beamed forth with a keener edge, or more distinct hue, than I had expected. My brain's memory for each of these objects obviously contained less flamboyance, less vitality, less vibrance. Not that my memories of these objects were drab; they weren't. But it seemed that on this day, STOP signs shone redder, the sky burned bluer and, within it, cottony clouds billowed with finer detail, each bunny-white bulge precisely demarcated as if cut from Heaven with a surgeon's scalpel.

*September 11ᵗʰ was like this!* I suddenly recalled with a start. *How incongruous! How diabolically ironic!: On a day of infamy with events so surreal, light optimized the perception of reality!*

I carried this thought as Meesha and I continued toward the restaurant. Meesha walked on the inner part of the sidewalk while I did the gentleman thing, shielding her against potential harm from the street. We did not talk much. I told myself that I felt more like thinking, while it appeared that Meesha felt more like window shopping. In truth, we did not talk because we were inhibited. It was too soon; things still felt awkward. Not until we'd killed some time, relaxed, maybe had some booze would we begin to converse. Drinking, of course, was against the hospital's rules, but I didn't give a shit. I was with my wife. I had just taken her out of the whacko ward. She wore a turtleneck to hide marks no turtle would ever become desperate enough to inflict upon itself. Only an intelligent being—-a human—could do such a thing, especially when betrayed by the only person she trusts. And, in this case, that human was my wife. So if I wanted a fucking drink, or she wanted a fucking drink, we were going to have a fucking drink. Maybe even two. Maybe even ten.

While Meesha glanced into the shop windows and the ubiquitous light spilled splendor all around us, I zoned in on this phenomenon: *What is this with my perception? Why do things look so different today? Has the whole world changed?*

*Of course not,* my head echoed.

*Then why does everything appear grander, more beautiful? Even ordinary objects, like glass lunch plates and aluminum radio antennae, scintillate as if heaven borne. And why should this affect my mood? I should be so far down in the dumps that no good thought could possibly rise to my brain. I should be grieving my ass off about my wife's mental state, but I'm not. I'm concerned, yes; and I know that there is a lot of shit to deal with, a lot of shit to work out; but the beauty of this day is preventing me from descending as low as I feel I should. Or am I simply relieved and happy that Meesha is still alive? Or am I just stunned as a motherfucker from all this shit going down in my life and in the world?*

I didn't know. So I went back to the concept of light with the restaurant still three blocks of Meesha-distracting-antique-shops away. In doing so, I realized that my notions on light were not new to me; I'd had such thoughts before and they began to trickle back: *When people rattle off that hackneyed phrase—"I know it's true; I saw it with my own eyes!"——Is the fact really imbedded in the focus? Can we really trust what we see? For what IS it that we see? Isn't our visual perception of every object simply our brain's processing of the light reflecting off that object, rather than the object itself? How do we know that our brain processes the light in a way that redefines the object precisely as it exists? Sounds weird,* I thought, *but how do I know that I'm seeing a park bench the way it exists in reality and not in some other shape or form? Maybe what I see as a park bench looks more, in reality, the way I currently view a phone booth. And maybe my ability to use the bench—which requires that I accurately interpret its shape, size, and texture—without an accurate visual image is simply a reflexive action of my brain, adjusting to non-visual sensory input. And what about my eyes? How do I know my eyes don't distort light in any way before feeding it to my brain? Who's to say? How would I know?*

*Now I'm getting really weird,* I thought, as I continued down the street. *Where the hell do these thoughts come from?*

Meesha suddenly stopped to study a cherry table that looked like it had been built when Columbus was a kid. I was too distracted by my thoughts to pay the table much attention, so I just stood a short distance away from the store window and let pedestrians pass. An elderly man with a Nikon around his neck and a wife on his arm strolled between Meesha and me. His wife's face was so wrinkled that it reminded me of newspaper that had been unraveled from a crunched ball. *Is her face really that wrinkled,* I wondered, *or am I simply imagining it? Does she REALLY look like an Oil of Olay model, but my brain processes her as old and haggard?*

We were now only two blocks away from Dominic's, the place at which we'd decided to eat. Shimmering light continued to dapple every reflective surface tilted toward me. Like tongues of flame licking the wind, leaves flickered on a sugar maple across the street, reflecting the star of our solar system with a neon-like glow. A muscle-head in a shirt too small walked aggressively past us with his arm around a bottle blond in black spandex. *Her head glows with or without the sun,* I thought. *Or is it just my eyes—or my eyes conspiring with my brain—making me think so?*

My gut told me that my eyes and brain were okay; they were allies, organs I could trust. But then I thought about a philosophy course I'd taken in college. I remembered that the professor had proposed that the only thing in which a human being could truly believe was his existence. Anything other than that, according to the professor, was suspect, untrustworthy, a product of one's senses, the result of perception and interpretation. *So what does that mean? That any or all sensory input could be fraudulent? That I can't trust anything I perceive? That my eyes, ears, nose, tongue, and tactile sensors could all send false data, thus give me false readings?*

I didn't buy it: *No way. Sure, some people have defective organs—those who are, to some extent, blind or deaf; who can't smell or taste properly; who hear voices or hallucinate; or who have lost feeling in an appendage, an arm or leg or whatever. But these are people with defective body parts; they're the exception. Most people have adequately functioning sensorial organs and, therefore, perceive stimuli the way stimuli is received by them.* To believe differently, I concluded, would be to agree with my philosophy professor, who doesn't trust his sensorial organs, only that thing which convinces him that he exists.

*But what is that thing?* I wondered. *It can't be the brain. The brain is also an organ. Why should I trust my brain, but not my other organs? That would be a contradiction. My brain can also be defective with mental illness, physical impairments, and other cerebral afflictions.*

No, I realized what my professor was talking about wasn't the brain, but the mind, something separate from the brain, something ethereal. According to my professor, a person could have a defective brain, but still know that he exists through his mind.

*So, then, what the fuck was my professor saying? That the only thing I can be sure of is my existence, by the means of something I can't see, touch, feel, hear or smell? And, as a result, the only thing I can trust is something I can't perceive; by definition, what most people would call "nothing", but what he called "the mind"?*

*Bullshit,* I thought. *No doubt there is a mind or soul separate from the body, just as there exists a God beyond the reach of our senses. But there's no way that this God would have given us bodies that we can't trust, bodies that perceive things differently than they are. A world with such beings would be a hoax, and THAT I can't buy. It wouldn't make any sense. There would surely be easier and more logical ways to control one's creation, which would be the only reason for some deity or power to create corrupt organs and distorting senses in the first place.*

Meesha ended her study of the cherry table whose construction predated the Nina, Pinta, and Santa Maria, and we started walking again. After a few steps, Meesha suddenly began talking about the table's design. Though her speech was soft and words hesitantly spoken, her talking jerked my head right up and to my left. *She's trying to break the ice!* I listened carefully. When sure she had finished, I asked her what she thought the chances were that the table's owner ever had scurvy. My inclination—as is my nature—has always been to tease Meesha, make a joke, try to make her laugh. But she just looked sideways at me and frowned. *Too early for humor,* I concluded, disappointed. Worse yet, I couldn't think of anything else to say. Meanwhile, something was still bugging me.

I, of course, didn't buy the theory that properly functioning human senses could not be trusted. That was my philosophy professor's problem, not mine. It was the phenomenon beyond our senses that bothered me—mainly light.

*I may trust my senses,* I thought, *mainly because they're a part of me and, therefore, I feel that I can accurately evaluate their effectiveness. But light, which is not a part of me, which is beyond my body yet impacts my senses, gives me the creeps. How do I know that the images my eyes receive are valid representations of what exists in reality? Is it possible that light, by nature, corrupts the representation of an object? Or, even worse, is it possible that light is just in representing an object; but something, somewhere, distorts the light during the split second it takes to reach my eyes?*

The restaurant was now just a block away. I could see a green and white striped awning hanging over a large window. Scrawled across the middle of the window was **Dominic's**, in the same shade of green as the stripes in the awning—a lush, grassy green. It made me think of pictures I had seen of rural Ireland. I imagined that the letters drawn, which I interpreted as Celtic scrawl, were actually stenciled sod glued to the glass.

Meesha had not stopped window shopping. Ordinarily, I would have shared my thoughts with her and strongly wanted to at the moment. *We need to start talking!* my brain yelled at me. But it just didn't feel like the right time to start. She seemed too aloof, too distracted, too distant. *Too early still,* I concluded. I felt it would be best if I left her alone to antique gaze, rather than bore her with my loopy views of light and reality—or the lack thereof. So I continued on my own.

During the final stretch of our walk, my brain must have hatched a thousand thoughts. *So strange,* I thought, *how I can think of so many things so fast sometimes, but not remember where I left my wallet when I'm late for work?*

I looked ahead at the grassy green moniker adorning the clean, sparkling glass. I could not see past the glass, for it shimmered with blinding light. But I knew that just a few feet beyond, people were munching food and slurping beer, as I would soon be. I knew this, for I had eaten at Dominic's before. *But what if I hadn't?* I thought. *I obviously would have no idea what existed beyond that opaque plane of eye scorching yellow. Pretty weird. So, what else? What else is out there hiding behind dark doors of light, beyond my knowledge? What else is out there hidden from view, but impacting my existence?*

We entered Dominic's. A thin waiter with a Newbury Street wiggle led us to a small table. Straddling the seats of two high-backed chairs that faced each other, it stood vacant by the front window my eyes had just been trying to penetrate. We sat down. I ordered two Heinekens. The waiter brought them. Then I asked Meesha about the antiques she had seen, wanting desperately to restart communication between us; but it didn't work. My mind would not stop. *What the fuck! Am I going insane! What is this with light!* Sipping the cold, green bottle, I nodded absently at Meesha's description of relics upon which humans once sat. *Something's going on here, damn it! But what is it?*

*It's the knowing, isn't it? Or, more accurately, the not-knowing. The not-knowing of what exists. The inability to decipher, explain, understand, interpret, or simply see—never mind, control!—what is right before my eyes. It's a strange and scary thing, isn't it? There we go, hip-hopping through life with so many things right before us, but concealed—like the inside of Dominic's—or Meesha's emotional pain.*

I tilted the green, translucent bottle upwards so that its flat bottom pointed toward the ceiling. A sudsy, tepid sip—what remained of my beer—rolled through the bottle's neck and into my mouth. The waiter saw me killing my first soldier and wiggled his way over. He made a joke about me being thirsty. I smiled, then ordered another round as well as food: beef ravioli for Meesha, penne pasta with broccoli and cheese for me.

*God is light,* I suddenly thought. *The Bible says so.* I could feel the slight beer buzz begin to kindle my skin. *From what I know about physics, if a person travels at the speed of light, he won't age. Explains how a being like God could exist forever. Light always is. But not always what it seems to be.*

My mind blinked back to Dominic's blinding window, the one outside. *So I might see light,* I thought; *but what it reflects, in reality, might not be what I see. I trust my eyes to see things as they appear to me—that assumption I've already made—but things that appear to me could be distorted.*

*Who could distort these things?*

*Well, God for one. How hard would it be for a being who is characterized as light to control light? Or maybe God is ALL light and ALL light is God, such as the sunlight reflecting off the outer window. As a result, God controls what all people see. That would certainly be a way to alter a human's destiny.*

*But does it have to be God? Couldn't it be another entity? Maybe from beyond our universe? Another supernatural being? Or even a human? Control the perceptions of the masses and you own the world, don't cha? Couldn't a government or other organization—criminal? terrorist?— distort or even create light, such as laser beams, to affect what people perceive? Not all the time possibly, but at critical moments to achieve a certain end? I should think so. Talk about mass manipulation! Psych-Ops, baby! You want to scare the shit out of some soldier? Just beam down several battalions of mouth-frothing Marines in front of him and watch him screw. No need for real troops. Light will scare away any enemy.*

Meesha finished telling me about the antiques she had seen just as our food arrived. She was already two gulps down on her second Heineken, which told me she was less than one beer away from tipsy. A heavy drinker, Meesha was not. A couple of cold ones and she was game for some pretty funny escapades, like the time we went to The Rogue before we were married.

We were living together, just south of Boston, and decided one Saturday night to go out for Pizza. The Rogue was a local bar with a big brick oven in the back. You could go there, tie on a good buzz, and eat some pretty decent Italian pie.

On this particular night, I downed my half of the pepperoni with extra cheese with my usual four Buds. Meesha usually drank half as much, while munching her section of the tomatoey sphere—but not on this night. On this night, she maintained her pizza consuming quota and matched me bottle for bottle, sud for sud.

Forget her hand, I had to hold her elbow while walking out of the joint. Initially, during the stroll home, she clung to my arm, her posture like a puppet's. Then, halfway to our apartment complex, we came upon an abandoned grocery carriage. It belonged to the food market located a few streets over.

Thinking fast and moving faster, I bent low and lunged my right shoulder toward, then gently against, Meesha's upper left thigh, before lodging it softly within her groin. Then I stood up straight.

"Ahhhhh!" Meesha wailed in an ascending shriek which descended from my shoulder, followed by, "What are you *doing*?" But she did not fight back the way she would have ordinarily. Booze had temporarily tamed or incapacitated her. And when I dropped her into the carriage's basket, she yelled, "Get me out of here!", albeit with gaiety that shouted, *I'm having fun!* So was I.

I immediately grabbed the cart's rear, horizontal push bar and took off. Wheels shook and squealed as they fought aged tar below but, though the rattling was raucous, it did not offset Meesha's howls. As I pushed, she laughed. The harder I pushed, the harder she laughed. She threatened me with every type of assault a drunken woman can imagine while being recklessly taxied in a grocery cart. She threatened to retaliate while I was sleeping. I told her I looked forward to the event. She yelled: "I'll use an egg beater!", to which I replied: "Ain't that a yolk! Torture me with a toaster for all I care!", after which I tried in vain to increase my speed.

Suddenly, out of the corner of my eye, I noticed movement. Still at top speed with the carriage wheels pouring continual cacophony into the night, I turned my head toward a middle-aged woman. She stood on the front porch of her house. She was watching us. Her eyes were wide, her facial features rippled. Losing not a second nor wasting a step, I head-gestured toward the carriage and yelled, "You just don't get much for your money these days!" The woman didn't blink. She just kept looking. She didn't say a word.

When we finished sucking pasta and slurping Heineken at Dominic's, Meesha and I re-entered the cascading brilliance and sat down upon a sidewalk bench.

"You've been quiet," she said abruptly. I smiled. I knew she would unwind. A little alcohol always does it. "What've you been thinking about?"

I hesitated, then laughed, a self-conscious chuckle. "Nothing much, really. Just some weird stuff."

"What kind of 'weird stuff'?"

"Ahh, just crazy thoughts about light and reality and perception—crap like that. Nothing important."

"Tell me about it."

I was about to say, "Nooo, it's stupid, just my brain trying to amuse itself," when I realized this was Meesha's way of saying: "Please talk to me! Let's be close! AGAIN! I need it! You need it! WE need it!"

So I told her, in detail, every thought I'd had while we were walking and drinking. I figured talking about anything, no matter how bizarre, was better than silence. *NOW*, I thought, *is the time for us to connect, to get started, to move on, to push forward with our lives.* When finished, I found my wife nodding pensively.

I laughed again, self-consciously again: "What's up?"

"Don't you see it, Luke? What your brain's doing?"

"Yeah," I cackled, "I'm obsessing on bullshit! Must be a bit stressed, still."

Her voice was soft and soothing, so loving and kind: "Obsessing, yes; bullshit, no. Your brain is trying to cope, but it can't. It can't accept. So it's searching, hunting, and grasping. Things have happened that were beyond your control—Hunter dying; me trying to take my life; even, to a certain extent, the World

Trade Center. You have to accept that these things happened; that they weren't your fault; that you, alone, didn't cause them and couldn't have stopped them. In a sense: forgive yourself. But your brain won't let you. Instead, it's analyzing every aspect of your existence to find a reason, a truth, an answer. It won't let go."

I now found myself nodding pensively. The old Meesha was back, the one who knows me so well.

"But some things in this world have no logical reason. Senseless things sometimes happen. Things sometimes exist beyond our sight and control, and you have to just accept these things, or you'll go crazy. Someday maybe, in another life maybe, we might find out the reasons—but not now."

I felt myself still nodding, though less vigorously. My throat was tight, my eyes heavy. Ivory bit my bottom lip.

"Don't you see, Luke, your brain is mining for logic to explain irrational behavior and unforeseeable events. You're trying to find a smoking gun where no shot was fired. The fact is: you can't. So you're beating yourself up. A part of you feels guilty for what I did—maybe even for what Hunter did—but you can't feel that way. It wasn't your fault. Yes, you did say some awful things to me. That, I must tell you. After your diatribes in the car and in bed, I felt pretty bad— very lost and alone. I got extremely depressed, fast. I felt worthless and unwanted—pretty hopeless—pretty much like dirt, to the point where I didn't want to exist anymore. Your words hurt me a lot, Luke. That, you have to know. But *you* didn't make me attempt suicide, hon. Only I can commit my own suicide. That's what these last couple of weeks have taught me. I, and only I, am responsible for my life. No one else. Only I can live it, and no one can make me end it. Life is a gift. I must cherish mine and take care of it. No one else will, or even can, if I don't. I can't always control what goes on around me, but I can control me, my actions and my thoughts. The same thing goes for Hunter and his reckless behavior. *He* did himself in, Luke. There was nothing you could do to prevent it. *He* did it, just as *I* did it. *We* did it.

Not you. You're not responsible. You can't be everywhere, stopping people from hurting themselves. You're a human being. You've got to accept that, forgive yourself, forgive your humanity. For me, it was my fear of abandonment, my phobia. You don't know what is going on in someone else's head and can't be expected to. It's just like looking at Dominic's opaque window. You can't see the other side, and you shouldn't expect to be able to. But because of what's happened—your losses, your pain—you feel you should have been able to, and can't accept that you can't. You feel guilty. And so you're doubting yourself, your senses, reality, the things you *can* know and believe."

I sighed through my nose. Looking down, my brow furrowed, I whispered: "I never—I never meant—God, I wish I didn't hurt you, Meesha. I'm—I'm so sorry. Please forgive me." As I spoke, the flesh framing my eyes filled with fluid sorrow.

Meesha's voice softened even further to meet mine: "I forgive you, Luke. I know you didn't mean those things. I know you love me. I know it instinctively. I should never have doubted it. The perfume on your hand—I—I should have known better! I *know* you! I *trust* you! We've been over it so many times now—the counselors, the shrinks, the sessions. You've got to *let go*! We both have to let go—forgive—move on. Remember the Serenity Prayer?: 'Accept the things we cannot change, change the things we can, let God show us the difference.'"

I nodded.

"We've got to live it. I've grown from this experience, Luke. I've learned. I'm addressing my baggage, trying to exorcise my demons. I've become stronger. You have to, too. We have to work together. Please come back to me, hon. I want my husband. I want my lover. I want my friend. Carpe Diem, Luke. *This* day. Today."

I pulled Meesha into my arms as a drop from my right eye cascaded down my cheek. It was still early in the day, but late in the year, this fact evident in the golden blanket worn by all things; and I felt that cyclical sensation, unique to autumn, that borders on sorrow for time passed.

# Chapter 4

We landed on Re'enev just after noon, but by the time we had retrieved our luggage, picked up the rental car, driven to the hotel and checked in, my watch's hour hand pointed toward three. Didn't matter; the sun still sizzled, and the cultural show for which we had reservations that night didn't start until seven-thirty. We unpacked and threw on summer clothes. Then I unlocked the mini-bar, pulled out a couple of cold cans, and passed through the sliding glass doors onto our balcony. On the long beach below, fluid blue turned frothy white as it rumbled onto a belt of coral powder, the same glistening shade as the sea's salt when dry. Thus, it was with this view and frosty brew that Meesha and I christened our room and toasted our trip, hugging and kissing, then making love panting ocean air, to begin a much needed getaway. "I feel like a newlywed again," my wife whispered in my ear from beneath me. I smiled, then smeared her neck with long, stroking kisses.

Later, after a stroll around the hotel grounds and a walk along the water, Meesha and I boarded a bus to the Re'enevian cultural show, which turned out fabulous; the food served, stupendous. The main course was tender pork peeled from a pig that had been roasted whole within a deep pit. Heating the pit were rocks that had been pulled from a fire, then dumped into the hole and covered with large ferns and other machete-cut plants. We also ate steamed yams, sweet corn-on-the-cob, mainland-grown potatoes, and more than a dozen kinds of fruit. In addition, I tried Uli'Koloo, a gooey sauce made by beating the root of the Hukakai plant. Uli'Koloo was served in a small bowl. With my fingers, I dipped clumps of rice and pieces of smoked beef and chicken into the pink-tinted condiment, then plopped the dripping concoction into my mouth. And to wash this all down, I drank many Mai Tais while Meesha stuck to creamy, stomach soothing Pina Coladas.

After dinner—which we ate at an extra-long, wooden, picnic table with a few other tourists—we watched a dance recital. All the while, we continued to slurp the endless supply of intoxicating Re'enevian beverages forced into our hands. Meesha smiled frequently, I noticed. I couldn't help but feel joy.

The show was good: young, beautiful, Re'enevian women draped in long, elegant dresses, swaying and gyrating to the acoustically hypnotic waves of a guitar and ukulele band strumming behind them. The night air was warm, but tempered by a relentless Pacific breeze.

About halfway through, the recital featured a fire dancer, for whom the band replaced their string instruments with drums. This crazy guy played with a rod that was several feet long, and flicked and lashed spiky tongues of orange and blue at each end. He wore nothing but two pieces of efficiently concealing fabric, though only the size and shape of wash cloths, suspended from cordage wrapped around his waist. Although chunky, he whipped that flaming rod with seeming recklessness and dazzling dexterity around the tight contours of his naked frame.

Following the dance exhibit, Bruddah Eze—short for Ezekiel—stepped on stage. Bruddah Eze was this gargantuan man with a gargantuan heart who sang and played the ukulele. Never before had I heard such a powerful, yet ethereal voice. And never before had I encountered such human incongruity: such a beautiful being trapped in such an unappealing body. He must have weighed seven or eight hundred pounds. And how irrelevant! As baritone as Pacific waves pounding lava tubes, yet as graceful and serene as an albatross in flight, did Bruddah Eze sing. It took Meesha and me no more than sixty seconds into his first song to agree that Bruddah Eze stood on earth, but performed from heaven. Heart of gold? Garbage. This guy had the thumping pump of Christ. His blood was type D—Divinity flowed through his veins. He was kindness personified, love layered in lard. Through his music and movements, he conveyed a caring as colossal as his body, as deep as he was wide. It gripped you, an anonymous soul in the audience, and pulled you toward him, making you feel like you were kin to Eze; that you and he were not strangers, but rather two people who shared a common existence in a beautiful world, and that there existed no reason why you and he couldn't celebrate that fact together.

"Isn't this guy great!" Meesha whispered in my ear. Smiling, I nodded enthusiastically.

Listening to Ezey—-his nickname and certainly an appropriate one, for it invoked in me the image of an "easy" rolling disposition, so characteristic of the big happy Re'enevian—ignited in my heart a dormant altruism combined with a unique peace, such that I longed to reach out to people, to God, and to nature. As a result, in bed after the show, I reached out and pulled Meesha against me. Smothering her with a hug, I said, "Hon, I gotta tell ya: that Ezey's performance sent a tingle up my spine. It was like the chill I got when we heard *Memory* on Broadway. In *Cats*, remember?"

A feminine "Uh-huh" rose up my chest from beneath my chin.

"It was like someone was rubbin' an ice cube along my back and neck. I got Goosebumps. The guy's voice is *incredible*."

"I agree," Meesha said, inserting her svelte feet between the bulk of my calves while gently squeezing the upper nape of my neck. "For me, his singing, his view of life—they reminded me of the way I felt as a kid, when I finished reading *The Catcher in the Rye*: that although there exists much bad in the world, much phoniness, there also exists much that is authentic and good—and probably a lot more of the latter than the former."

"Yeah, I can see that," I said, "Ezey made me feel benevolent, like helping someone in need." Thinking about it further, finding myself getting a bit pensive, I added: "His music clarified my focus—sorta reinforced my notion that maintaining harmony with God, people, and nature is tantamount to anything else I could ever do on this spinning sphere we so chaotically inhabit."

It was a wonderful way to feel, especially after suffering the grief, depression, anxiety, and guilt of Hunter's death and Meesha's meltdown. "It's like the door to a new room has opened," I explained to Meesha, "a new room in my existence, a den vibrant with life, happiness, and optimism."

I instantly embraced this room, this feeling, and sought to embody it for as long as I could, to make it my new outlook on life. Meesha understood my desire; in fact, felt the same. After further discussion, she asserted: "The Re'enevian culture vibrates with a goodness, kindness, wholesomeness, and authenticity that other places seem to lack." Then she wondered out loud: "Are these beautiful characteristics expenses of what we mainlanders call 'sophisticated civilization'?" I think she had something there.

Ignorant of its source notwithstanding, Meesha and I felt carried by this buoyant, Re'enevian spirit through each event and activity we enjoyed and situation we encountered over the next several days. These were things that either she, or both of us, had wanted to do: a botanical garden tour; car trips to remote parts of Re'enev few visitors ever see; lengthy dialogue with native Re'enevians about their lives wherever we went; a spectacular helicopter flight over the mountains, through valleys and canyons, and along the formerly volcanic coast; watching black Frigates and white Albatross majestically soar upon the warm, salty draft that gushes up the basaltic cliffs of Re'enev's northern tip; a motor boat cruise up the lushly rugged, but eroding mountainous shoreline; pounding beers and talking Re'enevian music with the friendly entertainers who played at our hotel; and plenty of body surfing in cool, clean blue to escape the midday heat while marveling at the velvety terrain beyond. And it was this terrain that interested me the most. While I churned the Pacific with gentle treading, my feet kicking, my hands weaving, I studied mountain sides that soared toward turquoise in at least a dozen shades of green. I could just as well have been dreaming. The fertile facades seemed superimposed. They appeared to emerge from Re'enev's soul just beyond the water's edge. I felt as though I could reach out across the waves and incongruous band of scorching, almond sand and grab a branch. A painted cardboard setting for a high school play would have seemed more real.

Our excursions and touristy activities were fun. They were also, for the most part, solitary. With September 11th recent history and World Trade Center rubble still smoking, few tourists existed. Crowds, as a result, never did. We felt like we owned the island—when, in truth, the fucking island owned us.

Our favorite event, Meesha and I concluded, was the door-less helicopter flight. Strapped to our seats, we hung our heads out the sides for stunning panoramic views. The young pilot, a former naval aviator, flew with as much daring as he did caution. He repeatedly swooped down—low, smooth, and nimbly—between the narrow sides of the rainforest canyons. It was so much fun! Making hard turns, the centrifugal force bending us left and right, I imagined myself one of the frigate birds I had studied along the cliffs. For short moments, which I tried to prolong and will never forget, I felt so free and autonomous, the pretension of self-propelled flight inflating my chest and exciting my soul.

But it wasn't just the flight, itself, that aroused Meesha and me; so did the land. How amazing it was to see abundant plant life growing laterally out of fissures in solidified lava at three thousand feet! Through the chopper's open sides, I felt like I had when treading water, but now my perception was real: I *could* almost touch the stalactite peaks—peaks carved from volcanic residue separating the green, furrowing valleys below. To see these sharp blades of eroded lava before my eyes, almost close enough for me to touch, and the tropical valleys of paradise-level lushness between them; and to understand that it took millions of years for molten lava, spewed from the ocean floor, to reach this state by the way of relentless wind and rain, cutting streams, and the occasional blast of a hurricane; simply boggled my mind. And I hadn't even gotten around to thinking about how any of the life had found its way there! *Who are we men,* I had to wonder, *who have arrived here in this last blinking moment with our flying machines and philosophies? How much,* I continued, *has this stalactite tip before me withered during my thirty-five years? THIRTY-FIVE years? How much has it eroded during the past thirty-five THOUSAND? Could it have already reached this point when the first Polynesian nomads navigated their way here aboard wind powered canoes?*

*Probably so.*

*And when the first hairy, cave-dwelling midget learned to shish kabob his turtle meat?*

*Probably then, too.*

*And to imagine that I think of the Napoleonic wars as having happened a long time ago!* In our sixty-five-mile-an-hour culture, it often seems that last week is viewed as ancient history. But nature, I have found, has a way of pulling me into the breakdown lane.

As spectacular as the chopper flight had been, it was only natural, given my fascination with the land, that my primary desire would be to hike. There were so many trails and so many places to see! And these places were accessible only by foot: lava tubes now hyped as dry or wet caves; all kinds of exotically enchanting vegetation; the nesting spots of beautiful birds that exist no where else on the planet; scores of hidden reservoirs fed by clean, glistening waterfalls; and ancient sacrificial altars, now covered by jungle growth, if we could find them! (as our chopper pilot had tauntingly couched it). I could hardly wait!

Not so with Meesha; she wanted no part of it. Despite the goodness, kindness, wholesomeness, and authenticity that she and I acknowledged in the Re'enevian culture, Meesha sensed something eerie about the island itself. I didn't share her apprehension about going on a hike, but I could understand why she—reacting to recent events, I surmised—might feel something odd about Re'enev per se. Ever since the World Trade Center tragedy and subsequent anthrax attacks, I had found myself a bit skittish, more sensitive than usual. And from the moment we'd set foot on Re'enev, I, too, had sensed something strange, a certain aura. I described it to Meesha one morning during breakfast.

"It's similar to the feeling I had during the days immediately following September 11th—a peculiar uneasiness—an elusive anxiety—like an untouchable, invisible, unnamable, but ever present vulnerability."

Meesha thought it might be "due to the near desolation of the island, the noticeable lack of tourists and," thus, "employed locals supported by tourism,"-—security personnel, life guards, hotel staff, police, etc.—both groups decimated in the wake of the World Trade Center's destruction. Of course, it could also have simply been our imaginations (though unlikely that we'd *both* be deluded). Regardless, a vulnerability was sensed. It was practically palpable. I'd felt it so far during our stay, though I'd tried to ignore it. And it was apparent that Meesha had felt it also, especially whenever we discussed exploring Re'enev's wilderness: "It's dangerous, Luke! You've heard the locals SAY so! Even the concierge and the bartender at the pool! Weird stuff goes on in that jungle. I don't want you going either! Especially with that secessionist movement, that independence thing. That scares me!"

I tried to console her, right up until the night before the hike: "Aw Meesh, these independence guys are harmless. They're just peaceful activists. They're not out to hurt anybody. Plus, they protest on the streets. In front of important buildings. Where people are. The last place you're gonna find 'em is the swamp."

"Listen," I said, "so far we've gone on every tourist event— every excursion—*together*. I don't want this to change. Think of the chopper trip and the boat ride by the cliffs. That was fun! And the culture show, the garden tours, the road trips we took up North, an' all the critters we saw. C'mon! We've had a ball! Don't make me do this one *alone*! I want you *with* me!"

Persistent as I was, I reached a point where I knew dialogue would not work. Thus, I executed my infallible contingency plan, one that I've had to employ several times at critical points during our marriage.

Early that evening, eight days into our Pacific retreat, Meesha had exited the shower and was towel drying herself just inside the bathroom door. I opened the door, entered, picked my wife up onto my right shoulder, and carried her out while she punched me and squealed.

"There are loud mosquitoes in here," I said, "didja leave the sliding doors open?"

"What are you *doing*?" she yelped—half yell, half laugh—as I tossed her onto the bed, "I'm trying to get ready for dinner and you want to play Cro-Magnon Man! You're timing's a bit off, don't you think!" She tried to slip beneath my arms, her wet hair flopping in front of her face; but I stopped her, swinging her back onto the bed. She was mostly dry, but purely naked and I was loving every visual moment. I pushed her fully down across the bedspread, then held her there by her elbows while she grunted with struggle, gritting gleaming teeth. I'm sure I saw a smile in there somewhere. Then I hurdled her miniscule waist with my right leg as if straddling a horse, pinning her fabulous frame to the bed with my lower body. I grabbed both of her wrists with my left hand and went for ribs with my right. Meesha, I knew, if not the most beautiful woman in America, was certainly the most ticklish. And I let her have it. And she went berserk. She screamed and struggled and squirmed while the fingers of my right hand pulsated with first-digit- frenzy against a cage of flexible bone flush with lean, sensitive flesh. Nothing could stop me. I dropped my left hand, releasing each of hers, then let her have it with both of mine. She went nuts, crazy, slapping me on both arms, hollering and twisting her torso, her impeccable boobs swinging in sync. So I went for the kill. I dropped my face between her breasts, not letting up on the tickling for one moment, then vibrated my lips within her cleavage producing a loud, long raspberry. She screamed even louder, then cackled and cawed while continuing to twist, swing, and slap as I blew three more obnoxious blasts from within her mammillary valley. Whether it was the pitch in her voice or the tears in her eyes, I'm not sure, but something told me then that Meesha had reached the breaking point. So I said, "Either you're goin' hikin' with me tomorrow, or I'm gonna tickle ya t'breakfast! The choice is yours."

She knew I was serious. She called me a "turd!", a "jerk!", a "schmuck!", a "moron!", and an "idiot!", then said "Okay! Okay! Okay! I'll go!", then slid her right hand deep inside my shorts to find me like a hot copper water pipe. She would need another shower before we went anywhere.

After dinner, we hit the sack early so we could rise, refreshed, with the sun. Meesha fell asleep first. As I lay there, my wife in my arms, my mind ablaze, I thought: *Things are getting good again.* Squeezing Meesha gently, gratitude billowing my chest cavity, I found it unusually easy to breathe. Listening to Meesha do so with heavy, feminine exhales, I turned toward her, watched her, appreciated her. *I said some crazy shit a few months ago, I* thought; *musta been temporarily insane—over the edge with anguish. Whatever. That's the past. What matters is NOW. I* studied Meesha's restful countenance, so innocent and serene. I studied her long and hard. *She's the true one, I thought, truly the one, and only one, for me. She must believe that. I must convince her of that.* Then I lowered my lids.

# Chapter 5

W hile we stood at the beginning of the path, a tent of Makoa tree canopy a hundred feet above us, my mind on the hike ahead, my eyes inadvertently landed on scars. *If you didn't know they were there*, I thought with irritation, *you wouldn't even notice 'em.* But my conscience knew they were there. God knew they were there. Satan knew they were there. And it seemed that the three of them conspired to ensure that I would never forget.

It wasn't yet eight A.M., we hadn't even started hiking, and I was already sweating bullets—a human machine-gun spitting rounds of brine. Being a woman, Meesha didn't sweat—she "perspired". But such semantics did not prevent her "perspiring" from resembling the green bottles I'd emptied a couple nights before.

A curvaceous, Re'enevian waitress had served us. We sat outside one of the restaurants in our hotel complex. Torches lined the three walls horse-shoeing us to the rear. The sanded stone surface of the terrace floor reflected flickering orange. The nightly entertainment had just begun. In the darkening distance, curling blue crashed turbulent white across a strip of beige. I could hear every wave.

I watched the waitress as she sashayed to the refrigerator behind the bar to pull out my first one of the evening. Her coffee skin gleamed in the soft blend of fire and twilight. Returning, she set the Heineken on a small table between Meesh and me. Then her lips parted. And from within a countenance so richly brown appeared a quarter moon of absolute white. What followed was involuntary. My mind immediately vaulted to the waves washing the beach behind her as I pondered the purity that seems to exist in all things naturally beautiful. *'Seems'*, my mind echoed, and I thought: *Now why did I think that?* But the notion was too tainted for my mood and swiftly dissipated. I doubt I could have held any negative thought during that moment, so tranquil was the terrace's ambience.

The Pacific's incessant churning, in harmony with the acoustic guitar and ukulele players before me, lulled my inner being. So serene did I become that I felt no need to guzzle the beer I had ordered; relaxed, I already was. So the bottle just sat there; but not without my noticing how quickly its glass exterior began popping water pimples. These beads of condensation grew until their weight pulled them down the container's curved sides, leaving streams in their wake. "Perspiring", the bottle had been. And now my wife was doing the same. *Women,* I thought: *pretty weird. They'd rather liken their body's cooling mechanism to the reaction of a cold piece of glass plunged into sultry air, than to a natural function of the opposite gender of their own species. No wonder we fight.*

The morning's rising fire felt pleasant but, at the same time, relentless and overpowering. Unlike the New England sun, it frightened me. Boston has its hot days alright; but there, the big ball simply shines down on you. Here, it seemed to exhale down my neck as if the inflamed coil of a giant thermal fan.

The path before me resembled a tunnel by the way it snaked beneath a natural arbor. A man made trail, it bored through various types of low lying jungle vegetation. Various shades of green bulged toward and engulfed me in overflowing layers, while flowers of a dozen vibrant hues randomly spotted the billowing enclosure.

To the right of the path and several feet into the brush stood a tall tree bearing dull green needles. The green of these needles lost its luster to a yellowish-brown, thus lacking the verdant sheen of a pine. In addition, unlike a pine whose needles bear a smooth and consistent surface, these needles were comprised of dozens of links joined end-to-end. I thought: *A botanical chain! A TREE chain!*

Then I noticed, protruding about ten feet up the trunk, a medium-sized branch fractured along its top. The limb had snapped, I presumed, from ferocious winds received during one of Re'enev's recent, devastating hurricanes. A V-shaped split opened the woody appendage skywards just a few inches from the tree's trunk. As a result, most of the branch declined from this crack, hanging from the trunk by a mere sliver along its bottom half. The pulp of the branch's interior had seasoned. It reminded me of the split oak I kept stacked behind my house back in Massachusetts. The pulp of this branch was darker than any other section of the tree. *Obviously dead*, I thought.

Wanting a walking stick for our hike, I tore the dead limb off. I had to exert more force than I had thought would be necessary. However, when the branch finally broke, it did so cleanly, its severed tip tapering to a sharp point. Despite its sharpness, though, the tip retained long, partially snapped, off-shooting splinters. I grabbed my guide book, identified the tree as Ironwood, and learned some interesting things about it. The jointed needles, I discovered, were actually branches, sprouts from the tree's trunk. In addition, the wood was tremendously hard; Re'enevian natives had once used it to create spears, hammers, and war clubs among other weapons and tools.

My new walking stick in hand, we stood before the path. Our intention was to follow this trail through the thick brush, inclining and declining for several miles, until we reached a cool, refreshing reservoir within the northern coastal cliffs. According to my book, this misty pool was the splashing collection of several vertical streams that rushed over a cliff from a gushing river more than a hundred feet above. But, first, we would read the sign.

Bolted to an unpainted magnesium stake impaling the entrance to the path, it was impossible to miss. The placard itself was composed of steel and coated with a reddish-brown primer only a shade darker than the iron-saturated clay beneath our feet. From this primer, superimposed in banana yellow latex, screamed the following:

<u>HUNTERS!</u>
While on the hiking trail, please keep your firearms
unloaded at all times.
(Access to Hellameena Canyon. Division of Forestry and
Wildlife.)
<u>NOTICE</u>
Hunting season is now open. Non-hunters are advised to
wear bright-colored clothing and stay on established trails.

"I don't like this."

"Aw c'mon, Meesh," I said, "s'long as you stay on the path, nothing's gonna happen."

"That's what I'm worried about."

"Whattaya mean?"

"Magnets, Luke; you're a bit deficient in those guys. Remember?"

I smiled. It was one of our running jokes; that is, one of our jokes from *before*—before our world imploded, before our life exploded, before every molecule of shit comprising our existence flew into the giant thermal fan. How profound, how pervasive seemed the darkness that followed! Whenever I look back at

Hunter's death and the aftermath, my memory projects a moonless night without stars. It's how my mind imagines the ceiling of Hell—all illuminating sources fully eclipsed—for it was a life seemingly without hope. I say 'seemingly' for above the pits of our depression, outside the caverns of our desperation, hope had faintly glimmered, begging to bend around the edges of our anguish. But we didn't know it. We couldn't see it. And we surely couldn't feel it.

Meesha had read in some magazine that the human brain contains magnets, and that these magnets are what provide man with navigational ability; that man, in effect, has a compass within his cranium. The article went on to note that some people possess more magnets than others and that, theoretically, these people have a greater capacity for finding their way around.

This was all Meesha needed. One thing she couldn't stand was my getting lost. It seemed to her I always was—while driving, while hiking, while strolling through a shopping mall. It drove her nuts. She would get exasperated and call me "directionally challenged!" Then she'd pull out some map, remember some landmark, or simply intuit her way toward getting us back on track. I must admit that she was pretty good at this. She seemed to remember landmarks better than I did and displayed an uncanny ability to find her way around unfamiliar places. But I'm not sure I buy the magnet thing. I think I was simply more oblivious to my surroundings and got lost in thought more often than she. Didn't matter. After reading this article, Meesha concluded that the contents of my cranium pulled fewer iron molecules from the atmosphere than the head of anyone else alive, or dead for less than a year. And she never let me forget it.

So it felt good to smile, and not just because it wasn't yet nine a.m., though the air I breathed was a sour mash dry eighty-five degrees without a single white puff dangling from the blue dome above. No, I smiled because Meesha and I were getting along—

once again. The vacation was working. We were reconciling. We were having fun. That morning, we had had sex, and good sex it was. Meesha had the most beautiful breasts I'd ever seen on any woman, naked or clad, in person or in print. They were simply stupendous. Firm, enormous bellies capped with nipples the size of raspberries protruding from silver dollar areolas of that fruit's color. Sucking on them evoked in me such a sexual rush that the orgasm which inevitably followed was always violently pleasurable, each one seeming to surpass any prior. Satiety was the rule, not the exception, though only temporarily. My desire for Meesha always resurfaced within a day or so—or, at least it had until Hunter died. After that, our sex life sailed into a sand bar. Lately, though, it seemed to me that Meesha and I had rediscovered our intimate bearings.

The path down to the valley was narrow and steep. The rubber soles of my old running sneakers securely gripped lava rock one second, then treaded precariously on loose sand or red, iron-rich dirt the next. The further we descended, the mistier the air became. It was through a vapor shroud that we were passing and it temporarily stole from my view some of the most beautiful scenery Planet Earth has to offer. These thick blankets of dew continuously descended into the valley from Mount Kilialioni, several miles to our left, and Mount Wili'a'inmea, several miles to our right, and merged. Such opaque condensation, interrupted multiple times daily by full throttle precipitation, is what nourished the valley and, with Re'enev's equatorial sunshine, turned it into such a botanical delight. The valley itself, as depicted in my guide book, was a large triangle that narrowed toward the mountains, its vertex squeezing between these rain magnets. At the same time, the valley's center served as a drain. Naturally, over the millennia, this triangular terrain had evolved into a swamp.

At one point during our descent, a gap pierced the dense mist to my upper left, providing me a view across the valley. The moment was precious. I knew it would last only seconds, so I stopped moving. This optimized my vision. Meesha caught up to me, wrapped her arms around my waist, gazed over my left shoulder and said, "This is beautiful. I'm glad I came."

Rain water streaked down the green, rocky face of Kilialioni in streams of silvery white. We saw at least a dozen streaks, despite our limited perspective. I could only imagine how many more were racing down the rest of the mountain side. Each streak seemed separated by only a few feet, though logic told me the difference must be greater. The overall image reminded me of the pearl necklace I had purchased several days earlier at a tourist trap. It was a spot where tall, whistling geysers blew from a spout in a lava tube, whenever the tube received a wave powerful enough to push sea water beneath it. Unlike Meesha, I wasn't impressed. So while she took pictures, I ventured up the hill to a street vendor who was offering her wares from beneath a staked tent. When Meesha finally caught up with me, I placed the necklace over her head. She was stunned. Then astonishment became appreciation and eyes moistened. Suddenly, my antennae vibrated and my buzzer wailed. I'd been married a while now; I knew what was coming. So, to avoid an emotionally silly scene, I struck preemptively: I grabbed my wife and kissed her. It was a success. When her eyes dried, Meesha noticed the length of the necklace and wrapped it several times about her, making each loop shorter than the one prior. The result was a half dozen gleaming streams flowing down her gorgeous front.

When the gap in the mist sealed, I restarted my descent thinking about the valley, the mountains forming it, and Hellameena canyon beyond. I had read so much about this part of Re'enev prior to the hike, and these parcels of information were now resurfacing within my memory.

Hellameena, I remembered, loomed to the rear of the valley, just beyond the last blade-like ridge joining Mount Kilialioni with Mount Wili'a'inmea. Dry, and deeply eroded by the river that snaked them, the iridescent walls of the canyon were horizontally striated with myriad shades of red. I remembered that, during the helicopter tour, the pilot had said each reddish layer was the residue of a volcanic eruption that had occurred, during the development of Re'enev, millions of years ago; and that the depth of each resulting lava flow, each adding further mass to the land, averaged about twenty feet. Scanning the remains of the volcanic layers that had eroded, via the river thus carving the canyon, I could see that hundreds of eruptions had been required to form Re'enev.

Our descent was steep, steeper than I had expected. I leaned on my Ironwood stick to maintain my balance. Meesha grabbed fists full of brush, jutting rocks, and reachable branches. Over real steep spots, I held her hand or arm. In the process, I noticed that my quadriceps never slackened. The skin covering them vibrated incessantly with the quivering sinew beneath. *I can handle this,* I thought, *I'm in pretty decent shape. But how about Meesha?*

I looked back. Her flushed face, so stunningly attractive, flashed me a dubious smile. I returned one, then asked, "You gonna be alright?"

"Ppphhh!"

*Was that a snicker?*

"I'm a trooper!"

*I guess it was.*

"You just concentrate on the trail and don't get us lost!" Then another smile; this one a little more loving, a little less tense.

I smiled back, thinking, *Damn! They don't come any better.* Then I turned around and continued.

To the rear of the canyon, I remembered, ran a coast-long wall of rippled rock, fertilely sheathed in cucumber green, several thousand feet above the shoreline. A terrestrial big brother, this wall shielded the inner island from merciless sea, wind, and rain. And while the perpetually eroding coastal wall served as rampart, Hellameena canyon simply hung loose, passively sheltered behind it—as if no destructive elements could ever reach it—as if a meek, little river hadn't been eating it for years.

Our descent began to taper. At the same time, the earth started oozing black water from beneath my sneaker soles.

Where the path was not worn, torn or muddy, it bulged. These were spongy bulges, lumps of ancient bog. Every inch of unadulterated growth perpetuated a jungle rug of moss, plants, grass, and fungi.

I spun my head right, then left. Flora was exploding all around me. I felt like I had stepped into some exotic, undiscovered Monet. Life in this valley didn't just exist; it burst from every crevice. Lichen gripped every rock. Mushrooms popped beneath every fern. Bracket fungi hung shelves on every tree.

I continued. Each step further drenched my sneakers. I didn't care.

"Good thing we wore old shoes, huh?"

"Yeah," Meesha replied.

My Re'enev guide book had recommended doing so. The iron rich dirt, it said, could not be cleansed from clothes no matter how often you washed them.

When our descent fully ended, telephone poles began. Lain successively end to end, they crudely demarcated each side of the path. As I sloshed between them, I marveled at the brush. The variety and uniqueness of the vegetation, and the bristling intensity with which all things grew, fascinated me.

But it also made me a bit anxious. Why? I didn't know. It may have been the flora's suffocating density, or the choking way the stuff engulfed our path. It may have been the simple fact that no other hikers existed, no other people were around.

Or maybe it was my fear of walking into an encroaching terrain I knew little about and, thus, had no defense for other than the limited knowledge my guidebook could provide. I really didn't know. I just knew what my book had taught me, augmented by the informational tidbits the tour guides had tossed during our earlier excursions on Re'enev.

My limited knowledge included the mountains. Kilialioni, I knew, was Re'enev's tallest with Mount Wili'a'inmea just a few hundred feet behind. Rarely visible was the peak of either. Rising into the trade winds, they were usually hidden by thick, hastily moving blankets of white and gray.

"Hey Meesh," I said, my nose in the guidebook, "says here that the ancient Re'enevians viewed Kilialioni's peak as an insertion point into the heavens—a sacred place. The sacrificing of young virgins upon this peak was a common occurrence."

"It also says," I read verbatim, "that Mount Wili'a'inmea was named by the ancient natives for the abundance of Wili birds that once made the mountain their home. Today, the Wili bird is extinct; but, for hundreds of years, Re'enevian natives had considered the Wili bird sacred."

I, however, had my own theory regarding the origin of Mount Wili'a'inmea's name. While walking through the thick jungle with a human sacrificial alter to my left, and the former mountain roost cloaked in an eerie mist to my right, I couldn't help but feel "The Willies". And I am sure the ancient natives had felt the same. To Hell with the sacred-bird-as-namesake theory.

Having reached the relatively flat floor of the jungle valley, I could no longer see more than fifteen feet in front of me. Yet, up above, just a few hundred feet earlier in our hike, objects in the distance had been so visibly clear. I remembered the warnings we had received at the hotel about how dangerous the jungle could be. Lancing alarm pierced me just below the sternum. I tried to ignore it and assuage my concerns through thought: *This is a documented trail on a map distributed by Re'enev's tourist bureau. There is nothing to fear. Many other people have already hiked it.* This satisfied me logically, but did little for my emotions. Regardless, as I strive to be a man who is guided by, and reacts primarily to, logic, I walked on.

The path had started wide, about four feet across between the prostrate telephone poles. However, as we had walked, it had narrowed. It did so gradually, imperceptibly, for I didn't even realize it until thick, green leaves the size of elephant ears brushed against my shoulders. It was then that I also noticed the perpetual awnings of clumped fern, ten feet and taller, bending over me from both sides. In addition, the spongy moss beneath my sneakers had become mossy sponge: thicker, mushier, and with greater capacity for holding brackish water to flush over my feet. And I heard music. A symphony of bird song harmonized the almost impenetrably dense flora surrounding us. But under the conditions, harmonious song did nothing for human nerves. So, when it came, I wasn't surprised. I had been expecting it.

"Luke, I don't like this. This is freaky. Are you sure you know where you're going?"

"Yes, Meesh. Don't worry. We'll be alright. Just trust me."

How I would soon regret those words.

We marched on. The deeper we went, the denser—the wetter— the more lush everything became. Standing trees spawned vines, flowers, and nettles. Fallen trees spawned standing trees—what died soon rotted and became soil for the living. Beneath what lived, plants and bushes competed with lichen and other fungi for every open inch. At one point, an eerie moss began hanging from every vegetative appendage. It looked like a gargantuan spider web that could entangle a man until its hungry maker was ready to feast.

"How far have we hiked?" Meesha asked.

"I don't know," I said, "but in this terrain, it'll feel farther than it really is." In any case, I felt as though we had plodded for several miles.

Although we were now, technically, in the swamp, beyond the descending entrance trail, the going at times was hilly. The narrow trail snaked up and down and around right angles that offered no warning of, or protection from, precipitous drops, of which there were many. Several times my sneakers slipped on loose rock, or a patch of sand, and I almost went flying; only my good balance saved me. Some inclines were so steep that Meesha and I had to pull ourselves up using the moss clad trees anchored to the mountain. The first time I grabbed the branch of one, I was startled by the cool water that oozed over my hand from its thick, super-saturated sheath.

It was about 10 A.M. when, after covering, according to my guide book, two long and treacherous miles—it seemed like so much more!—we reached a sign that split the path:

This sign disturbed me. Unlike the professional looking, reddish-brown placard with yellow markings that we had read at the beginning of the hike; and similar ones that we subsequently passed, assuring us that we were still on the right path; this sign was amateurish. It was nothing more than white paint scrawled on plywood, using what I assumed had been an artist's brush. *An artist's brush*, I thought, for the strokes were narrow and choppy.

I read in my guide book that heading right would take us just outside the edge of the swamp and the foot of Mount Wili'a'inmea. Then, it would lead us to a triple-pronged water fall that we had seen during our chopper flight. The distance would be another one-and-a-half miles.

Alternatively, going left would bring us into the swamp, which we could cross upon a raised boardwalk. According to my book, the boardwalk had been built to accommodate hikers and save the bog. Peat bog, it explained, takes ten thousand years to form and a single footstep to destroy. Re'enev's wild boar proved difficult to control. Vacationing humans posed less of a problem.

Reading further, I learned that after spanning the swamp—across which it zigzagged for more than a mile—the boardwalk ended and the trail returned to raw earth. It exited the swamp and ascended the coastal wall protecting the west side of Re'enev, then ultimately wound through these cliffs to Re'enev's northern shore. From our helicopter tour, I knew that the coast's tall, sharp ridges and rounded spires were spectacular. This was due not only to their element-sculpted physiques, but to their ferocious fertility. My guide book said that, throughout the cliffs, dozens of fern types fought each other and a myriad of other plants for survival. It also described the cliff-top trail. This intrigued me immensely. Centuries earlier, Re'enevian natives had deliberately cut this amazing path. It ran along precarious terrain, roughly a mile above sea level, and sometimes narrowed to less than a foot. Yet, despite the hazards of trekking this trail, my guidebook said the view more than compensated for the risk. *This* was something I wanted to see.

My guidebook also described the birds that could be seen from the coastal trail: the red breasted, cross-billed Supawannae, an incredibly long-winged Albatross, smooth soaring Frigates, Red-Footed Boobies, Red-Tailed Tropics, and sea skimming Shearwaters. "Can't wait to see those guys!" Meesha said. Bird lovers, we looked forward to seeing these rare and beautiful creatures.

We went left and were soon slogging through ruptured bog, sucking mud, and an uneven rug of tangled grasses, flowers, and weeds. How thick! How pungent! And this was *prior* to the boardwalk.

At two different spots, we passed plywood signs with

<——— SWAMP TRAIL

choppily stroked in that same picket-fence white. These signs were not ambiguous, certainly understandable, and correlated precisely with the directions given in my guidebook. They were effective in confirming our terrestrial navigation, which was vital considering the number of unmarked paths we encountered. But their appearance—the way it so drastically differed with the cosmetic professionalism of the reddish-brown and yellow signs we had encountered earlier along the path—bugged me. It sapped me of some confidence. I felt that in a government owned park of a US territory like this, the rangers could have—and should have!—used better material to direct their guests, the paying tourists. They should have done so if only to fortify the hiker's trust in the directions they had to follow, thus providing them with a vacationer's peace of mind. Now, granted, I wasn't walking point in some third-world civil war. But this wasn't my back yard either.

By the time we reached the unpainted, pressed-wood walk, our sneakers wore cola-colored muck like rubber galoshes.

It took us an hour to walk through the swamp. Without a boardwalk, it would have taken us a day, maybe more—if we could have gotten through at all.

"This place is amazing," I said, "eerie, yet amazing."

"I know," Meesha said, "I feel like I've entered another world or, at the least, landed on another planet."

It wasn't that the composition of this vegetation was radically different from that of the secondary jungle surrounding it. What it *was*, was abundant. *That's* what bludgeoned my senses. There were just more of things—more of everything. The swamp was so much thicker, denser, wetter—so much more severe.

Our guide book said the swamp was classified as a "dry rainforest", though I couldn't see how any place that gets thirty feet of rain a year could be considered "dry". What would it take to be "wet"? Seemed to me that the next notch on the moisture scale would be titled "lake".

Two hundred feet above the boggy earth hung several canopies. These were continual covers of broad-leafed green that

I never saw. In fact, I was lucky when I could see farther than twenty feet. Most of the time, water vapor obscured everything beyond that; but, what I *could* see was surreal, a bit ghostly: misty white sheets drifting through the sprawling green.

"According to the guidebook," I said to Meesha, "the tree-topped canopies are layered." Since I couldn't see them, I tried to imagine them. They appeared in my mind as tents within tents. *No wonder so little sunlight makes it to the forest floor. Yet stuff still grows down here like crazy!* My guidebook had an explanation: "The swamp's under story consists of vegetation that requires less sunlight, but thrives in soaked soil." Wherever I looked— wherever I listened—oxygenated hydrogen dripped onto plastic sounding foliage. It never ended. I heard intermittent bird song and relentless drip. Otherwise, the swamp was silent, eerily silent; and, of course, wet—very wet.

Using our guide book, we identified much of the flora and fowl we saw during our boardwalk stroll. "Look at these!" Meesha would say. "And what are those?" I would counter. Flowers with shapes and color schemes—sunrise reds, early dusk yellows, dirty blood blues, and hallucinogenic purples—I had never seen before, nor could ever have imagined, competed for real estate every inch of the way. A chorus of fowl peeped and cheeped throughout the organic theater, their shrieks heavy with dense valley echo. This snagged my attention.

"Sounds down here are muted. They seem farther away than they really are." Meesha nodded. I noticed that a stepped on leaf bent with a lesser crinkle; a stepped on branch snapped with a lesser crack.

From every tree hung twisting, woody vines. To every tree clung dense, iridescent moss—some so thick that I wondered if moss could grow on moss. I saw ferns of every imaginable dimension and of every imaginable green; no size, shape, or shade seemed implausible. I saw fiddleheads bigger than fists. I saw flat ferns, tall ferns, wide ferns, and short ferns. I saw stalks so thick they reminded me of human backbones. I saw dead ferns so large their cracked fronds bent like lean-tos among the living. *A guy could camp under one of those*, I thought. I wondered if Hunter ever had.

But my favorite discovery on the entire lava lump was the Ula ahi. Ula ahi was Re'enevian for "tree of fire tongues", a name so evocatively appropriate I doubt Shakespeare could have coined better. Meesha read from the guidebook: "It's an endemic plant, found only in the rainforest, and only at an elevation greater than one thousand feet." This astounded me. This gorgeous plant, with its holly colored leaves and clumps of flaming bottle brushes, existed no where else on the planet; yet, it flourished here, before my eyes, with what I perceived as human-like contempt for the boorish plunderers who bore no impact upon it. The goats, pigs, rats, and cats could do whatever they liked, but they couldn't taint one oral organ within the flaming red canvas that permeated the otherwise green swamp, as if the lush terrain were ablaze. "Tree of fire tongues", yes; but also, thought I: *Tree of Fire God*, for it seemed that no less than a deity could have protected a vulnerable organism so well. If only that deity could also have protected vulnerable *people*.

Reaching the end of the boardwalk and the exit to the swamp, I stopped and gazed. "Look at that, Meesh." She looked. In the distance, through a gap in the upper tree canopy and diffusing mist, rose the fern-coated facade of Mount Kilialioni. Again, I saw at least a dozen streaks of glittering white. They hung at irregular intervals, the way my gift of strung Pacific pearls had across Meesha's chest.

Like the path to, the path from the swamp was also deeply muddy. It tenaciously attempted, though again in vain, to pry off my sneakers as I stomped, spawning in me the irrational feeling that the spooky jungle basin was trying to get me any way it could.

When I finally reached dry ground, I glanced down at my feet. *About an hour has passed*, I thought, *since we initially stepped onto the boardwalk. Swamp must be a couple of miles wide.*

Despite its beautiful fauna and the way its exotic composition bombarded our senses with endlessly intriguing detail, we were thankful to be working our way out. Dry dirt now felt like soil from heaven. Even the raised walkway had been muddied enough to sully a hiker's shoes. There had been no way to get through without getting messy.

But our thankfulness was short lived and without warrant. For it was not much later that Meesha, the woman I so thoroughly loved—my Goddess, my buddy, my queen; my soul mate, with whom I had so recently fortified our original bond, re-cementing it with forgiveness, acceptance and understanding; my true equal, my kindred spirit, my partner and companion for life—stepped unwittingly into the jaws of the jungle, the evil behind the good, the ugliness within the beauty.

# Chapter 6

After fighting our way through the sucking mud and ruptured peat to harder, drier, redder ground, I realized we were ascending Mount Kilialioni. The ascent was slight, for the valley was large. We still had much farther to go until we reached steep incline.

The sun reappeared with its former intensity. While it dried the swamp's mistiness from my light-green T-shirt, it pulled sweat pills from my forehead. Then it ducked behind hasty shrouds of white for several minutes before reappearing. This ducking act would occur over and over.

The path beneath me had narrowed. This tapering must have been gradual, like our ascent, for I hadn't noticed it until now. But it was definitely narrower.

It also appeared infrequently used. Grass and weeds grew where, it seemed to me, a regularly traveled route would have been stomped clear. *The drop in tourism*, I reasoned.

A slight breeze caught me on the upper back, cooling my shoulders and flickering leaves in the tall trees. The lower brush surrounding us simply waved. This soft wind cascaded the mountain side during the following hour, though not nearly enough to comfort us. Out of the swamp, we now trekked in secondary rainforest. That, combined with the sun being almost directly overhead, placed shade on the deficiency list. Bird song now rang through the trees with a lighter, crisper shrill. And my breathing was less labored, though I moved faster. *What a difference dry air makes.* We walked on.

Reaching another sign is what truncated our hour of little wind and less shade. This one, like the last three, was amateurish: white, artist-brush strokes, fine and choppy across a piece of plywood. Unlike the last three, however, this one read:

CLIFF TRAIL

<————

I looked left, to where the arrow pointed. I found a path which, like the one we had just traveled, appeared infrequently used. Vegetation sprouted where on an often-used course the red dirt would have been bare and tight.

But then, I noticed, another path veered to my right, yet no arrow pointed that way. This path was hardly worn at all. In fact, calling it a path was generous. It was no more than a swath of bent grass through unadulterated brush. My brain clicked.

"Hey Meesh. I betcha this is the path to the Erkasakal the helicopter pilot was talking about."

"The Er-*what?*"

"Er-kas'-a-kal. Re'enevian for sacrificial altar. Remember?"

"Oh, yeah," she said. "The religious sites made of lava rock."

"That's right. The pilot said there was one down a path off the cliff trail. Remember?"

"Yeah."

"Where the trail went ninety degrees to the left while another path, an unmarked one, went ninety degrees to the right. Right?"

She agreed, then added: "He said most tourists don't know about it. The locals like to keep it a secret, so that it stays pristine. That's why the path's not marked."

"That's right. I think this is it. I think this is the path. It's hardly used. And it's the only fork we've seen that branches so drastically—a hundred-and-eighty degrees. The pilot said there was only one on the trail that did so. You wanna check it out, see if we can find the thing? I'd like to see it."

Eyebrows drop. "Uhh, I don't know, Luke. It *would* be nice to see, but do we have the time? It's a long way to the cliffs."

"Yeah. It won't take that long. We'll just take a few pictures and come right back. I'd like to see one of these things. I find this stuff interesting."

"So do I, but I don't want to get lost. Everyone we've met has said to stay on the trail, never to get off."

"And we'll do just that. The path starts right here. We'll just stick to it until we find the site. You wanna see it? Are you game?"

"Are you sure this is the path the pilot was talking about?"

"Ahhh, no, I'm not sure, but I'm pretty sure. I think it is, based on his description. If it's not, we'll just come back. No big deal."

"Uhh, I don't know, Luke. I'd like to see this artifact too, but I don't want to get lost. That wouldn't be good. I wouldn't like that."

"Ah Meesh, don't worry. We'll be all right."

With smug defiance for convention numbing my undisclosed apprehension, I ignored the

sign and headed right. The going wasn't easy, but difficult in a way diametrically different from that which we'd endured in the swamp. Now, we had to push through vegetation so thick it required that I, leading the way, plow through each step. I would stretch my legs as far in front of me as I could, turning my foot sideways, my toe inwards, to gain maximum stomping width. Then, stepping on the lower portion of each plant, I'd flatten it. *Yeah*, my inner voice naively chimed, *Keep on Truckin'*.

Then my chime fell out of tune: "Are you sure about this, Luke?"

We had progressed about a quarter of a mile along the skimpy trail. The vegetation was thickening around us the way I imagine ants feel when they venture onto a lawn that hasn't been mowed in weeks. I shot my eyes skyward past tall brush dangling tennis-size balls of red and green. The concave dome still reflected an impeccable blue, while its blazing chandelier broiled my neck. Mount Kilialioni loomed to my left, a silent overseer of the valley, as we now walked parallel with her. And I knew Mount Wili'a'inmea, to my far right, watched me from across the swamp; but, I couldn't see her due to vegetation and fog. I still felt a bit anxious about venturing off the established path, but this was offset by my newly acquired Re'enevian spirit, though I'd only been on the volcanic mass for little more than a week.

"Just *hang loose!*" I shot back over my shoulder, lacing the latter two words with sarcasm. Following the trail my stomping feet widened, Meesha snickered. She did so loudly, the gesture obviously intended for my ears.

I laughed. And because I did, I again felt good. *Yeah*, I thought, *just "hang loose"*. And this took me back to the bus ride home from the cultural show Meesha and I had attended our first night on Re'enev.

On the yellow school bus that would return us to our hotel, the strangers with whom we had started the trip were now less strange. People were talking and laughing, producing far more noise than they had while riding to the secluded cove. This, I credited to shared experience, the infusions of Re'enevian spirit with which our hosts had injected us at every opportunity, but mainly the booze.

Meesha and I sat a few rows from the back. As soon as our carefree driver hopped on, he took a head count. The front of his white T-shirt, I noticed for the first time, shouted:

## RE'ENEV
## HANG LOOSE!

in rich, tropical green. Satisfied that his entire herd had returned, the smiling driver grabbed a microphone off the dashboard and started singing a song, which prompted everyone else to start singing along:

"Don't try to fight it,
it ain't no use;
when you're on Re'enev,
you just gotta hang loose."

There were additional stanzas, but I don't remember them. I just remember that the second line ended invariably with a word that rhymed with "loose". This way, the last two lines could remain constant. I must have heard them sung a dozen times.

With about forty cocktail-oiled tourists wailing, my libido, loosened by booze, suddenly wanted Meesha. My left hand gently clutched her right thigh; but, in my mind, it caressed farther up her leg. A bit mai-tai'd, I found my thoughts floating and desires unraveling:

I lead Meesha to the end of the white, sandy beach that we had strolled prior to dinner. Carefree and sexy, Meesha swings her head leisurely as she walks, her straight brown hair sashaying across her back as her full bottom sashays down the beach. I lead her into the midst of some clustered palm trees.

Despite the discordant singing and bumpy bus ride, my mind has no problem maintaining the voluptuous image of Meesha's naked, bikini-tanned flesh beneath me. Likewise, her firm buttocks face little resistance in indenting the bits of bleached coral upon which they swish. So full-bosomed yet lean with forefinger-to-thumb sized nipples that bear the tiniest bumps, always and again reminding me of raspberries, Meesha gently pulls me toward her by my extended, pulsating desire.

She smiles up at me as I enter her, a painfully pleasurable grin, exposing teeth whiter than the sand beneath us. Her eyes are closed and mouth still open when I lower my head and slip my tongue beneath hers. This surprises her; her eyelids flick open, but close just as quickly, all at camera-shutter speed. Twisting my head sideways, I sink my mouth's organ deeper and tongue her entire cavity, sucking and swallowing her carnal succulence. My tongue slips over her inner cheeks, their tissue soft, wet, and smooth, while fleshy lips betray salivating passion as they press and pucker against my own. And her breath, so hot and sweet, invokes in my mouth a burst of the most deliciously erotic flavor—what sex would taste like were it candy.

Her breath is heavy now and becomes heavier the faster I pump. Suddenly, my loins fill with a slight pressure, which increases incrementally with my every thrust. At the same time, hot lubrication soaks my groin. When the pressure in my pelvis becomes so agonizingly wonderful that I feel out of control— that I would drink fresh cement to simply bring closure to the sensation—I cup her buttocks and lift her off the sand, sucking and kissing her smooth, tender neck as—

*Her neck.* Here I was, ready to explode—hot, excruciating pleasure—when the thought of her neck ended my fantasy, and I found myself sitting on the bus with my left hand on my wife's leg and an erection for her image in my shorts.

My fellow bus riders were still chanting about "hanging loose", so I started to lip sync the words. But guilt-laced dejection killed my enthusiasm, so I just sat there. *Why the neck? Why the FUCK'N neck? It always came back to that! Why did I have to think of her neck? DAMN it!*

I snapped back from the aftermath of the drunken feast to the edge of the sober swamp, still a bit jovial from bantering with Meesha about "hanging loose", but also tainted from having thought—once-a-fucking-gain!—about her neck.

*Scars and Stripes Forever!*

As usual, my inner voice tried to numb my pain with sarcasm. However, this just invited more guilt—guilt that masqueraded as a conscience, but which admonished with emotion only, no logic. I wasn't in the mood.

*Oh no? And why not? Words fit the picture, don't they?*

My mind paused a moment before blurting: *Damn it! Things are good again between us! I've got to stop thinking about this shit!*

I stepped harder on the crunching stems, purging my angst and anger through the stiff stalks that buckled beneath my feet. *Will I never be able to put the past behind me? I thought THAT'S what this trip was all about!*

I pushed forward about a quarter mile—then another—then another. Up above, the Gas Burning God was slipping from, then back behind, clouds as often as our pseudo path had been zigzagging around obstacles. I wasn't sure what all these obstacles were, for I couldn't always see them. But this was par for the course, for I couldn't always see the path either. Sometimes, my eyes would snag nothing more than a bent piece of grass, or some broken brush. Had I not been so determined to find the Erkasakal, I would have stopped at one of these points and headed right back.

However, I wanted to find this sacred site. So much, in fact, that I tolerated moments when my eyes snagged nothing at all; when I actually found myself off the damn trail and breaking my own, simply to get Meesha and me back to a trace of the one we had been following.

Meesha didn't notice when we were temporarily lost. She couldn't tell whether the trail beneath her had been broken by me, or had already been trodden upon when I had reached it.

Then my stomach sizzled. The burn lasted as long as the fact that the path I had been following was right around me, except that *this time* I couldn't find it. Trying not to panic, I looked all around, cleared brush all around, even jumped up and down—while ensuring Meesha didn't see me—but the trail was nowhere to be found.

I glanced up. The sun burned directly overhead. It was noon. Furthermore, in the northern hemisphere, I knew, the sphere traversed the sky with a southern slant. It currently hung to my right. Thus, I was heading East.

*Noon*, I thought. Then I remembered the spectacular sunsets Meesha and I had enjoyed during our vacation thus far. This was occurring around eight o'clock, I recalled, maybe a bit earlier.

*But what is important are the shadows. The brushy coastal areas start to dim between five and six.* I remembered walking down wooded paths to the perimeter beaches. Raised characteristics upon each tree's face displayed as a two-dimensional blur. This was not the vision I wanted for exploring a rain forest.

So I had a good five or six hours left. *No problem*, I thought, *plenty of time*. I would just truck on, find the path, see what I could see and, when I'd had enough, head back and onto the cliffs. At that point, the path would be further trodden by my size twelve's, providing an easier trail to find and a familiar, thus faster one to follow.

While searching for our trail, I thought of Hunter. *HE would have no trouble finding the path. He never would have LOST it.* This bugged me, though I knew it shouldn't. I had never been a Force Recon Marine. I had never been trained for jungle travel. I was a city boy. I was trained for the office: aggressive deadlines, crashing systems, jammed copiers, and snappy secretaries. I didn't go my father's way, didn't conform—I was the alleged alpha. But I have to admit that I envied the fact that my father and brother possessed rugged military knowledge, such as outdoor survival skills, that I did not. It caused a remote capillary within my ego to throb whenever the thought arose. What this signaled, I'm not sure; just that it taunted me occasionally with doubts about my ability to perform in dangerous, unconventional situations.

Of course, over the years, it was impossible for me not to pick up tidbits of gung-ho know-how, simply from the military conversation and documentation that polluted my upbringing. My mother called our house "The Barracks".

I looked over my right shoulder. Meesha was struggling through grass and vines I had parted just ten feet earlier. Birds fluttered in the trees above her. A butterfly danced in the humidity by her head. I stopped to watch.

She wore white shorts cut at mid-thigh. Her brown hair jutted from beneath a white painter's cap, which shouted BIG RED from its frontal crown in stenciled, blood-vibrant bold. But the Cornell cap could not vaporize the estuaries that streamed down her heated complexion and tendon-striated neck. Nor could they impede the blotchy red that had crept from her face, down her neck, and across her chest. As she approached, her thigh muscles bulged femininely with each step.

I did not have to ask. Her expression spoke volumes. But I did anyway.

"How ya doin'?"

"How much further?"

"Answer the question. Don't ask one."

"Shut up and tell me how much further I have to go."

I smiled. When Meesha caught up, I took her hot body into the cusp of my right arm and gave her luscious frame a tight squeeze. I held her for several seconds longer than I typically would—that is, longer than the span of my usual hugs—and she acquiesced to my embrace for as long as I held her. Then, as soon as I released her, Meesha raised her right hand to her forehead. Her index finger and thumb like pincers, she deftly whisked perspiration from her eyebrows.

"Just a little further," I said, "I wanna see what's up ahead. I think the terrain changes a bit. If it's not there, we'll turn around."

Meesha nodded, leaking a barely perceptible reluctance, and I again took the lead.

The terrain did change, and just after I rediscovered the trail. How faint the damn thing was! Nothing more than a few blades of broken grass. *No wonder I lost it! Gotta be more careful. Can't lose it again.*

The trail lead us through more thick brush, muddy bog, jail-door bamboo, and trees of myriad variety. We zigzagged through this dense wetland, referencing our guide every so often to identify nature we encountered. It was a lot of fun, despite the apprehension I felt about moving so far off the main path, so deep into brush so infrequently traveled—practically virgin territory. Nonetheless, I kept going, propelled by adventurous curiosity.

I've always felt that to truly experience and enjoy a foreign land, one must visit spots other than the tourist magnets. One must travel the real terrain, meet the real people, and experience their customs. In that mode of thought, I felt good, for I knew that Meesha and I were exploring off the established route, seeing things that we may never have a chance to see again. And had I known ahead of time what these things were, I would have stayed at the hotel, plopped by the pool, guzzling beer, sipping Mai Tai's, and slurping Pina Coladas all day long. But because I did not know, Meesha and I ventured forth, deliberately consuming the beautiful wild life within our vision; while, at the same time and to an even greater extent, that wild life consumed us. For it was when the tree canopy began getting a little taller and sparser, the underbrush a little higher and thicker, and the ground a bit drier, that something metallic *clinked!* and Meesha's agonizing scream ripped through the hot jungle air. It was a howl seared by pain. And when I spun toward her, terrified, I found within a cloud of dirt, dust, and vegetative debris, the most beautiful features I have ever known contorted into the most hideous face I have ever seen.

# Part 2

# Chapter 7

I rush through the brush on feet with no nerves. Were land mines exploding beneath me, I wouldn't notice. I'm too consumed. Meesha's screaming has completely sucked me in: eerie screams, terrifying screams; at first, high-pitched shrieks—vocal darts that plunge into my heart—they become guttural, polysyllabic utterances I cannot interpret.

I reach her. I look down. I find an eye-bulging, cavern-mouthed, tortured fish face glaring wildly, but seeing only pain. I want to scream, but know I can't.

*"Survival rule #1,"* Hunter says suddenly in my head, *"Stay calm. Keep your composure, especially when caring for casualties. Don't want 'em to panic."*

A subdued metallic glint shimmers from the inner, biting edge of one of the triangular teeth snarling at me. There are at least a dozen. I can see all of them except for those that are imbedded in Meesha's right calf—imbedded just below where her shin bone protrudes from her mangled appendage, which now bends at 45° in a spot where the human leg should not bend.

*A TRAP! What the fuck is this DOING here!*

Fully open, the half-circle jaws would extend well beyond a yard. *Big enough for bears. FUCK IT! Doesn't matter! Can't waste time!*

I look at Meesha, her pain-rippled face oozing screams, tears, and agony. *I have to act!* My body begins to tremble. *I have to act NOW!*

A ton of despair detonates within me. *Oh Meesha! Oh fuck! Oh, my honey!*

I cry, not recognizing my strained, frenzy-tempered tone as I frantically scan and analyze the trap: "Don't worry Meesh! Just hold on, honey! I'll get you out! Just hold on, sweetheart! Just hold on!"

During the century-long-second, I identify the Slicing Satan's key components. I see two teeth-bearing iron bands, each a half-circle, widest in the middle and gradually narrower toward the ends, where they hinge to form a full circle. My screaming senses tell me that the right band——the one nearest me—had hit Meesha's leg first; a direct smash to her fragile, unprotected right shin, thus demolishing it. Then, a millisecond later, the opposing band swinging upwards from the left had bit into the outer portion of her calf, its sharp, crude teeth sinking into her flesh with merciless, mechanical anger. I also see two V-shaped steel, diving-board-like springs lying on their sides as such: < >, each with its open end facing the hinged bands; and a thin, steel pin permanently fastened to an extension of the trap's underlying base on one end while hanging loose on the other, but only when the trap is idle. When the trap is set, the loose end hooks beneath a notch in the iron neck supporting the trap's trip pedal.

I square my shoulders with the V-shaped springs and the hinges that join the jaws. I plunge the Ironwood stick's pointy end into the moist, cakey earth just beyond the trap's circular perimeter. My body, arms, and stick arch over the metal monster ensnaring Meesha.

I raise my right leg until my thigh ascends away from me. My quadriceps tremble with anxiety; their enveloping skin weeps liquid angst. Against the vibrating black-ground of my mind, I imagine Meesha writhing and screaming as I rock the trap, further mangling the bleeding, S-shaped appendage that had once been her leg. This screws me all up. I am panting in a natural, outdoor sauna, but with thoughts that feel more like frozen steel ripping gray strips from my brain. My aching soul begs: *Please God, throw her into shock!*, knowing well the severe consequences such a state can produce. Doesn't matter. Fuck the consequences! I'd give a kidney and a lung right now, on the spot, for a single hypodermic of morphine; but such bargains exist only in my dreams. Instead, I hope desperately that, somehow, Meesha's body can generate enough endorphins to deaden the pain, if only a little.

Meesha screams as I pull the Ironwood stick's upper girth against the semi-circular jaw farthest from me, straightening the trap vertically. Actually, they are more than screams. They're audible shivs that pierce my eardrums to puncture my brain and impale my heart. But they fail. I ignore them. *To get Meesha out, I have to repress my emotions! I have to push on!*

I squeeze the Ironwood stick as I step onto the V-shaped spring to the right of the shark jaws, placing my foot on its descending top arm. Tension stiffens my own arms as I hold myself aloft. I sort of feel like I'm floating. But the spring barely descends. *Damn!* I was hoping that one foot would be enough.

I squeeze the Ironwood stick harder. I lift my left foot up, onto the spring to the left of the shark jaws.

The springs sink several more inches. It's enough to release the teeth from Meesha's leg, but not enough to extract the limb. I have to fully open the jaws.

*Damn*, I think, *these springs deliver some force!* Two hundred pounds, yet I'm still almost a foot off the ground. Below, to my right, Meesha writhes and moans. My darting eyes catch her leg bleeding copiously from gashes where iron teeth have punctured, and her own shin bone has ruptured, her skin. I have to figure out another way to flatten the springs. And I have to do it soon! *But how?*

My arms still stiff, my hands still clamps upon the Ironwood, I slowly bend my knees. I try hard, as I sink, not to wiggle or tip the trap. My only objective is to minimize, then eliminate, Meesha's anguish.

I don't know exactly what I am going to do. However, I know that my standing upright hasn't extricated Meesha, nor has it provided me any insight to how I might.

I descend slowly. Through the pressure of my clutch upon the Ironwood stick, I feel my body's leverage increase. I keep my head up. To preserve my balance, I focus my eyes on the broad, ridged trunk of a Makoa tree a few yards in front of me. It takes a while for me to descend. As I do, Meesha groans. Inch by inch, I lower, slower than a clock's second hand.

When about halfway down, I lower my eyes. I want to know how much farther I have to go. And it is then that I figure out how to extricate Meesha. The solution is simple; but its execution, difficult.

I move the Ironwood stick inside the perimeter of the trap's circular jaws, then use it as leverage while lowering myself to a full squat. I make sure that I maintain even pressure, thus motion, through my hands and arms, so that I don't jerk the trap in any way.

Hamstrings on calves, I lower my head sloooowwwwly. Chin on chest, I scan the ground directly below. Fearful of tipping the trap, I press harder on the stick whenever I feel the slightest forward momentum. Meesha moans without pause.

I lean the Ironwood stick against my stomach, then reach down with both hands and grab the trap's underlying base. Squatting stone still, I focus on Meesha. She continues to writhe and moan, but with even less intensity than just minutes before. *Is she drifting into shock?*

Every nerve in my stomach flickers, every muscle in my body flexes, as I pull upward on the trap's base. The longer I pull, the deeper I sink. And I don't stop pulling until I stop sinking, until I have reached the base, until the top arm of each spring lays upon the bottom arm, until I can pull no more.

Maintaining pressure upon the springs with my feet, I move my hands to the trap's circular face. I push down hard. In the process, the Ironwood stick slips from my abdomen to the ground.

But I feel good. I have the beast under control. I grab the stick, place both hands on it, turn to my right, and shove it into earth. Leaning on the stick, I reach over, grab the pin, and lay it across the jaw between the trip pedal and the extension to the trap's base. Then I fasten the pin, hooking it in the notch indented for it within the trip pedal's neck.

The trap is now set. The shark jaws will snap only if I step off the jaws and pressure is applied to the trip pedal. But with Meesha's leg still in there, I'm not taking any chances.

I scoop mud, grass, dirt and other debris lying along the ground and push it beneath the trip pedal. To fill this space requires several dozen scoops. When I can push no more beneath the pedal, I pummel it with the Ironwood stick. Confident that the pedal will not sink one millimeter under substantial pressure, I move on.

Head down, I slowly step off the trap—then abruptly look up, to my right. *What was that?* I scan the green canvas a few yards beyond the Makoa tree, where my senses tell me the vegetation had moved. *What moved it? What caused that branch-breaking sound?* I peer beneath curtains of hanging moss and dangling vines, between trees and plants so profuse with parasitic life that I wouldn't blink were a talking snake to offer me an apple. Something had moved in this dense flora just a few yards from me, but it was no snake. Snakes are too agile for the sound I heard.

I turn toward Meesha. I study the bloody bone jutting from her calf. I can't tell, due to the flap of skin enveloping it, but I'm hoping it's a flat crack, relatively even across the top.

I look down at her face. I implicitly know it is beautiful. But, at the moment, it seems so irrevocably contorted. *Oh, the*

*PAIN she's in! Why did I take her DOWN HERE? My WIFE? My MEESHA? My HONEY? Oh God, please STOP it! Please HELP her! She's in such AGONY! Oh God, no MORE! Pleeaasssse! No MOOOOORRRRREEE!*

I suddenly think of all the pain that Meesha has suffered during our marriage, and this gives me the urge to sweep the dirt from beneath the bear trap pedal and trip the fucker with my head. *HOW COULD I HAVE BEEN SO WRONG? SO SELFISH? SO FOOLISH? SO STUPID?*

Then I feel an abrupt change, a tilt to my mental equilibrium, as different as the eye is to the rest of the Hurricane: *STOP IT! You're RUNNING! DEAL with the situation! Don't dodge it! DEAL with it!*

I fully comprehend the task before me. That's the problem. *DAMN! Why is it that so many things that are best for people—the right things to do—are the most difficult?* I actually think about knocking Meesha out. *Unconsciousness is better than pain. But that's a state she'll probably end up in anyway. Why add concussion to her list of problems?*

*Look at the bright side,* I suddenly think, glancing at Meesha's lower calf—I have been monitoring Meesha's calf with such glances from the moment her leg snapped—*it's not pale, overly swollen, or excessively bruised. Could have been worse: bone could have torn an artery. Then you'd be making life or limb decisions with a tourniquet, a simple toggle twist determining her fate. Thinka THAT. You're lucky! So stop fuck'n whining and do whatcha gotta do!*

# Chapter 8

I knew I would have to do this to poor Meesha the instant I saw the dull white streaming viscous red poke through her skin. *Fuck!*

It would not be prudent to do while she still lay in a lethal trap. But whether she lies in a trap or not, I have to act and act now—I have to seize the opportunity—before the sharp splinter cuts a vessel, or the skin it impales becomes infected. *We're in the jungle. Infections thrive. You can't wait. You've got to do it now! Right away!*

Damn Hunter! Of all the things a guy can pass on to his brother! Some guys might get money; others, family heirlooms; some, even, nephews and nieces to raise. But what does my brother leave me?: Knowledge of how elite Marines survive in the wild. For crying out loud, I work in the city! I make my living whacking QWERTY! A vice-president with hemorrhoids is the meanest thing I'll ever face!

Or so I had thought. Shit, if I had only known.

But I never thought I would have to use this kind of knowledge. And, especially, not on my Meesha.

I slowly step off the mud-muzzled trap, then gently slide the camera strap off Meesha's neck. I lay the 35mm Canon on the ground behind me along with the flimsy nylon knapsack I had dropped when Meesha began screaming. With the oppressive rainforest exhaling thermal fumes into each and every of my dilated pores, and my wife becoming paler, colder, and more detached by the second, I am not ignorant of the colossal task before me. So, as I kneel to pick up Meesha, with sweat raining from my head and face, I clench my teeth, praying: "Dear Jesus, please help me. If never again, at least this once! Please help me."

I look down at Meesha. Tears blur my vision. Several drop and swiftly merge with hers, cascading her cheeks. My lips tremble. I fight back convulsions that beg to break my precarious composure. I feel so impotent. I can't stand to see Meesha in such pain. It kills me. I'd give my soul to trade places with her.

"Honey," I whisper, my mind pre-executing every step I will have to perform, my throat salty and tight. "Please hold on, sweetheart. I'll get you out. Just please hold on. I love you, hon."

I wipe my eyes on my shoulder sleeves, then lift Meesha as gently as I can—first up, then away from the lock-jawed shark's mouth. But my gentleness is in vain. Meesha screams with such agony that I mentally seek, again, some way to numb her. But I can think of nothing other than physically knocking her out; which, of course, I could never do to my wife.

"It's okay, Meesh." I say softly through a mouth dry with fear. "Don't worry. I'll get you outta here."

I carry her to a forked tree, the closest I can find whose trunk splits at a level lower than my waist. I lay her gently on the ground with her legs straddling the tree and her head in my hands. Just a few feet from us grows a patch of ferns. These ferns sprout large fronds, broader than the shutters on our house. Continuing to hold Meesha's head with my left hand, I lean with my right and rip several fronds from their stalks. I place these fronds on the moist earth beneath Meesha's head. Then I gently lay her head upon them.

I stand up. Reaching full height, I study Meesha's mangled leg. I don't move my eyes, but my peripheral vision notices that her left leg extends beyond her broken one—not a whole lot, but enough for me to detect a difference. At the same time, I hold my breath for a count of ten. When slowly exhaling, I feel my pulse decelerate. Paradoxically, my anxiety suspends briefly while reddish still frames flash in my mind. I chronologically foresee infection—pus—maggots—gangrene then amputation, if I don't administer the necessary aid punctually and properly. And these are just my red thoughts. I don't peek at any black ones. They would bring my angst hurdling back at Olympic fifty-meter speed.

I glance at the tree. I know it's a tree, yet I cannot see one square inch of bark or wood. Rather, I see a stout trunk with jutting limbs, all sheathed in moss equal parts green, brown, and yellow. Thicker than a shag rug and appearing just as soft, the moss assuages my anxiety a bit, despite its eerie look: *It'll provide cushioning.* I had planned on lining the fork with fern fronds or something similar, but decide the moss will sufficiently serve the purpose.

I glance down at Meesha. I see a stranger. She spits forth a shriveled countenance that hideously squeezes a distorted mouth, swollen eyes, and clamped lids—lids that shroud the wells of endless tears. Beads of the latter continuously merge with perspiration to push streams down every slope of her face. I wonder what she is thinking. I wish she would talk. I think maybe I should speak. Then I feel the desire to cry. So I stop thinking altogether and throw myself into the task.

Meesha howls when I place her calf within the tree's fork. Her shriek shaves my entrails, but I ignore it. I have to. I have to keep going. I lower her ankle just beyond the wooden V, so that her upper Achilles tendon fills the V's pointed joint.

"Okay, Meesh. Bear with me, honey. This is gonna hurt a bit. I gotta fix your leg. Just bear with me, sweetheart."

I grab the broken shafts of Meesha's shin as gently as possible, but with an objective to meet; and I am going to meet it as quickly as I can, to minimize Meesha's trauma and pain.

But the instant my left hand touches torn skin, I think about sanitization: *Hey asshole! This is an open wound! You're in the jungle where shit thrives. You wanna kill her with your germs?* I am in such mental chaos that I haven't considered cleaning my hands.

It is too late already. I know that. I'll have to address the antiseptic thing later. Right now, it's more important to deal with the leg itself, before its muscles freak out on me.

"Okay, Meesh. Hold on, hon." My bottom lip quivers, making it tough to talk. My eyes continue to water, making it tough to see. "I have to tell ya: This is gonna hurt. Just stay with me. Okay? I love you."

I inhale deeply. I do not exhale, though I hold my mouth open. An observer might think cellophane seals my lips. Then my arms move.

It is not a tug, but a slow——firm——pull and I can feel the severed bones slip past each other. Meesha's body tightens as if she were hoisting a great weight, then her voice box blows at an octave fire engines fail to reach. My stomach clenches with the squeal of her pain, my tear ducts burst a squall of compassion. I try to speak, but salty saliva gags me, though it doesn't matter: Meesha goes limp before my caressing words could have reached her ears.

I maneuver the bones through Meesha's calfskin, pulling them back so that their broken ends do not extend beyond each other. Then, I reconnect them, sliding the severed edge of one across the severed edge of the other. I press my fingers firmly. Only skin separates my hands from broken bone. I press along the fractured circumference to align the bone surfaces as perfectly as I feel possible—to minimize any overlap. Each time I squeeze Meesha's bones, I feel and hear their surfaces grind. The waves of my pulse repeatedly slam against the hull of my ears, yet the distinct *grating* remains unmistakable. *Thank you, God, for removing her from this pain.*

The distinct *grating* continues. *Damn, this sucks!* However, I am tremendously thankful that Meesha is unconscious. *God, please keep her this way for a while. Don't let her suffer. Please.*

I glance at my arms. Sweat coats each the way butter layers a hot pan prepared for frying. My eyes sting. My scalp itches. I am thirsty and scared, and I've only just begun. Nonetheless, I feel relieved, having successfully reconnected Meesha's bone. *Thank God it wasn't a compound fracture!* That might have been too much—a bit too hard to set.

I rush to the tall, Makoa tree a few yards before me. I find the end of a broom-handle-thick branch hanging a few feet off the ground. Reaching as high as I can, I break the branch. I yank and twist it free from the tree's trunk. I pull off all its leaves, fruits, and twigs. Branch in hand, I rush back to Meesha.

I scan the jungle around me, though I know I won't find any. *And even if you did, you'd have to boil it first. You don't have time for that!*

*Damn!* I know the alternative. I've heard it a dozen times—*fuck you Hunter!*—but shudder at the mere thought of subjecting my wife to it.

I scan my visible vicinity once more. It isn't much—about fifteen or twenty feet in each direction. Suddenly, my eyes stop. *Not bad,* I think, *considering I wasn't even sure what I was looking for.*

To my left, beyond the moss smothered tree holding Meesha's leg, rises another. In addition to moss, inch thick liana spirals up this tree's trunk in a suffocating coil. The vine not only rises up the tree, but creeps beyond its base onto black dirt, fungi infested boulders, iridescent peat, and rotting logs.

I grab the vine with both hands above my head and yank. I should have known better. Vines don't proliferate in a jungle because they are flimsy.

I slosh over to the spread of fungi-covered boulders over which the vine sprawls. Along the edge I find a small one. I dig and tug at its front with the heel of my right sneaker. It moves a little. I bend over and pull it from the earth with my hands.

I am in luck. About a foot in diameter, relatively thin, and smooth along the surface, the stone bears an edge.

I slosh back to the vine-coiled tree. One hand grasping each side of the stone hatchet, I raise it above my head. My thighs quiver. My stomach clenches.

I lower the stone with a motion similar to, and with as much force as, I would use to split firewood. A dozen whacks puts me through so that I begin denting the tree trunk below.

I pull the lower piece of severed vine from around the tree. I tug at it along the ground, yanking its hooked arms and tendrilled fingers off other jungle life.

Reaching the fungi-covered boulders, I replicate the wood-splitting motion I had used against the tree. Now pounding against stone instead of wood, I am able to slice the vine in half as many strokes.

I cut the vine into many pieces, several groups of varying lengths, then begin rushing them back to Meesha. Along the way, though, I stop at the patch of humungous green ferns and break off at least a dozen fronds.

At the moss covered forked tree, I whip off my sneakers, then my socks, then throw my sneakers back on. To keep them clean, I place my socks next to Meesha, along the edge of the fronds on which her head lay. Then I cover my socks with the fronds I have just gathered.

I grab my Ironwood stick and the Makoa branch. I notice that the former is twice as long and twice as thick as the latter. *Doesn't matter. The Makoa stick is good enough for what I need it for.*

I grab my green knapsack and pull out the rental car keys. I run the sticks, car keys, and chopping stone back to the cluster of boulders. I lay the sticks side by side. Using the trunk key, I begin sawing. I saw into one end of each stick, my intended notch parallel with the stick's length. I saw until the notch in each stick is deep and wide enough to insert the sharp edge of my chopping stone.

I grab the stone. I place its sharp edge within the notch of the Ironwood Stick and begin pounding. I bang the stick as if I'm trying to split it in half lengthwise. I pound the stick progressively harder each stroke, careful not to overdo it, until I extend the sawn notch with a two-inch crack.

I grab the Makoa Stick and replicate the task.

I rush back to the moss-covered tree. I pick up the camera by its black nylon strap. The middle of the strap bears a thin, oval, rubber pad for neck comfort. Each end of the strap loops through a plastic ring welded along each side of the camera; each loop closes when it weaves back through a plastic buckle.

Quickly but carefully, I undo each loop. With the neck strap free, I place the camera in the green knapsack. Then I recreate loops at each end of the strap.

Along the lip of the knapsack's neck, the satiny green enfolds a thin nylon rope. I pull the rope out of the knapsack's neck. It is about a foot and a half long.

I grab the Ironwood and Makoa sticks. I place them side by side, their split ends together.

I grab the camera neck strap. I pull one looped end up the slit of the Makoa stick, the other up the slit of the Ironwood stick. Then I yank on both loops to ensure that they are tightly wedged within their respective stick slits.

I place the Makoa branch along the inside of Meesha's mangled leg, then lay the Ironwood stick along the outside, both within the tree's fork.

Grabbing the neck strap a hand's distance up from the rubber pad, I create a double-looped circle. I slip the circle carefully over Meesha's foot. Then I slowly adjust the neck strap by its plastic buckles, closing the circle gently but firmly just above her ankle.

Using four of the shorter vine pieces I have cut, I tie the splints to Meesha's leg. I place the first around her ankle, just above the camera neck strap. The rest I wrap around her upper shin, lower thigh, and upper thigh. I fasten all with temporary overhand ties, not wanting to knot them just yet.

I grab three of the longer vine pieces. Using simple overhand ties again, I fasten the Ironwood stick against Meesha's lower torso.

I pick up the thin nylon rope. I am glad I have this. I don't feel fully confident in the retaining integrity of the vine strips. Had I more time, I would strip their fibers and reweave them into stronger cordage, using a more complex braid. But, time I don't have. I have to make do with raw vine. *I'll just use extra.*

I tie the knapsack rope around the sticks by Meesha's lower knee. Though I use a single tie, I pull them together fairly tight. Then I check the vine strips, pulling a couple that are too loose for my liking, and further tightening the camera-neck-turned-ankle strap.

I stand up straight and reevaluate Meesha's position. Then I grab some of the fronds that lay on my socks beside her head. I place them side by side, along the ground next to her body, covering the strip of mud that stretches from below her raised foot to beside her right hip.

Then I bend my knees. I place my left hand beneath the sticks just below her right, upper Achilles tendon and my right hand beneath the sticks at her mid-thigh. I am extremely careful, deliberate with each move. *Her shinbone CANNOT slip!* Barely breathing, I lift her right leg from the fork in the tree; then I lower it upon the mat of ferns I have just laid, as slowly as I can while continuing to move.

I turn toward the forked tree. Using both hands, I rip thick, iridescent moss from its trunk until I have stacked a pile more than two feet high.

I loosen the vines and nylon rope that are single tied around the splint sticks and Meesha. I grab the rest of the ferns lying by Meesha's head. Between each splint tie and Meesha—each spot where her skin could get chafed by vine or rope—I place a fern, then stuff it with moss.

I grab one of my socks. *God, this is awful!*
*Don't THINK about it! Just DO IT!*
I unbutton my pants and pull them below my groin. The hot jungle air greets my genitals with an unexpected coolness. I press my right hand against my lower belly. I feel the pressure; I know I have some. My left hand fumbles with the sock to ensure that I am holding it by the lower, dirtier portion, that which had contained my foot. Then I release on the upper portion, which had covered my ankle and calf.

The white cotton discolors immediately—an ammonia-reeking, sunflower yellow—but I don't waste it all there. When the upper sock is soaked, I attempt to arrest the flow, but cannot. So I fuse my fingers and fill my palm cavity. My hand is just about to overflow when I finally run dry. Moving slowly, trying hard not to spill any, I pour my concentrated urine along the ridged bone of Meesha's shin. I pour slowly and deliberately to ensure that I cover each inch of skin around her wound. Then I gently message my warm, body fluid all around her punctured skin as well as over the flaps along the open gash. I spread the precious antiseptic as efficiently as I can.

I grab the sock. I pass it over the same areas, rubbing with its sanitized end. To meticulously clean Meesha's wound, I fold a soaked portion of the sock over my forefinger. With my finger, I brush away every speck of foreign matter that I can see. Then I pass the warm, soaked sock over all damaged skin to ensure that I disinfect every impacted spot, regardless of what I can see. *Thank God she's out! Though I guess this would have put her there, if she hadn't been.*

I place the antiseptic sock on top of the wound. Actually touching Meesha's skin lays the side of the upper sock that I did not use to cleanse her. I place my other sock on top of the soaked one. Then I cover both with moss and a fern, and tie it all down with a piece of vine.

I go back over all the splint ties and retie them with a square knot. "A square knot's good for first aid," I heard my father once say, "It lies against the victim's body. Doesn't bug him."

I go back over each tie as well as the ankle brace again, and tighten them as I see necessary. I need Meesha's leg snug. It can't move; that, I have to ensure.

I stand up and look down at Meesha. I find it hard to believe that I'm in the middle of a jungle, on an island in the Pacific, and that the woman lying unconscious before me is my wife. It's so fucked, seems so surreal. I don't think I'd be anymore surprised to see Jell-O clocks drooping from branches on the moss-covered tree.

*Infection.* I can't stop thinking about infection. I have to get going. I have to get Meesha out of here! We're in the middle of a tropical swamp, my wife unconscious with a fractured leg and gaping surface wound; and we have no first aid, not even a fucking Band-Aid.

I pick up the camera and knapsack and throw them into a patch of congested, waist high ferns a few feet away. The fern canopy hides them well.

I curl my right arm beneath the small of Meesha's back and my left arm behind her knees. As I lift her belly onto my shoulder, I thank God again for having rendered her unconscious. *Unconsciousness, though it presents its own potential consequences, is so much better than the pain she was suffering and would have suffered.* Or so I think.

Holding Meesha tight, I start back, intending to follow the trail on which we had hiked in. I think of infection again. *Damn! I have to stop thinking about this!*

# Chapter 9

After roughly a dozen steps, I stop. Meesha lies too loose. She sort of flaps as I trudge. Knowing the journey ahead is hot, long, and hilly, I need her in the best position, the way my father taught me to carry casualties.

My right arm currently clasping her upper thighs and lower buttocks, her right hand in my left, I twist her body clockwise upon my shoulders as gently as possible. Then I pass her right wrist, across my chest, from my left hand to my right.

I start walking again. Meesha lays across my upper back, shoulders, and neck. Her head hangs to my left; her feet dangle to my right. A pendulum, a catalyst for locomotion, my left arm swings freely to propel my body out of this sweltering quagmire as quickly as possible. At the same time, my right arm hugs Meesha's lower thighs, strapping her against my frame. It also pulls her right arm across my chest and presses her wrist against her right thigh, anchoring it.

She now flops less and I push on. For about one hundred steps, I'm fine. I see a clump of slanted grass here, a faint foot print there, a dent in mud ten feet later; thus, I know that I'm on track. But then it stops! Just like *that*! Nothing more! *What the fuck!*

I go back a few yards and start again. There isn't much to begin with; but, after a few steps, there is *nothing*! Not a single trace. Any impressions Meesha or I had made in the terrain have been absorbed by resilient turf, have blended with previously corrupted earth, or remain hidden. The trail is dead-—cold—silent. *Shit!*

I retreat and try once more. I search hard, desperately hard, back through the same opaque brush, slurping mud, mutilated bog, and jail-cell bamboo. Such thick flora! Such copious moss! Such ubiquitous fungi! Zigzagging through muck, my wounded, unconscious wife on my back, and I can't find my fucking way! Just as I had sometimes lost the trail on my way in, I have now lost it on my way out. *Damn! Will ya give me a fuck'n BREAK!*

It's funny how, all of sudden, the birds no longer sound pretty, the flowers no longer look beautiful.

Suddenly, I feel Meesha move. A slight tension reconfigures her frame. I stop walking and glance down to my left. Her eyes open briefly. Then they close. Then they open again, this time a little longer; then they close again. This goes on for a few moments: open—close—open—close. At the same time, Meesha starts to moan; not loud, just a gasping murmur; the respiratory struggle you'd expect from someone waking to intense pain. It kills me to hear it, kills me to watch her. *She's gotta be in agony.* "It's okay, Meesh," I say, swallowing salty spit, my throat retightening, "please bear with me. We'll get outta here. Just try to hang in there, sweetheart. I know it hurts, but just try to hang tough. Stay with me, hon. I love you." I pull my head back up and resume searching.

Then it hits me. The symptoms snag my eyes faster than would a male Northern Cardinal perched on freshly fallen snow. However, I think optimistically: *maybe she isn't in shock, or at least not that much.* But if she is, I unfortunately know it will, regardless of the degree, cause other problems.

I stop and look around, hoping: *just a broken twig—a flattened flower—ANYTHING!* My eyes search, my eye teeth grind, my mind gropes. Nothing.

With my free hand, I swat beads from my face, but this is no more than a mere interruption to the myriad of salty rivers rushing down. I haven't walked more than a quarter of a mile and my ribcage is already heaving, gulping oxygen to douse the blaze in my lungs.

*C'mon, you fucking pussy! Meesha isn't THAT heavy! Go! Move! Go!*

But I'm scared and confused. I reply in thought: *But the path? Where is the path?*

My mind strikes back: *Find it you asshole! Find it! Your wife is brutally wounded! Just GO! GOO! GOOOO!*

So I go. I don't know where the path is, but I will find it. I MUST find it. I move with the dry-throated notion that Meesha is now in shock. She whimpers less and more softly now than she did prior to passing out. It's as if she's feeling less pain when, it seems to me, she should be feeling more. *How could she not?* As much as I try to prevent it, her mangled leg suffers a jolt with each of my lumbering steps. Her right wrist—the one I press against her thigh—has become clammy, while her lips appear to have lost color as if they are suffering from poor circulation.

*God, please help me!*

I am tired, hot, thirsty, and scared—especially scared, for I cannot find the path. I stop walking.

*What should I do? What CAN I do?*

*What are the options?*

*What is the objective?*

*The objective is simple: I gotta get Meesha the fuck out of here, and FAST! And to do that, I need to find the path. But how?*

I've tried carrying her. This causes Meesha too much pain and isn't practical; I get nowhere. To find the path, I need the ability to bend, stretch, twist and turn, to maneuver freely, to scour the terrain like a bloodhound. And as much as I hate to face it—damn, do I hate to face it!—I can't do this with Meesha on my back. It just doesn't work. It also consumes too much time while Meesha requires immediate care. I need to get her help soon!

*But do I just leave her? She's unconscious, seriously wounded, and exposed to the wild. What if some animal catches wind of her, some carnivore?*

I know from reading literature about Re'enev, as well as from the tours Meesha and I had taken, that the uninhabited areas contain feral pigs. I've seen pictures of them. These beasts are nasty. They weigh up to two-hundred-and-fifty pounds and bear long, upward curling tusks. Seeing these tusks in the pictures reminded me of the swiveling, hook-like pincers I've seen fish dock workers use to move large blocks of ice. Bullhorn sharp, one tusk protrudes from each side of the pig's ugly, blunt snout. I envision the squat, powerful beast impaling my gut with its curled tusks, their points puncturing my intestines before exiting my back. Definite death.

*They can smell blood real well, like sharks, can't they? Wouldn't I be leaving her in danger?*

My mind flies back to the branch-breaking sound I had heard in the dense flora while I was removing Meesha from the trap. *Was that a pig? Wouldn't I have seen the sucker move? Freaking two-hundred-fifty-pounds is BIG! I would have seen it run away, wouldn't I have? And hey! Is that what the trap is for? Is the thing meant for pigs? Is someone out there trapping wild pigs? If so, how come there are no warning signs about traps?*

The wart of worry on the emotional plain of my brain grows faster than the bamboo around me. *What should I do? How can I ensure her safety?*

I can't. I mentally know that. I just have to emotionally accept it. Nothing in life is definite—fool proof—child safe—a sure thing. And this situation is simply an extreme that exemplifies that notion. I just have to do the best I can, and that best requires that I search the ground without restraint. The circumstances suck, but my only chance of saving Meesha is to find a way out, and I can only do that if I am able to crouch, crawl, reach and run—which, unfortunately, means searching without her. So I have to simply go—leave her for a short time, just until I find the path, then come back and get her. *I'll only be gone a little while. Nothing should happen in such a short span.* In addition, I'll move fast and smart, and pray as if her life depends on it; which, I hope, is true, for there would be nothing more assuring than knowing that Meesha's well being rests in God's hands. Unfortunately, I am beginning to feel that this cosmetically beautiful island contains no fingerprint of God's presence more recent than His fossilized hand in its creation.

A few feet ahead lies an oblong mass of green, its top edge slightly convex. *There's probably a boulder under there.* I walk over and kick-dig the moss with my right heel.

I am correct. I place Meesha on top, so that her stomach covers the rock's slightly rounded apex and her right side faces me. I lay her down gently, ensuring that I do not jar her splinted leg. Then I run to a patch of ferns nearby and rip out an armful. *I'm gettin' pretty good at this.* I realize that I have learned to automatically grab the ferns at the spot along their stalks where they will most efficiently break.

I book back to Meesha. Gently lifting, I lay a fern mat between her and the long, mossy rock. Beneath her splinted leg, I place extra fronds. Parasites are my reason for the ferns—those that thrive in moss. I'm hoping that laying ferns on top will help prevent crap from getting on Meesha. I know it isn't a great cover, but it's the best I can do at the moment.

With the ferns in place, I bend Meesha's healthy left leg. I turn her head so that her face points in the same direction as her left knee. I pull her right arm beyond her head. Then I lift her head and slip her upper right arm, the biceps and triceps, beneath for cushioning. I leave her left arm cuddled in the crevasse created by her bent left leg and abdomen. With her stomach covering the rock's rounded summit, her upper body descends slightly toward the rock's edge. *If she vomits, it'll just run off the rock. She won't choke the way she's lying. Her breathing'll be okay.*

I rush over to the fern patch and rip out dozens. I rush back to Meesha and cover her entire body. I rush back to the fern patch. I repeat the process. Then a third time. I want her as camouflaged as possible.

I kneel at the rock by Meesha's head. I gently push sweaty hair away from her eyes and wipe her forehead. Her eyelids seem to bounce, begging to stay closed. She's barely conscious. While whispering, I gently massage her scalp the way I often do at home in bed: "Meesh, honey, I've gotta go find the way out. I won't be gone long. I just gotta find the path. I'll be right back. Don't worry. I'll be right back to get you. Don't worry one bit. Just hang in there, honey. Just hang in there. I love you, Meesh." Then I kiss her long but gently upon her moist, salty forehead.

# Chapter 10

My heart hatchets my throat as I rise from Meesha's side. It tomahawks against my wicker-tendoned neck, whacking the strained striations with woodpecker rapidity.

*Damn! How am I going to get OUT of here? I still have MILES to go. And that's only if I can figure out which WAY to go!*

*Dear Jesus, please God, please give me strength and wisdom. Help me to make the right decisions. Please help me take care of Meesha, Lord. Please help me to not screw up.*

Salt stings my eyes. The burn is relentless. I repeatedly try to shake the sweat from my sockets, but the effort proves futile. I walk with one eye open, switch to the other, go back to the first. Nothing works except crying, but then I can't see.

I sink as the moist cushion of the earth descends beneath my weight. The bog water seeps through the fabric of my sneakers, soaking my feet. I know my socks are serving a greater purpose, but it would have been nice to have kept them where they were. The wet chafing, I know, will soon wear away skin. This will cause pain; then, with the swamp water, infection.

*Infection.*

*Damn! The fucking thought is killing me!* And I know why. All I've done is put a splint on my wife, then cleaned her with piss— *cleaned her with piss: how oxymoronic!*—hoping I could get her out of the jungle in a relatively short time. But "relatively short" does not correlate with the pace I am making. As a result, I now realize that if we don't make it back to civilization soon enough, I may have to take some drastic measures. Wounded human flesh decays quickly in the jungle. Left to rot, the corrupted tissue develops gangrene, which kills its victim. I remember both my father and Hunter telling me what soldiers have had to do when in life or death situations involving infection, heat, and rotting flesh. The thought of it repulses me. The only time I have ever seen the short, slimy, white worms is when they have infested our garbage cans during the summer months.

However, my father and Hunter had introduced maggots to me not as enemies, but as medicine. "A guy's leg is rotting," Hunter had said, "and there's no medic around with tools and meds to get rid of the dead tissue, you just expose the guy to flies. Maggots develop, and you watch 'em while they eat away all the junk flesh. You know they've hit good flesh when the guy starts bleeding bright red and feels a lot of pain. Then you wash the maggots away with good water, or piss if you can't boil the water, then bandage him up. Gotta make sure you get rid of all the maggots, though, cause they'll just keep eating the guy up."

I pray with the fervor of an abducted child's parent that I won't have to expose my wife's leg to maggots. Sterilizing her with urine was bad enough. But time, I know, will be the determining factor: either I will promptly make my way out of this jungle without having to perform more first aid, or I will submit to the insufferable and execute the unthinkable.

*Hey asshole! Whether you gotta perform more first aid or not, you still gotta get Meesha OUT of this garden from Hell! AND to a hospital as soon as you can!*

Suddenly, for several seconds, every fluid in my body—every molecule of mobile matter that is electrically conductive—rushes toward my brain with the intensity of movie-goers exiting a flame engulfed cinema. I feel as though my head is going to blow off. Could NASA physicalize this feeling, rocket science would advance fifty years.

I catch myself. I do the breathing thing again: ten, then another ten. I feel a little better. I close my eyes. I think deeply. I know what I have to do: find our tracks in, follow them back out, and don't get lost. That's it. No other option exists.

*But what about traps? How do I know there aren't more? Of course there are! Why would some asshole just place one? Better yet, why did the asshole place any? There aren't any bears on this island. And if there are more traps, I could easily step into one. Then we'd really be fucked. That would be it. We'd both die. Predators, gangrene, starvation—*

*Stop it! Ya gotta stop this! Forget it! Forget traps. Think about something else—other than traps and infection.*

Something then bludgeons me: *how will I ensure I find my way back?* I remember the terrain in: *some parts were kinda dry, others swampy. Even if ya find the trail out, you won't be able to retrace your steps. You'll lose the path like ya did, at times, coming in. Ya can't let that happen. No fucking way! Ya need to be able to find your way back to Meesha as efficiently as possible. No getting lost. No losing your trail.*

*Okay, so I need to mark it.*

The terrain engulfing me is pristine. *I'm probably the only bonehead to come down this way in months, if not years.* Thus, it comes to me fast; the solution is simple: I will beat up vegetation along the way. *Anything freshly torn will be your mark and ONLY your mark.* I feel good about this. I spin around and walk back to Meesha. I kiss her again and tell her I love her again. She feels and hears nothing.

I start out strong though I'm hotter than a Jalapeno, as if my blood has somehow been transfused with Tabasco sauce.

My tongue has begun to swell. Saliva coats my throat with the consistency of tissue paper. Swallowing is as easy as gargling cotton balls. Drenched in liquid salt, my arms and legs radiate a dark pink. The color originates from their inner versus their outer sides, similar to the difference between a bruise and a tattoo. Mud splashes up my shins and thighs and splatters my shirt, which clings to my skin. I go back to the blinking bit, one eye at a time, for my hair is now supersaturated. Every sweat bead my scalp pops immediately slides to my face as if my hair were skull grass impaled with a KEEP OFF sign. Many beads pop.

However, my eyes grip the trail—the one I'd lost with Meesha upon my back. This makes me feel good. I'm still on track. I'm going to break the spell this lava zit has cast on me. *I am going to beat it!* Confidence inflates my sinew, toughens my tendons. *I'm going to get us out of this shit!*

I pick up speed. A burst of strength, like a second wind while jogging, surges through me. *I am going to get through this. I am going to find my way back. Get help. Help Meesha.*

I press on. My progress is good, though the trail is bad. I am breaking branches, ripping off ferns, kicking down bamboo. *How far have I gone? A half a mile? A mile?* I'm not sure. *Don't go too far! Can't leave Meesha alone too long! Just need to get confident with the trail, so that you know you can find your way out.*

There barely is a trail. *No wonder I lost it so often earlier!* Most of the time, it is hardly visible; other times, it isn't at all. When the trail disappears, I can sometimes follow brush that I, myself, trampled on the way in. The rest of the time there is nothing to follow and I have to retrace my steps, or search farther ahead, to find the path. *No problem. Just keep your eyes down. Don't take 'em off the ground. You've been down this way before. You won't lose it this time.*

So I do just that: I keep my eyes down—on the ground—on the proverbial road. I scour the terrain surrounding me for every possible alteration, every conceivable nuance. And every third step, I snap a branch, tear off some ferns, or knock down some bamboo. I try to trash the trail, pound the path, stomp as much as I can. I HAVE to find my way back.

Then it hits me——a baseball bat in an alley—a brick wall at midnight. I don't know how it happens; it just hits me. One second, I have the tangible track of human travel beneath me; the next second, I don't. *What the fuck?*

I jump back a few steps and restart my tracking. The same flattened flora retreats beneath me. The brush I have just broken passes by my sides. Then nothing. *Damn!*

I jump back again.

Then again.

Same thing each time. *Fuck!*

I push through trees and plants to my left, into swampier terrain. I find nothing. All is pristine.

I push the other way, first back to where I had started, then farther into drier, less swampy terrain. Again: nothing. All is untouched, so maddenly unadulterated. How I yearn for scuffed soil, a bent branch, a candy wrapper, a rusty beer can, a lousy footprint, some ecological destruction, some sign of man!

*Oh God, please! Where is the path? I need to find the path! I need to get back to Meesha!*

ORANGE! ORANGEY-RED! As if the lamp beneath my eyelids suddenly illuminated the world beyond me, all I see glows with a fiery-tint.

My body downshifts, my mind engages both axles, and I rip. A human Humvee, I spit shredded jungle in my wake. Cranking, I am, for I have had it. Urgency rifles through me. Never reckless, always in control, I torpedo vegetation, spearheading thicket with my skull and shoulders. I don't run blindly. I navigate my course, searching for tracks. Finding none, I change direction, seeking different ground. With eye sockets stretched and eyeballs scouring, I plow, charge, grunt, and swear. I am desperate—in control—but desperate. I just keep going and going and going. Oh, the heat! And my thirst! And this fucking BRUSH! *It'd be easier to run through a tornado tousled lumber yard.* I had never known how thick and constraining a jungle can be.

But I keep driving. The jungle seems as seamless as my angst-addled determination is myopic. I start feeling dizzy and nauseous. My legs begin to ache with the muscle soreness one feels with the flu. The dizziness is the worst. It clouds my perception and rattles my motor skills. The ground beneath me seems to move.

But everywhere I look, vegetation stands erect as eighth-grade boys thumbing through a Playboy! *Fuck!*

I barrel through endless green while bright red oozes from every unclad spot on my body. I shoot left, then right, then left again. I go under stuff, over stuff and through stuff. Some things I break; those that I can't, I go around. I charge on and on and on and on.

Then I stop. I breathe deeply, counting to ten. I perform the exercise three separate times, thinking with each digit: *I'm fucked—I'm fucked—I'm fucked....* Then I change tack and pray for a miracle, banking my last desperate grasp on the redemption value of my final—and apparently expired— coupon for mercy, begging that I stumble upon some hidden route out of this garden of evil.

*Oh? And what makes you think you can find one now? You've been hunting for a while! But now, you hope you might "stumble" upon one?*

Praying with all my might, as if pressing my lips and furrowing my brow will enhance the chance my plea will be heard, I beg God: *Please help me find a way out! Please help me get to a path, some way I can get help for Meesha!* Hoping, still praying, I move. Large leaves brush my face. Tree arms try to trip me. Twigs take swings at my head.

Then I trip. I fall over a rotting log. My right hand lands in some ferns. My left arm grazes a tree.

*Dear God, please help me!* I mind-scream while rising. An auger bit spins into my chest; I can almost see red curls of shredded flesh fly off in every direction. A shaken can of Coke incurs less pressure than does my body from the tension. *What am I going to do? I've got to get outta here!*

I've been so preoccupied with simply navigating that I haven't noticed, until now, that I've been bitten at least a dozen times. Unlike birds, mosquitoes are not an organism I thought might fly in flocks, that they could form their own air force. I was wrong. Dozens fly sorties by my head. But, as with water, I have no time for bugs or itches.

I fall again—then again—over a fallen tree. It is so unexpected. From the tree juts a splintered branch. I fall upon the branch; its dull point jabs my left breast. I feel much pain, but even more fear. *What if I had taken that in the neck? Or the eye? God, please help me!*

Then I see it. Standing, I would not have. Lying, I do.

# Chapter 11

That was a small print, I think, only half my sole. Good thing I fell down. Wouldn'ta seen it. Might not've found the rest, the way out, though it was right in front of me. Gonna have to stay sharp going forward—head down, eyeballs to the ground. Not every print is obvious. Gonna have to look hard, double check, scrutinize, persevere. But at least I know that I'm on the trail, that I can find my way out. Gotta get back to Meesha now. It's been a while. Can't leave her too long.

I am almost there—almost back to the oblong rock. My markers are great. I really hit this vegetation hard. No problem finding my way back to Meesh. Wish the same were true about the trail going out.

Time worries me. I musta been searching for about a half an hour. But it only takes me about fifteen minutes to run back. God, please let her be okay! Please let nothing have happened!

Twenty feet before I reach the oblong rock on which I had left Meesha, I suddenly stop. It is my first opportunity to see the spot, the jungle's density having obstructed my view until then. But I don't see Meesha.

It's my eyes, I think, I'm tired and sick and seeing things. I walk closer, but I still don't see Meesha. My stomach flares. My eye sockets widen. My brow descends.

I walk all the way up to the rock, then fall before it. If the impact hurts my knees, I don't feel it. Though sweating in the jungle, I am frozen meat.

Off the rock, from among scattered fronds, I lift a piece of nylon rope, camera neck strap, and vine. I study the truncated ends of each. Each bares an even edge. *A fucking knife!*

Then I remember the branch breaking sound from the brush when I was working on the trap. *And I was worried about PIGS! Fuck! Where IS she! Oh God, where's Meesha? Who took Meesha!*

Rapid breaths steal through my petrified features as I try to organize my thoughts. But my brain doesn't want to work. *Someone has stolen Meesha!* I have trouble believing it. *This is fucking INSANE! Where is my wife! Who's taken Meesha!*

I slowly scan the vicinity, the dense green flora, the tall trees and suffocating brush. *Am I being watched? Who is out there? WHAT is out there? Why would someone take Meesha!*

While scanning, I see it: White. Some red. Not big, but couldn't miss it. Sticks out too much. Left right in the open, and too white against the jungle.

I stand up, walk over, pick it up. And with my wife's blood-spattered, leather sneaker in my hand, I realize I have encountered Satan.

*This was left so I could SEE it! Someone's FUCKING with me! Is it the bastard who placed the traps! I gotta find her! I gotta find Meesha! Shit! Fuck! Damn! I gotta FIND her! Oh Meesha! Oh God! Meeeeeshaaa! Hold on, honey! I'll find you! I'll find you, sweetheart! Just please hold on! Oh God, please take care of her! Please don't let her be harmed! Please help me to find her! Please God, please!*

*I gotta use my head. Gotta be sensible. Can't panic. Can't fuck up.*

I think of the neck strap, rope, and vines. *Whoever took Meesha has a knife. I gotta be ready. I gotta find her, but I gotta be prepared. Gotta arm myself. But how?*

A strange though not unpleasant sensation invades me: I suddenly feel my brother by my side. I don't see him, of course, but I know Hunter is there. And I know he will be with me for as long as I need him—till I find Meesha, till we get out of this suffocating hell-hole. That, I know. I feel his presence—his spirit? his soul?—as if he and I are a two-man team on a commando mission.

How quickly life can change. It happens so fast, sometimes, that you have reason to wonder whether time really passed while the event took place. Just a few hours earlier, I was on a nice little hike with my nice little wife on a nice little island in the middle of the Pacific. I was feeling good; things were getting better; we were reconciling. Now, I'm standing in the jungle with eyes swollen from crying, my throat raw from muted screaming, and my brain wracked with fear for my missing wife's well being. Nonetheless, I don't stop thinking. I know what I need. And as I scan the visible vicinity for a rough surface, I remember the rock on which Meesha had been lying.

I run back to the oblong boulder. On the ground in front lies the Ironwood stick. I kneel down in front of the boulder and start scraping moss and fungi from it with one end of the stick. When approximately a square foot of rough surface emerges, I begin rotating the shaft slowly while continuing to scrape its end against the course stone. Every few minutes, I gently glide my thumb over the stick's end. Every few moments, I scan the jungle surrounding me for movement or change. When I have formed—that is, feel—the sharpest point I believe possible, I stop. I know that it will be dangerous to use the shaft as a walking stick with the sharpened end jutting toward me, but I don't want to dull it with repetitive thrusts into the ground. *I'll take my chances.*

I shuffle over to a patch of bamboo. Bamboo, I remember my father telling me, can be dangerous. It grows fast, in bunches; and although strong, tough stuff in short lengths, it is somewhat flexible when long. *Sort of like plastic*, I think. Bend it too far, though, and bamboo will shatter into sharp, piercing splinters. *Vegetative shrapnel.*

I find a shaft that stands isolated, unencumbered. It is about ten feet tall and yellow with green stripes. Its base swells to about an inch in diameter.

I rip out a bunch of ferns and large leaves, then scoop handfuls of dirt and cover the base of the shaft. Then I grab the shaft above my head with both hands and pull down with all my weight and strength. Being extra cautious, I close my eyes and turn my head. The shaft breaks at a node just above where I'd placed the shielding vegetation. Luckily, no shattering splinters shoot into my legs.

I run the bamboo shaft back to the oblong boulder. I still feel dizzy. My throat and mouth burn. My stomach twists, a wringing rag. I remember that bamboo clumps often hold potable water, but I don't have time to find and extract any now. *When I find Meesha.*

I shove the thicker end of the bamboo pole into the soft earth beneath the rock's front lip. Spinning the shaft, thus grinding the dirt beneath its end, I can force the pole in about a foot-and-a-half.

I step onto the rock. I place my hands, clutching the shaft straddled by my legs, as close to the rock as possible. Then I turn my head and pull. The shaft bursts a bit higher than the spot at which I had hoped. Splinters fly; but, lucky again, I remain unscathed.

I pull the broken end of the severed shaft from beneath the rock. Had the pole snapped in the location that I had intended, I would have a bamboo piece consisting of three ring-like nodes capping the ends of two hollow, cylindrical internodes. But the break occurred just below one of the nodes; so, instead, I have a capped cylinder- —a canister—on one end and an exposed cylinder on the other. The exposed cylinder is a bit narrower than the sealed one.

I grab the thicker internode with my right hand, my favored one, and squeeze it several times. It feels natural, as if nature had intentionally shaped it to be a handle.

I have chosen bamboo because of the lecture my father once gave me regarding its usefulness: how you can steam cook with it and make a wind instrument out of it, as well as a variety of utensils and tools. "Bamboo," he said, "is the only wood that can hold an edge." I would learn later that it is actually a grass.

My legs straddling the portion of the rock on which I had sharpened the Ironwood stick, I wonder: *Can I put an edge on this long tube I now hold?*

The cracked end of the bamboo shaft bears a slight slant. I push this slant down against the surface of the rock and drag the shaft toward me, applying firm pressure. *SSSSCCCRRRAAAAPPPE!* sings the stick as its cracked slivers bristle. I pull the bamboo stick toward me several times, pressing firmly, dragging it in one direction only. Then I touch the cracked aperture I am shaving. The slant reveals slight wear. *This will work,* I tell myself. *But hurry, you can't waste time! Gotta find Meesha!*

I continue dragging the bamboo shaft toward me—one time— ten times—a hundred times. My body bleeds sweat. My heart sweats blood. My mind will not stop. As the edge on the cracked piece of jungle grass turns lethal, so does the edge of my mind. I ponder the evil that lurks within the jungle surrounding me. *Am I being watched? Should I hide while I do this? Who or what am I dealing with?* But for all the fear I feel, I seethe with just as much anger. *Someone has taken my wife and there is nothing I won't do to get her back—NOTHING!*

As the shaft's narrower end gets more so, a point and edge form. The exterior of bamboo is very hard; the interior is not. It is the inner section that I am wearing away. The outer side holds the edge.

When I have worn the blade down sufficiently, its angle from tip to handle approximately thirty degrees, I grab a flat but course stone, the size of a quarter. I stroke the inner side along each of the blade's two edges, honing each edge from handle to tip. Again, as I had on the larger, stationary rock, I stroke the bamboo in one direction only.

After a few minutes, I pull my thumb across both edges. Very little pressure is needed to sense the sharpness, to invoke the pull on my skin. Were I to pull my fingers along one of the blades, rather than across it, I would certainly slice a deep gash. *This is about as sharp as I am going to get any piece of wood,* I tell myself (remembering that bamboo is not wood, but a grass).

I grip my knife's handle just below the node nearer the twin blades, grab my Ironwood spear, and begin walking toward the enemy. I am a fire fighter engaging the wild forest blaze, a bounty hunter confronting the homicidal fugitive, a Siberian hunter entering the domain of the great striped cat, and I am afraid. But I am also angry. *I have to find Meesha! I need to find Meesha! I must find Meesha!*

I head toward the spot where I'd found her bloody sneaker. Farther to my rear, I leave civilization and its safety. I clutch my weapons tightly.

# Chapter 12

I walk slowly, carefully, vigilantly, past the spot at which I'd picked up Meesha's blood-spattered sneaker. I precede each step with a sweep of my Ironwood stick. The handle of my bamboo shank is curled within the short left sleeve of my shirt the way punks sometimes carry cigarettes. This way, when I need it, I can grab it quickly.

*Where the fuck would someone have taken her?* I'm breathing slowly, walking. *Someone wanted me to see her sneaker. Someone is trying to lure me. But where the fuck to?*

Suddenly, I stop. The contrast in color catches my eye. Twenty yards to my left, a white sneaker hangs in lush green. For a long moment, I stare at it. The moment does not seem real.

I venture forth, continuing to sweep in front of me for fear of traps. I consider crouching, bending over as I move in the high brush, but decide against it: *Why bother? Someone obviously knows I'm here. No sense hiding. I just gotta find Meesha!*

I leave the shoe untouched. I look at the earth beneath me and a thought ignites in my head, but I have to make sure. I creep forward. I go about fifty yards before I see it: twenty feet beyond hangs a torn strip of white sock.

*Okay,* I think, my breathing labored, *it's a game! They know I'm here and want me to know they're there—somewhere. They're not hiding—not fully anyway. They want me to find 'em. And they know I don't know the land, so they've put me back on the trail. Probably ambush me along the way. Sick bastard! Who IS this? My wife is HURT! I gotta use my fuck'n head!*

I scan the jungle thoroughly, left to right, right to left, and all around me. My senses are screaming. I could hear a flea fart a mile away. The leanest wisp of jungle mist wouldn't escape my eye.

*There's a mad man out there. He's got my wife, and now he wants me. Fuck! I gotta be smart. Gotta find Meesha, but can't get suckered into his trap. Gotta play this smart—smart, carefully, and with stealth.*

Hunter rushes through my mind along with my father and things I've learned from them, as well as things I'd once contemplated with an imagination that Meesha often called amazing—strange—even sick. "Creative," I would retort on those latter occasions. "Sick," she would relentlessly maintain.

On the male, USMC-influenced side of my family, much emphasis was placed on improvisation. I must have heard my father say it a thousand times: "If you got a job, get it done. I don't care how you do it. Dig a ditch with your freakin' hands, if you have to. Just get the job done!"

Hunter and I grew up with this. "Adapt! Improvise! Overcome!" It became our credo, stamped upon our brains, hard coded within our psyches. And it served us in numerous ways, some of which I am still discovering.

I change my mind regarding crouching. Whoever is out there has erred: they've given me directions. Before, I was at their mercy, looking for markers. But now I know it is the trail they want me to follow. "Never take an existing path," I can hear my father saying, "it is likely a trap." Either they are stupid and don't realize the upper hand they've forfeited, or they just don't care. I hope it's the former, but in either case I have to take advantage of all opportunities, optimize all advantages.

Back and knees bent, head lowered, I retreat to the oblong rock, then past it, moving farther into the brush. Staying as low as possible, I go in about fifty yards, trying to minimize any noise I make.

I stop. The earth below me is soluble and runny; the orbit around my head, buzzing with bugs. I bend down, place the outer edge of my hands at shoulder width along the ground. Moving my hands toward each other while pressing down, I scrape together a mushy loaf of coal colored mud. *Kill two birds with one sweep*, I think. First and foremost, I will camouflage every exposed piece of wet skin whose alabaster luster, through the verdant vegetation, could betray me. In addition, I will layer myself with the best insect repellent this store in the jungle can hawk.

I look down as I smear muck over my light green T-shirt, black nylon shorts, and old running sneakers. I'm hoping layered thickness will keep the biting bastards at bay while I blend further with the environment. Immersing myself in the terrain, I assume the essence of the land. I am becoming one with the jungle.

I resume walking, parallel with the path fifty yards to my left, my vigilance maxed. Amplifying the *thump!-thump!* cadence of my quickened heart, my ears also evaluate every sound external to me. Hoping to catch foreign scents in the sultry air, I breathe only through my nose. And, as if sensors within an electronic surveillance system, my eyes flicker repeatedly, back and forth, back and forth.

But it is the change in my walk that is most noticeable, even though it was not intentional. I just happen to catch myself doing it. In addition to crouching, I find myself testing each step with my heel, making sure there is nothing potentially harmful beneath the turf on which I am about to press. Then, when confident no traps or other obstacles exist, I softly roll through my step from heel to toe. I am balanced and deliberate, careful and cognizant. And not until I have fully completed my roll and stand perched on the tip of my toes do I hesitantly insert, into the soft earth, the heel of my other foot.

*You've gotta become more immersed in the vegetation,* I tell myself. *You need to merge with the environment, make you and it one. You're an animal—a wild pig, a feral goat. You need the senses of hunted deer. Develop them! Think like one! Get spooked!*

I slither almost silently through leaves the size of elephant ears; grass taller than me; vines, nettles, briar, and bramble so tangled and dense I think of sloppily piled barbed wire. All the while, I keep myself within viewing distance of the pieces of clothing marking the path.

As if a periscope, my neck twists my head left then right, left then right. I squint as my vision reaches farther into the brush. The longer I look, the more precisely I see; the greater the detail that emerges, the sharper the outlines become. But I also notice that my eyes become weary very quickly. Too much detail analyzed with too much intensity causes my vision to blur.

So I start to look at things indirectly. I don't gaze right at a tree or bush, but slightly off its center, thus taking in only its shape. In effect, I am studying silhouettes. In this profusion of plant life, a human silhouette will stick out like a poodle in a fish tank. By looking at each object indirectly, taking in shape in lieu of detail, I can study my surroundings for as long as necessary, while seeking that which is most important: the presence of man. *I gotta find Meesha soon!* my brain screams.

Several yards to my right, overgrown by moss, fungi, and dense vegetation lies a fallen tree. This one is deciduous—mahogany or acacia or something. It's wide, circular base flares dead, knurly roots and clustered black soil at an angle forty-five degrees to the ground. I've seen several fallen trees similar to this one along the way.

I look beyond the fallen tree. The vegetation surrounding me is so incredibly dense. Not only do I doubt anyone on land could see me, I doubt some guy in a helicopter hovering above could either.

It is when I pass another strip of white sock hanging far to my left that it happens. For all my vigilance, I should be prepared. I *had* expected it could happen, but I can't say that I am ready for it. It certainly takes me by surprise.

I'm rolling slowly through each step, placing my Ironwood stick in front of me, carefully scanning the increasingly eerie, jungle canvas with nervous eyes. Yet, despite my tactile vigilance, I'm not really in tune with the ground ahead. I am more alert to things that are, or could be, at eye level: vegetation, birds, animals, humans. As a result, when I lunge, swinging forth my Ironwood stick through tall ferns and feel its dense end strike solid matter, I simply think that I've hit a rock. But that thought lasts no longer than the fraction of a second that sound requires to travel four feet, for what follows the bump of my stick and changes my opinion regarding the object I have struck is the horribly familiar *screech!* of slicing steel.

The steel bands bite into my walking stick like a ravenous lion upon the leg bone of a dead elephant: with awesome power, but not enough to break it. The punishing shock from the powerful bite sends vibrating shivers up my right arm and a wave of fear through my skull. *Another trap! DAMN it! That coulda been my LEG! WAKE UP, Luke! Ya gotta get Meesha! Ya can't get hurt! Watch where you're going! Keep alert for EVERYTHING!*

I pick up a long, not-yet-rotten stick lying nearby and lift off camouflaging vegetation. Unlike the one that butchered Meesha's leg, this snare is smaller and has no teeth. *Probably used for wolves or mountain lions.* The trap is also newer, its steel a dull satanic-black. No rust exists; none even nips its edges. *This was laid recently. What the fuck is going on? Who the fuck is out here? And what the fuck are they doing?*

I extract my walking stick and move on. *How many more are there? How many have I inadvertently missed? And are there only snares? What other trap types could this mad fucker—HAS this mad fucker—put down? And what about him, himself? Couldn't he just be sitting in a tree somewhere with a high velocity rifle, watching me the whole time, patiently waiting for the right moment to rip a hole in my heart?*

*Maybe. But, if so, why hasn't he done it? Why is he playing games with Meesha's clothes?*

*No,* I conclude, *this sick bastard wants me alive.* Why? I don't know. But he definitely wants me alive.

Glancing around, I don't see much but ferns and Ula Ahi trees; except, to my far left, where there dangles another strip of white within rich green. *How fucking far are they gonna take me? God, please help me find Meesha SOON! Oh God, she's hurt so BAD!*

I scan the ferns; thousands flourish. Beyond the ferns spreads a tangle of vines, grasses, and assorted jungle plants. The density of it all invokes in me the image of jungle warriors whacking their way through using long, broadening machetes, so wide at the end they could feasibly chop down trees. I think of the stories my father told me about Marines in the Pacific during World War II, and how thick the jungle was that those guys had to battle. In the Pacific, my father said, the elements themselves were an enemy, and often fiercer and deadlier than their human counterpart. I wish I had a tree-leveling machete.

I sneak forward about a hundred feet, my throat feeling like I've been gargling cold, gray ashes from a dead fire. I see another piece of white hanging in green to my far left, and it is when I see this white strip that I stop. It's my nose. It tells me to.

That smell. I know that smell. *What the fuck is that smell? And where is it coming from?*

My head—my body—all perfectly still, I breathe deeply. *Sweet—faint—almost pungent.* My mind's a bit cloudy. I'm having a little trouble. But I know that smell. *What is that smell?*

I bend my head to the right and drool a thin line of gooey, dry mouth spittle onto the first digit of my right index finger. I raise my finger and confirm a former thought: *yes, I am downwind—if you want to call this baby's breath a wind. I've been in saunas with a stronger breeze.*

This is good, being downwind. I'm concerned about my body odor. I know that the strong signals of synthetic deodorant and civilized cooking still emanate from my mouth and pores. To a naturalized jungle dweller, I might as well be lighting stink bombs as I strut.

But this smell I detect isn't natural to the jungle either. It's an odor with which I am familiar. *But what the hell is it? Damn it!* My mind won't work.

I glance carefully around me, staring through the brush, not looking directly at any one piece of vegetation. *How much further do I have to go? Where the hell is Meesha?* I am looking for movement, profiles, disturbances in the terrain: a branch out of place; a patch of grass lying a way it shouldn't, contradicting the pattern of its pals; maybe even some tracks. I can feel myself getting more and more vigilant, more and more paranoid, more and more...*aggressive?* Yes, more and more aggressive. I can't help, nor can I stop, the hot tastes of fear and anger I feel boiling in, and rising from, my gut. Had this combo a color, it would be dark, sulfuric yellow—napalm mixed with mustard and whiskey. The emotional equivalent of burning bile somersaults within my psyche. My wife is missing. Her abductor is out there, and I don't give a fuck who he is. I'm going to get her back.

I suddenly think of weekend nights during high school when my friends and I would break the law. The reason is the smell. I *knew* that I knew that smell. It isn't as strong now as when dried, chopped, rolled in thin paper and smoldering beneath my nose, but it is still the same smell. As far as I know, nothing else on this planet smells like it; and once you've smelled it, you remember it. And I'm remembering it now.

My eyes scan and penetrate the jungle as my nose sucks it in. It is pot. I am sure of it. But it doesn't smell smoky, unless that is how pot smoke smells when filtered through the carbon-dioxide-sucking green of moist, lush jungle. *Is someone near me smoking reefer? Is the fucker who took my wife getting stoned?* My anger flares molten-lava-red, as does the end of the rolled ganja I imagine some bastard is toking. *I hope he IS stoned. I hope he's WASTED. His mental agility will be diminished. He'll be slower—sluggish—much easier to handle, should he try to stop me from taking Meesha.*

If I was alert before, I'm now wildly wary. Every muscle in me is taut. My teeth grind. My jaw hinges scrimmage. Tendons quiver along my bones like plucked guitar strings. I can feel my heart whapping my chest at a rate that rivals a sewing machine. Far reaching, ventricled fingers tap my inner neck with each stitch-like pump. I don't realize how much I'm sweating until I see the balls drop. Not beads, but balls, they free fall from my forehead; wet, momentary obstacles to my vision.

I venture forward ten cautious steps—then, another ten. There are no more markers along the path. *Am I there? Have I reached something? Where's Meesha!* My eyes are straws that suck in every molecule I pass. Birds relentlessly slice the silence that would undoubtedly drive me cuckoo considering my level of tension.

I pick up my head and glance left, toward some tweeting, but abruptly stop. My eyes tell me to. They see ferns, a whole patch of ferns, but not ferns like those that I have seen thus far. These are not as full, their surface canopy not as opaque. They remind me a bit of the sweet fern bushes my mother grows in her front yard. *Funny*, I think, *I haven't seen this kind of plant until this point. Has the jungle terrain changed? Is there more or less sunlight? Have I ventured into an area with a different level of annual rainfall?* I look about me for other clues: additional plants I haven't seen before, a difference in the upper jungle canopy, a change in the color of the soil. But I find nothing.

I stand still for a moment—listening, looking, breathing, thinking. My brain tells me nothing is different, but my gut tells me something is. *What is it?* As I listen, look, and think, I begin to breathe deeper, hoping to smell a change in the fermenting jungle fragrance—a change beyond that of, and possibly responsible for, the ferns. Almost Zen-like, I try to *feel* my way to a clue. But my actions are superfluous; I needn't do any of it. There is no way I can miss the eagle. Were my eyes covered by cataracts—were my sight that of a ninety-year-old man with eyeballs yellowed from a lifetime of drink—I would see the eagle. I would see it easily. There would be no way I could miss it. It is *that* big. And this bird of prey has been waiting for me.

# Chapter 13

My brain has a hard time believing the image my eyes send it. For a moment, I seriously wonder if the heat and humidity have corrupted my sense of vision. Unfortunately, the weather is not responsible for what I see.

I see an eagle—a large eagle—in flight—no more than thirty feet away. What I do not see is my wife. *Where the hell's Meesha!*

I'm standing, camouflaged, behind a clump of Ula Ahi trees. The knuckles of my right hand, squeezing my Ironwood stick, gleam French vanilla as blood dissipates beneath the skin. Through the jungle canopy above, gradually thinning since I stepped off the boardwalk, fractured sunlight cuts the green earth with sporadic slices of jagged yellow.

*What the hell IS this? WHO the hell is this? And where the fuck is Meesha?*

I kneel as quickly as I can without giving myself away. I don't move jerkily like I would grabbing *The Globe* from a vending machine in Boston. Instead, I find myself moving like water: my body, a narrow six-foot stream; my physical being, the incarnation of fluid mechanics. It feels weird, like I don't recognize my own flesh—or maybe because I know it better now than I ever have—

like I've become a robot. Anger and fear power my parts; yet, at the same time, an intense patience I have never previously felt, with the viscosity of oil, lubricates their movement to a lethal, swiveling smooth.

*I have to find Meesha! I've GOTTA find Meesha!*

But before I can search for my wife, I must deal with the eagle. I have no choice. *Who is he? What does he want?*

The eagle, I know, was chosen as Uncle Sam's national bird and symbol for its regal head and fierce demeanor. Fierce? Hell, even when fed and nonchalantly soaring over the safe haven of its nesting grounds, its scowling countenance reminds me of an Apache warrior lusting for European blood. The one in my sights is no different, except that its yellow mouth is not clenched with that inimitable eagle fury. Rather, the pointy, descending curl of its upper beak hangs high enough over the petite valley of its lower beak that the bird appears to be screaming. Embedded in the royal white headdress capping a body blanketed in brown—brown, that is, until the tail which, again, gleams as white as the head—are the invariably demonic eyes. Blaring pale yellow, these scathing spheres, I can readily tell, would rip me to shreds had they teeth. But since they don't, they intimate that their ally, the gaping beak, would be delighted to bite off my head with a single chomp.

*I can't believe this! This is fucked! I gotta find Meesha!*

The eagle is glaring at me, screaming at me, dive bombing my way. Its yellowy-orange claws reach for my body from below its white, howling head. Long, black talons curl inwards and cut the air before my face. Reaching for me, the claws tug on the bird's fuselage, bending it slightly forward, a little above the tail. Resembling adjoined scythes, these daggered hands virtually stab at me in a covert way as they lunge from beneath the eagle's broad winged awning.

*Damn it! Did the eagle take Meesha?*

And what an awning! From low on the eagle's stout neck, where sheeny white meets rich brown in an abrupt but jagged edge, the feathers begin to layer. They start short, their layers thick; but with each layered retreat, the feathers lengthen while their cascading thickness thins. The thinner each layer, the lighter its shade of brown. These feather-layered rows consume an impressive expanse. But even more impressive is the medium on which these wings spread, due to their daunting width.

*It is a canvas draped over bones!* I think, while realizing that I have never before thought of human skin in such a way. The wings begin where the thick clavicle ends within the man's gargantuan left shoulder, and reach the symmetrically corresponding spot within his gargantuan right. Around the long, fleshy curve of each shoulder's deltoid muscle, the eagle wings flare, the feathers spreading so much that gaps appear between their tips.

*If the giant took Meesha, where is she? Why'd he lead me here with her clothes?*

I don't think he knows that I'm here. If he does, he certainly doesn't care, or he'd be looking at me. Instead, he just leans against the center pole supporting his shelter, staring at the marked trail as if waiting on a friend.

*But he isn't waiting on a friend! He's waiting for ME! What should I do?: Attack him? Try to confront him peacefully? Either way, I've gotta decide fast! Can't waste time! Gotta get Meesha to a hospital!*

The giant suddenly moves. He steps away from the lean-to, bends to his right and pushes aside several shoots of thin, green, elongated leaves. *What's he looking for?* Moving ahead, toward the path, still bent over, he pushes aside some more shoots. Then he lifts a hand that must measure twelve inches in length and slides it from his forehead to his neck over straight, sweat-slicked, black hair. Thick, and spurting above a straight line vigorously close to his brow, his hair lies trim above his ears. It is a professional cut, albeit stylishly rogue by the exclusion of an inch left streaming down the back of the man's burly neck.

To say this guy is big is to say the sun is hot, a neutron is small, or that Great White Sharks can be unfriendly. As he moves toward the path, bent over, I notice that dark brown marks his upper back also. It is the same chocolaty shade as the wings that span his broad chest and engrave his mahogany desk-like shoulder girdle. *What is THIS? Whatever the pattern, its ink is pretty damn dark.* I think this, for the tattoo is readily apparent despite the giant's deep, tropical tan, a tan seared into skin already dark by nature—Pacific Islander dark—and now richly brown like the fertile soil between the green ferns he continues to tend.

Suddenly, the man stands upright. A shiv pierces my sternum and arrests my inhale as huge wings unfurl toward me. They are so broad, I feel enclosed, as if trapped. It is the eagle again; but, now, it is not facing me. Rather, it is facing the same direction as the image attacking from the man's chest. It is the same eagle, only its back side. Like its front side, the eagle's back side also sprawls impressively, wide and deep, with power-spewing intimidation. It also looks as though it's attacking. Eagles can dive-bomb prey at one-hundred-and-fifty miles-per-hour, and every inch per second of that velocity whistles malevolently from the giant's ink pricked, muscle-bumped back.

I sense myself slip deeper into fight-or-flight mode. The adrenaline rush is wicked. I feel as though someone just stuck a long needle into my belly and injected a vertigo inducing dose of caffeine. My insides scream and churn. My organs react like Wall Street traders during a market plunge.

I study the man as he studies plants. He's about six-seven, maybe more. His shoulders are not just muscularly big, like that of a bodybuilder, but structurally colossal and square the way I would imagine Paul Bunyan's, or the Biblical Goliath's. And his back spreads so freakishly wide, his oblique muscles with such flare, that it appears as though he, too, can fly.

*Why an eagle?* Something bothers me about this tattoo. *What does it mean? Does the giant simply like eagles? Or does the raptor represent something more? A religion? A cult? Some sort of movement or belief?* In addition to eeriness and fear, I feel a sense of knowing, sort of like nostalgia, or deja vu; but I can't place it.

Looking into the ferns, the giant stands still, arms loose by his sides. Long limbs of inflated sinew, they veer away from his torso as they hang, the bulky wedge of his upper back placing pressure against them. A letter V—the size of which could beam neon red in Times Square—the man's back, symmetrical to his front, bears wing tips that fully fill the epidermal posterior of his hypertrophied shoulders. As they do on his front, the wings here also flare: two feathery hands with fingers spread so far that the giant's upper back contains little unetched flesh beyond. But unlike his front, where the eagle's head reaches toward me, from the giant's back it is these wings that do. And there's something else, something freaky: this howling bird appears to flap its wings whenever the giant flaps his. *Did the artist intend this? Or are the reciprocal movements merely fluky consequences of his needle?* In either case, the screaming, dive-bombing, talon-wielding raptor flickers its bent, sprawling span every time the giant moves.

Electricity sizzles through every nerve in my body. I feel buzzing from the centralized sciatic running through my groin to the thread-sized endings pricking my scalp.

*Should I move out now? Confront him? Why is he waiting so restlessly?* My gut tells me to study him a bit longer, collect a little more intel. *But I can't! I need to find Meesha NOW!*

I step out. Sweeping the Ironwood in front of me for traps, but watching the giant, I wade into the ferns. They brush my lower body. The sound they make is slight. *Doesn't matter. It's still sound. Will he hear me?*

He spins! Speed whips his movement. *He heard me! Now he sees me!* Surprise dilates his face. *He didn't expect me here.* Black balls boil, eyes sadistically simmering—arrows from Hell with heads of hate, they impale me from across the field.

With no hesitation and uncharacteristic quickness, he barrels toward me—*What the fuck!*—a crazed prize fighter bursting from his corner at the bell. *What's he doing!* He sees my weapons, doesn't care. I can barely react. A left jab *snaps!* at my head. I duck, slide right, look up: furious delight spews from the malicious mug. *The bastard's grinning! What the…!* Another jab! I try to slip left. Not quick enough! The huge fist grazes my right ear. Cymbals clash in my head; bass drums pump blood to the bruise. Smiling malevolently—perfect teeth framed by a handlebar moustache—the misplaced gladiator twists at the waist, jabs again! I pull to the left. Ferociously relentless, undoubtedly demented, he throws his whole body behind each punch. I duck and slide, but he jabs! jabs! jabs! I duck, slip, slide, block, retreat. I parry with my Ironwood Stick—but his reach is just as long! *Snap!* shoots his left, straight from the shoulder; immense weight steps into the thrust. I back peddle with panting breath. *This fucker's had some training!* Fear taints my taste—metal in my mouth. I duck, dodge, slide, block, run, retreat, pull and parry—anything to evade this maniacal assault.

"Your slut tasted good!" I hear it above the ringing cymbals and thumping blood. I can't believe my ears. My injured right one must not work; my uninjured left one must not want to.

He says it AGAIN! *So wicked! So malevolent!* This time the words sting—puncture my being—though sound far away, like at the end of a tunnel. *Is he for real! Oh God, noooo! Please! Noooo! Oh God, what have I done! Oh fuck! Why did I leave her? Oh Meeeeshaaaa!*

He jabs. I duck and slide. Nothing seems real. I'm dreaming; I'm living a daymare. He jabs again. I pull to the right. *He's hardly trying! He's playing! The fucker's having fun! Oh Meesha!* I hear

baritone laughter—far off, yet right before me. *What the fuck!*
*What does he want from me! What the fuck has he done with Meesha?*
*Oh God! What am I gonna do? How am I gonna get outta this? I gotta*
*get—gotta find—Meesha!*

Sweat rains from the giant as he strikes. Airborne, it glistens
in the jungle luminescence before spraying me. He smiles as he
jabs—*snap!*—toys with me—*snap!*—fucks with me the way a cat
does a mouse—*snap!* I duck and run, dodge and slip. *Gotta watch
my feet! Gotta slide! Don't cross'em! And look out for traps!* For a
fractured moment between punches, I catch the white flash of the
dark grin. *Fuck his face!* I concentrate on his shoulders: *when they
move, a punch will follow. But how am I gonna get away! What the
fuck! How am I gonna find Meesha!*

Suddenly I trip. *Shit!* I'm off balance. A jab flies at my face! I
duck behind my forearms. The five-fingered boulder bludgeons
my skull. Pain hammers my head, echoes in my ears. I see snow:
a sudden, blinding squall. Then I fall.

Hitting the ground, I roll—a quick revolution through the ferns.
*Traps! Look out for TRAPS!* Cuddling Ironwood, head aching, eyes
blurry, I stumble to my feet. He is on me instantly: another jab! I slip
left. I see blood on his hand. *Is that from me? Didn't know I was bleeding.
OR COULD THAT BE FROM MEE—? NOOOOOOOOO!* Another
jab! I pull right. Then a straight right that would knock down a tree.
I'm lucky: it misses—just brushes my right shoulder—spins me—
hurts, but does little damage for I roll with the motion, retreating a
few steps. I use the seconds gained to strategize. Thoughts scream
through my mind: *He's huge. Knows how to box. Kidnapped Meesha.
Claims to have…. Aahh man! Why! Playing games with me. Wasn't ready
for this. Will probably kill me—could easily—just jabbing now. But I have
weapons—where's his knife! But he knows the jungle. AND where Meesha
is. Gotta be smart. Gotta find a way. She's gotta be around here. But where!
HE isn't gonna tell me. Maybe I'll hear her. Or can track his trails to her. But
not with thunder punches raining down. No. Gotta stop that! But how?*

He's coming! Land leaping. Legs like trees. Clydesdale strides. Breath quivering, stomach somersaulting, I shuffle to the right— duck—but the jab lands! My forehead explodes! Head snaps back! Fire fills skull! More snow smears vision! *Oh God, please help me! Please stop this so I can find Meesha! Please God! Pleeeeaaassssssse!*

"I had fun fuckin' ya wife, ya little shit! Now I'm gonna have some fun fuckin' wid you! Har! Har! Har!...."

I rush backwards. *Gotta buy time! Get back my sight!* I don't look for traps. *No time! Take a chance! Fuck traps!* The giant follows me—straight on—jabs! I raise both hands. Monster fist ricochets off Ironwood. The giant jabs! I block with the stick. The giant jabs! I block. Then, a right hook! *Shit!* I didn't expect this. I raise the stick. Too late! SQUARE ON THE SKULL! JUST ABOVE LEFT TEMPLE! I go down. Hit hard. Vision fades: in—out—in—out. I stumble through ferns—*Traps! What about traps! Fuck traps!*—to my feet. *Get away from him! Get away from him!* Scrambling now. *Gotta buy time!* Expecting to get kicked, punched, but the giant lets me go. He's in no hurry. *Wants to proLONG my agony! Keep me alive as long as he CAN!* I hear laughing: "I tell ya, chicken shit, ya wife's pussy iz sweet. I musta licked her for a half hour straight."

My chest heaves lead air. *Gotta get away! Need time! Need some time!* I can't believe my ears. *No, God, no! Let it not be true! Oh, how could I! How could I have left her? Oh God, Meesha! This bastard! I'm gonna kill this bastard!* Blood no longer flows through my veins; something flammable and combustive has replaced it. *Don't care how big he is! I'm gonna kill this motherfucker! Castrate this prick! Gonna cut him to pieces!*

"Didn't think I wuz gonna get good motion goin' wid her leg all busted up, chicken dick, but once I got goin' the fuckin' wuz good. Very good, I gotta say, ya wife's very good! She knows how ta please a man! Har! Har! Har!...."

He's coming straight at me. But I'm ready. I know his combos now. I back quickly away, gain daylight for a second. I gaze up—at the face-—through the black holes—-looking for a conscience. I find none.

"Where's my wife, you evil bastard!" I don't hear my voice. I hear a man insane with rage, wild with fear, crazy with grief, yearning to kill.

"In my den of sin, where her big tits belong!" the giant bellows, smiling, his scintillating grin burning a hole in my heart. He snaps out another two jabs. I jump back, duck, and slip to my right.

*I can't keep running away! But I gotta find the right moment.*

Laughing, he comes at me fast—TOO fast! He jabs. I'm too late! My hands, too slow! The knuckled boulder pummels my skull again. I stagger. Ferns and trees swirl in my view. Then comes the right! I duck again. But this time, I get the stick up a bit higher. Granite knuckles connect with a sharp *crack!* Ironwood slams my forehead. I stumble back while the giant roars with pain. And as blood trickles from my scalp down my face, I suddenly see my way out.

Again—immediately—the giant attacks, but I don't retreat. I thrust my left foot forward, lunge at his right shoulder. *I gotta find out for sure.* He screams in rage. Throws up a dangerous forearm—like a linebacker—attempts to smash my face. But I am ready for it. I back away quickly. A thrill of relief permeates my being: I am correct. *I just have to DO IT correctly! Oh God, help me with this! Please help me!*

"Ya shoulda seen ya wife suckin' my dick!" the giant wails with unbridled anger, "She SMILED when she done it! Gimme dese big eyes. She likes me. Says I'm more of a MAN den you! Then she choked when I blew my load, so I stuck my dick in more and she REALLY choked! Har! Har! Har!...."

But the taunts, I notice, aren't free of pain. *His right hand's hurt! Can't punch! I'm gonna kill him! Gonna waste this bastard! Gonna cut off his fuck'n head!* The scintillating smirk is gone; a forced grimace remains. *Stay cool, Luke. Ya gotta wait for the right moment. Ya gotta play it smart.*

He jabs! But, again, I don't retreat. I duck and slip, shuffling to my left. Then I quickly lunge forward! As if attacking his right side! Again, the linebacker forearm flies up! Elephantine elbow aims for my head! But I anticipate it! Pull back! Drop under! Now squatting, I see only up. The colossal forearm swings over my head. My legs vibrate, though I can't feel them. I feel nothing—nothing but the need to rise.

My thighs fire! Buttocks push! Pelvis swings! Ribcage heaves! Shoulders lift! Arms pull! Head jerks! And lower throat groans: "Suck on this, you fuck'n asshole!"

I plunge the Ironwood stick into the eagle's screaming mouth. I shove it in as fiercely as I can. It *pops!* through the giant's bread box like a toothpick through shrink-wrapped cheese. The big man gasps, mouth and black holes agape. Hollow wails and bubbled blood follow. *Perfect!* I think.

"You're fucked now, you cocksucker! Where's my WIFE!"

I'm looking upward—into the black holes. They're flickering downwards from what seems as high as nearby trees. They spew hatred and surprise. But I quickly realize the hatred is not the giant's, but rather the essence of my reflection in his eyes.

He doesn't answer. I push the stick in further—harder. Twenty inch arms come crashing down. The massive right hits my left shoulder; the massive left, my head. The shoulder hit does little, but the smack to my head dazes me further than I already am. *Good thing he's shishkabobbed! Lost his power. Gotta hurry! Find where Meesha is before he dies!*

"Where's my WIFE! Tell me where my wife is, or I'll cut your balls off while you're still conscious you big, ugly son-of-a-whore! I'll SKIN you while you can still fuck'n FEEL it!"

The black holes are now supernovas. They exude visible evil as illuminated rage. He gasps faster though weaker, but his blood no longer exits as such. It now pours from his mouth. Oxygen bubbles still percolate the surface. His moustache, now supersaturated, drips copious crimson. The eagle is practically gone, its head and legs annihilated by the rupturing Ironwood. Its wings and body, themselves, are now canvases, though not for ink, but for dark red blood.

"Where's my wife!"

He doesn't answer.

"Where's my WIFE!"

No answer.

"Okay. Fine! Keep bleeding, you pig! I like watching you suffer! If only I could shove this stick up your mother's ass, this picture would be perfect!"

I gaze into the giant's eyes, relishing the fight still left in him. He knows he's going to die, but he can't give up; it's not his nature. And I know he's going to die; and I feel that it is my right to watch him and, if so desired, to enjoy it. *The bastard took Meesha. Says he raped her. Pay him in kind.*

And so I do. I've got him impaled on the end of my walking stick. He's bigger than huge. I couldn't pick him up if I wanted to. But I don't have to. He's standing mostly on his own. Only slightly do I support his stance with upward tension on the stick. But with that tension, I get my revenge.

In I push, until my front hand, my right, jams flush against the man's open belly. Warm blood gushes from the entrance wound and floods my grip. I pull back, far back, until I no longer see the bloodied tip of the Ironwood stick above the wings twitching upon his back. Then I quickly reverse direction. I thrust the long stick back into the giant's abdominal cavity until my hands join with a gushing *splat!* against his secreting body.

This thrust ignites the last spasm of vigor left in the giant. He opens his mouth to howl, but a red river usurps the medium any audible output would have ridden. "I like it!" I blurt, "Choke, you murdering fuck!" He lifts his beefy arms again, but gets them no higher than his shoulders. From there, he attempts to strike at me with open hands, as if to grab my face. *No fucking way dude!* The result is nothing more harmful than a dying man's flailing.

I pull the stick back out until I can no longer see its tip over his increasingly bent shoulders. Then I shove it right back in. I repeat this movement again, then again, then again. Each time, I whisper into his left ear: "How does the stick feel, pal? Ya like being done by the stick?"

It is on approximately the tenth repetition of my thrusting the stick into the eagle-twitching giant that I can feel his structure fully give way. He is not dead, for his black holes continue to rotate and his limbs continue to flinch, but he has become too heavy for me to hold up.

I let him drop. He falls forward. His right side brushes against a thick patch of Ula Ahi trees, then he slams into the earth. The pointed end of the walking stick pops farther out the man's exit wound from the weighty force of his fall upon the end I had been holding. I stand there, still lethal with rage, watching the giant's last breaths heave his mighty frame, while the Ironwood stick pokes flagpole-straight up through his torso and beyond. I think: *He never told me where Meesha is!* Jumping as high as I can, I land with both feet upon the back of his neck. The *crack!* is definite and distinct. I enjoy hearing it. I wish I could break it again, but necks only break once. So I jump upon the dead man's head until gray brain squishes out every orifice in his face and the fissures I crack in his skull.

When finished——satisfied?—I stand back and observe the scene with awe. Panting, I can barely believe I am here, in the middle of the jungle, watching warm blood dry on a man I have just killed. I see red spray on the green bush to the giant's right, which also bears undiluted smears from his fall. I notice that a couple of flowers on the tree have died; they are wilted and have lost their vibrancy. I also notice how close the color of the giant's spilt blood is to the color of these dead flowers. For a moment, I wonder if all death manifests itself in red, one way or another.

The heaving, of course, has stopped, but I kick him anyway. I want to. It is like kicking a large, rolled rug. I kick him again. This time, his left arm moves forward, a reflexive action from my booting his ribcage. The bastard's deader than dead. No doubt about it. *Big clunk of shit!*

I put my right foot on top of the eagle's tail, which just a few minutes earlier was a sweat-sparkling white. Placing both my hands on the Ironwood stick, I hold it tight, for the wood is slippery with blood. I pull the stick fully out of the giant's back and place its blunt end on the ground, its red-soaked upper shaft in my left hand, liquid scarlet flowing over my grip. My foot still on the giant's back, my lungs gulping rain forest air, I think: *Alright. Now where is Meesha?* Then I push off the carcass with contempt and march further into the sweet ferns, whose pungency scents the jungle around me.

# Chapter 14

I run over to the giant's lean-to shelter. There's nothing there but bamboo poles rain-proofed with large, green leaves. *Fuck! Where IS she?*

I drop my hands to my knees. My throat gulps air almost as fast as it pounds with my pulse. Sweat rains off me. *Alright. Gotta think. Be smart. Can't waste time. Gotta find her fast! Soon! She's gotta be SOMEWHERE around here.*

Starting at the hut, I circle outwards. With each revolution around the hut, I stray farther, maximizing the terrain that I can effectively scan since my previous pass. My body begs for water. Fire scorches my lungs. Each pass, being a broader circle, takes me longer to complete than the last. By my fifth revolution, I am beyond the sweet ferns and into indigenous flora, yet I still haven't found Meesha. Her shoes and socks, yes; her, no. *Fuck! Where IS she God? Oh God, please help me!*

*If she isn't here, then where could she be? Was the giant just fucking with me when he said all that shit? Was he just taunting me when Meesha really is somewhere else? But where could she be? Did he hide her farther away, then come back here to hassle me?*

*"Hassle you"? Cut the shit, Luke, he was going to KILL you!*

*Alright, "kill me". But where could he have hidden her? I wasn't gone that long. How far could he have taken her?*

I don't know. But there seems only one logical strategy: follow the sweet ferns. If the giant hid her somewhere else, he would most likely have kept her within the domain of his operation.

*But what if it wasn't him? There might be others running this show. It's gotta be a lot of work to manage this operation.*

My hunch is that others are involved. Operations like this are not usually run by a single individual. Security elements are required beyond that of immobile man traps; that, alone, would necessitate more men. Then there's the tending of the plants. If many plants exist, so must multiple field workers. Right now, I don't know how many ferns are out there. But I will find out.

A chill seizes my sweating frame: I clearly comprehend what I'm probably up against. It ain't pretty. These types don't fuck around. They're not just tattooed ex-boxers with attitude. They're merciless killers. And the odds are that somewhere, out there, they've got Meesha. *Fuck! I HAVE to find her! I have to find her SOON!* But, to do so, I must properly prepare myself.

I rush back to the dead giant. *Maybe he has matches—wire— something I can use.* I bend down and check the pockets of his green khaki shorts. The worthless shit isn't even carrying a wallet. His entire carcass offers nothing more than shorts bound by a black belt, white socks and black, shin-high boots. Then I remember the cut nylon rope, camera neck strap, and vines. *Where's his knife? It's not in his shelter! Damn, I could use that.*

I pull off the shorts, then remove my bamboo knife from my shirt sleeve. I grip the rear, belted portion of the Khakis firmly within my fingers. Beside my pressing thumb, I stab the bamboo through. Then I hear him: *"Never cut rope, or any other cordage, unless you have to!"* How often I still hear—and sometimes even listen to!—that paternal, militaristic, inner voice. As a result, I begin cutting as though I am peeling an apple and wish to remove all the skin as a single piece.

The fabric is tough and resists my sawing, which makes me saw all the harder. I stop when I have shredded the section of the shorts above the zipper fly and all of the left leg. It is the zipper that prevents me from continuing my single piece any further. *That's okay,* I think, *I've preserved a good portion as it is.* Then I finish shredding the remainder.

*In this heat, the giant will be fermenting in an hour.* I would like to bury the corpse to hide evidence of our encounter, but I don't have the time. *I gotta find Meesha!*

I take off. Though thirsty and exhausted, I walk fast, bent over and searching, the khaki fabric in my hands. I proceed roughly twenty steps before I stop and kneel in waste high foliage. Ahead of me, swaths of sweet ferns weave randomly throughout the jungle flora. Behind me, the searing gas God smirks as he bakes my back.

I scan North, South, East, and West. I scan well—thoroughly—deliberately. I look up and down, in between things, over things, and under things. I look directly at objects; then, at those same objects indirectly, a bit off center. I look for an image, a silhouette, or some movement. But I see nothing.

Slowly, I lower myself into the tall grass. Buttocks on the ground, I begin to cut. *I may have to sharpen this again,* I think, glancing at the knife's edge, but I continue. My strokes are short and minimal, just enough to sever pieces. I sever seven: one for my head, one for each shoulder, one for each calf, and one for each thigh. Then I tie them. I use an overhand knot, so that I can untie them as quickly as I may need. I make them tight, but not so that they restrict blood flow. When finished, I re-sheath the bamboo in my left shoulder sleeve, grab my walking-stick-turned-spear, and set out to follow the ferns.

Searching briskly for Meesha, I notice how they plant the sweet ferns in narrow swaths, in and around existing vegetation. You literally have to be within ten feet of the indigenous ferns to distinguish them from the introduced ones.

I also notice that the planted areas aren't huge. But this makes sense. They can't be big. They can't be detectable from the air. The DEA or FBI would pick them off with a single pass over in a chopper. They've got to be kept small and hidden within the indigenous flora. Never before have I thought about camouflaging plants with plants, but that is what these guys have to do—and have done.

Searching, I look to my right, to my left, behind me, then back to the undulating rows of "sweet-fernish" plants before me. *Barely discernible,* I think, *and it's broad daylight! The most visible time!* Not only do these plants blend with all the other fern types, but with all the other flora as well: the myriad of trees: tall, short, light green, dark green; the variety of palms of so many shapes; the waste high grasses of so many colors; and the flowers: blue, orange, purple, red, yellow, with berries and without.

But the jungle's most effective characteristic for hiding these fern-resembling weeds is its density. Looking around, I get the feeling you could hide the entire population of Rhode Island in here, tucking people beneath elephant ear leaves, overflowing moss rugs and the multi-layered tree canopy. And this feeling makes me hunt for Meesha as meticulously as I can.

Tapping into my energy reserves, I move forward, bent at the waist, as low as possible, keeping my back and head below the height of the tall grass. I bound in multiples—if not strides of three, strides of two; I go by how I feel. When I stop, I drop right down into a squat; my head up, perked like a Golden Retriever's, but inconspicuous below the grass line.

After several bounds, I am farther into the fern fields, the "sweetish" ones, the ones worth much money on the street. These introduced swaths flank me, while another patch of the indigenous kind appears in front of me. It is the latter that I seek.

I stop again. I grab only the large, mature, green fronds. Beautiful as the younger, smaller, red fronds are, they would be conspicuous, the opposite of what I need.

I uproot many and stick them in the khaki strips tied around my head, shoulders, thighs, and calves. I fill each khaki strip with as many fronds as I can and still move comfortably. My primary objective is function; my second, comfort; knowing, however, that both are necessary if I am going to succeed. After the giant, I'm not taking any chances.

I work quickly, though carefully. When I finish, I have used every fern piece that I've picked, save two. These two bear broken fronds that I damaged while trying to insert into khaki strips. I cannot use damaged camouflage. It will not look right. It would not look real. It could give me away.

Continuing to kneel, I scrutinize the horizon, spinning a full circle. I see nothing.

Carefully, I rise, bounding upwards, inch by inch. Facing Northeast, I look down, just beyond my feet. I am pleased. I do not see me. I see a bush. My human silhouette has been replaced by a jagged clump of shadow—a jagged clump no different than the vast stretch of other jagged clumps I see eclipsed across the jungle floor.

I spin slightly to the right while kneeling back down. *I am now there. I am now IN their territory. While searching for Meesha, I must be extremely cautious, vigilant to the max. Every move I make must be deliberate; every action, for a purpose. Otherwise, I've gotta be a clump of ferns. Ferns don't move. Ferns stay still.*

I rise again, but then I quickly retreat, without ever stopping. I recoil half-way, my hands sinking to my knees. I hadn't seen it before; yet, there it is, just a few feet in front of me. Not well worn—no mud pops through its vegetative carpet—it is only about two feet wide, simply a line of trampled grass and flattened ferns through untrampled grass and unflattened ferns. I can barely discern where it cuts the terrain as my eyes track its course. First, it borders the swaths of introduced ferns before me, to far left and to far right. Then, it angles up and away on both sides. I watch it parallel these "sweetish" ferns, while meandering between trees and other obstacles, before it meanders out of my sight. *Where does it lead?* I wonder, *Where do these introduced fern fields end? And, oh God, where is Meesha!*

I don't know where the fern fields end, but my gut tells me that somewhere between there and here I'll find my wife.

I don't use the path. That would be stupid. *Might as well wave red ferns and whistle. I've gotta stick to the dense brush.*

Knees bent, back hunched, eyes just peeking over the high grass, I, again, begin to bound. Now, though, I take just one step at a time. First, I probe the ground with my walking stick, tapping it every few inches, sweeping thick growth from left to right. Then, when sure the footing is safe, I move my right one forward, smoothly, consuming as much ground as I prudently can. Never do I pop above the jungle floor canopy. Never do I move too fast, jerkily in any way, or without full confidence that no one exists within my panoramic view. I am no longer in an office, wing-tipped and paisley-tied, hunting for paper strips in a jammed printer. I am now in a jungle, on an island in the Pacific, camouflaged and cautious, searching for my wife. And I'm looking for her everywhere, zigzagging through the fern fields, lifting every piece of concealing foliage. My only objective is to find Meesha before her abductors find me. I must use my brain to its fullest potential and just hope my untrained body can keep up.

I continue forward—ten steps, twenty steps, thirty.

After roughly forty steps, the introduced fern field to my left suddenly bends further that way. I swing my head to the right. The introduced field there is doing the same. I glance up, same direction. Several hundred meters ahead, a wall of eroding rock abruptly rises, stunning the continuity of the flat jungle floor. It's face is sheer, and through hundreds of layers of cooled, hardened lava, it iridescently displays the geological progression that created Re'enev.

The cliff is forcing me to veer left, just as it is bending the lucrative crops. I look at it again, then back over my left shoulder. In the rear distance, I see another range of cliffs. These are much farther off, a few miles to the South. Their hills reflect continual sunlight in various shades of green.

*So we are in a valley,* I think, pondering the cliffs. This makes sense. It's the best place to grow things. There's plenty of fertile earth, sunshine, and water; and, of course, though no less important: obstacles, abutments, coverings, and concealments behind which, or under which, to hide from legal authorities and poachers. *A POACHER! THAT'S what they probably think we are! And THAT'S a reason to KILL us! To them, we're just other criminals. No one cares about the death of a poacher. Certainly not the Feds. Hell, one less to follow is one less to catch. Makes their job easier. And with one less to catch, there is one less to feed. Penal system benefits. Judicial system benefits. Law enforcement benefits. Taxpayers benefit. What the hell? Everybody wins.* Except my wife, of course, who wasn't a fucking poacher, but simply a hiker who happened to have a careless husband. *OH, WHY THE FUCK DID I BRING HER DOWN HERE!*

*STOP IT! FIND HER! NOTHING ELSE MATTERS!*

I resume bounding—one step, two steps, five steps, ten. I'm now in the middle of the turn, yet nothing has changed. Swaths of introduced ferns still meander on both sides of me, in between trees and throughout the lower jungle canopy. The stuff undulates in patterns not unlike the black portion of Holstein cow hides. I can barely tell the lucrative weeds from the indigenous ferns and I'm marching right beside them. *No way some helicopter or fixed-wing craft could pick this off. It's too well hidden.*

*But where the fuck is Meesha!*

I go another twenty steps, then stop. I stop because the introduced fields, between which I am walking, are suddenly ending. I stop because a path cuts ten yards in front of me, connecting the end of these fields. I stop because this break in the terrain's continuity unnerves me. *What's happened? Is this it, the end of the clandestine plantation? Was the giant the only operator? Then where is Meesha!*

It just doesn't seem right. I just can't believe that that brawny giant was running this whole show, nor can I believe that this show ends here. You got a good operation that can make shitloads of dough, you don't keep it small. Man, if you're gonna take the risk of twenty-plus years in the joint, you go for it. And what I've seen so far isn't really going for it. *No, I bet my ass there's more ahead. There's GOTTA be more ahead. And that's where I'll find Meesha.*

So I move. I continue forward as I had been: bounding, one stride at a time. At the path connecting the ends of the two introduced fields, my insides surge with vigilance. I scan panoramically, then cross quickly.

*I have to be smart,* I suddenly think—*proactive. Like a Boy Scout and Force Recon Marine, as Hunter had liked to say, I've got to be prepared.*

So I turn right, but stay down, hidden within the ferns. Bounding toward the cliff, I cover my trail. *Can't let'em find me— surprise me—while I work.* As I strut, tears merge with sweat and slip down my face.

I move about an eighth of a mile. The rich, sweet smell of perpetual decomposition hangs heavy in the humid air. Songbirds flit about. Buzzing insects incessantly orbit my head. My grip punishes my Ironwood stick for the pain I suffer in my heart.

Near the cliff, a point so close I have to strain my neck, I stop. *God, please take care of Meesha. Please let her be okay.* I can't stop thinking about my wife. I can't stop worrying.

I begin scanning and gathering. I don't take from just one spot. I space out my cutting, slicing, and uprooting; I try to minimize the marks I leave upon the land. I grab vines from behind a tree, behind a leaf, under some ferns, beneath a bush; I leave nothing conspicuous. Where vegetation has been mauled by a feral pig, I further maul the area; let the boar take the blame. When I am finished, my shorts' pockets bulge, stuffed to their maximum capacity.

I bound back toward the sweet ferns, away from the cliff. Not once do I release my vigilance; never do I let down my guard. I cannot. I am both the hunter and the hunted. I must maintain my stealth and camouflage. My mud will always be thick. My strut will always be smooth. My ferns will always be fresh. Plants don't wilt in the wild; thus, they will not wilt upon me. I will relentlessly maintain my appearance as a bush and my noise discipline will remain severe.

My mouth is dry. I think of fluids. While gathering vine, I'd noticed a Traveler's Palm growing a few feet from me. It was the second one I've seen thus far in the jungle. I remember this tree from our botanical tours, though not for its looks, but its name. Pacific island explorers appreciatively called it such for the precious rain water that collects in the vortex where its gutter-shaped appendages join its center stalk. While gathering, I'd also spotted a raspberry bush and a tree similar to the Ula Ahi, but with pinkish, half-inch balls hanging from its branches. These balls, I remember being told, are edible apples. With my tongue feeling like sand, my throat tasting like wood, my breath the flavor of mustard gas, and my saliva the consistency of napalm, my flesh felt the urge to indulge in these jungle offerings; but my mind would have none of it: *Not until you get Meesha to safety!*

Back within the introduced ferns, at the spot where I had turned right to gather vines, I resume bounding, hunting for Meesha. At the same time, pulling three pieces of vine from my shorts' pocket, I begin to weave. Knowing the hike out with Meesha upon my back will be long and arduous, I want to tie her to me, keep her from moving as much as possible, for both her sake and mine. Thus, as I bound, I no longer check for traps. *Haven't seen any in a while, anyhow.* Instead, I pay the ends of three separate strands of vegetation through my hands, while they clutch my Ironwood stick. Initially, the task is difficult. I must pass each strand over the one beside it—right over left, left over right, right over left…. As three distinct pieces of plant fiber feed into the upper portion of my hands, a single braid emerges from the bottom. While my hands thread vine into rope, my eyes scan the perimeter. I become better at this process with every plait. Soon, I am performing the function without even thinking— diagonally overlapping each piece of severed vegetation with precision, effectively tightening the tangled strands just enough, then starting immediately on the following pleat.

At one point, I wonder if I'll have enough vine to meet my needs. I briefly consider returning to the giant and skinning him with my bamboo knife. He's very tall. I could cut out pieces of ligament and tendon and slice long strips of his skin. Then I could dry them all on a rock in direct sunlight and twist them together in sets of two or three. The final product would be strong and supple and work just fine, but I decide against it. Drying the dead man's flesh would take way too long; I can't allocate that much time. Plus, it would be too risky. The act of dissecting the body; the putrid, far reaching smell; the slicing, tying and drying—I could easily get caught unaware by one of his fellow farmers, who I believe must exist. *No, I conclude, it wouldn't be worth the risk. I'll stick with the vines and simply slice more if I need to.* I continue bounding. I continue hunting. I continue braiding. I continue thinking.

# Chapter 15

As I strut and braid, a sobering tsunami of cold reality washes over me. My short term memory, a wrecking ball, drops from my mind into my gut: *The trap. Meesha hurt. Meesha screaming. Meesha unconscious. The path out hard to find. Meesha gone. The giant. Blood. Pot. Pain. Oh God! If it could only be a dream.* But it's not. It's a truth that's just begun. *Shit!* I feel like puking, but I keep moving. I keep braiding. I keep searching.

The notion of Meesha in pain is a swift kick to my balls. But it is not a thought I will relinquish.

*Gotta be sharp, ignore pain. Gotta concentrate, overcome my anguish, operate like a machine, like a robot.* I have no idea who, or what, may be in the vicinity. *Everything I do must be done with stealth. I can't afford to make a mistake. There's probably a few hundred grand of planted revenue down here whose wholesome farmers wouldn't think twice about putting a bullet in my brain—especially when they discover what I did to their tattooed giant.*

Then suddenly: *I can't believe this! I'm carrying a spear, covered with mud, and decorated with leaves. Am I losing my freaking mind? What's next? Should I stick a mailbox on some cave and call it home? Should I become like Adam, toss my shorts, and wear only ferns?*

Pushing through the verdant density, I think: *I must use stealth. That is true. But that's only half of it. To find and get Meesha outta here, I'm gonna have to use ingenuity too. Supplies aren't gonna just fall out of the sky. I'm gonna have to be creative and innovative. I'm gonna have to use the skills Dad tried to pound into my head when I was a kid. If I can just remember some of the survival shit he and Hunter threw my way over the years.* And so, as I strut to the Northeast, I try to recall my father's and brother's words. It isn't easy, for I was never all that interested in learning how to survive in the wild—why learn junk I don't intend on using? But for some odd reason, I remember quite a bit. Maybe it's because they taught so well, or maybe because they spoke about it so frequently, or maybe because most of this crap is commonsense and the rest simply blank canvas for the creative. I don't know. I just remember.

I press on, each step a search, a hunt, each thought a razor scraping memories from my skull. However, I no longer physically feel. I'm sort of numb, as if I'm staying sane through Novocain, as if I'm overdosing on endorphins. The only thing that now penetrates my existence is thought, and the only kind that matter are those concerning Meesha.

*Am I losing it? Is there something wrong with me?*

I don't know, and I don't care. I feel as though my entire nervous system is frostbitten, that my brain no longer gives a shit what happens to my body. I simply want—NEED!—to find Meesha.

*But is that really true? Didn't I care that that giant might have killed me? Wasn't I nervous when he started coming my way?*

*Yeah, I was nervous,* I think, *but even more so, furious. Adrenaline-fueled rage inflamed every cell comprising me. I really didn't consider whether the giant was going to waste me per se. Didn't have time. My only concern was getting rid of the bastard, so that I could find Meesha; and, I must admit, punishing him a bit in the process.*

I'm at the bend now, the middle of the curving cliff to my right. I can see that the paths, which have been paralleling my flanks, still do. *Oh God, where IS she!*

I move on. *The giant. If he has partners—like I think he does— like I think he must—won't they try to make contact? Come looking for him? How do these guys work? Seems they would keep tabs on each other. If one guy doesn't return—return to where?—they'd start searching for him. Or maybe they don't. Maybe taking off for a morning, or an afternoon, or a day or two, is normal. Hell, the jungle is big enough; a guy could sleep anywhere if he's used to it. Or maybe the others don't want to track him down because they're afraid he was hit by some other growers and don't want to get wasted themselves. Maybe this is not a collective thing, but rather an every-man-is-on-his-own type of operation, sort of like fishing, like lobstering, and these guys just tend to their own business and leave everyone else alone. If that's the case, it would make sense: why would someone come looking for the giant? No one is responsible for him. In fact, if the giant did encroach on someone else's turf and got knocked off, the last thing anyone else would want to do is associate himself with the dead man. They'd want to distance themselves from him as much as possible.*

*So,* I think, *maybe it's okay that no one's come looking for the dead monster.*

*But then,* I wonder, *how do you explain Meesha? The giant didn't have time to move her far, but I haven't found her yet. So SOMEONE must have moved her. But who? When? How? And why?*

I feel uneasy. Regardless, I push on. The jungle becomes thicker, the under canopy denser, the upper canopy taller. I move parallel with the curving cliff, breaking my own trail, until the cliff abruptly ends.

To my right, about twenty feet away, stands a tree with large palm fronds sprouting from its top. These fronds shoot outwards from about fifteen feet above the ground and do so in a circular pattern, similar to the rotor blades atop a helicopter. From the tree's trunk descend multiple vines. Some reach all the way to the ground. The rest dangle above it.

*Another reservoir*, I think. *Just grab a vine and my blade, then cut high, then low. Gotta cut high first*, I remember, *so the fluid moves downwards. Cut the bottom first and capillary action will make it move up the vine. And drink it only if its clear.*

Now past the tree, I think: *I can't believe I remember this shit. Wouldn't Dad be proud?* a different part of me snickers.

But then I wonder: *What about MEESHA! Has SHE had water! In her state, she DEFINITELY needs water. Oh God, please help me find her! Don't let her suffer any more!*

I scan. I braid. I bound. Though I see nothing but green, I know that I am in the middle of it all and that somewhere, close by, I'll find Meesha. *I just gotta get there!* I also have this feeling that if I don't keep a constant watch, something will constantly watch me. I feel as though I can't drop my head for one second, or I'll lose my head before the following one begins. I know there's someone out there. I just haven't seen him—them?—yet. And there's no way in fucking hell that I can let him or them see me before I find my wife. That, I just can't let happen.

I periscope. See nothing. Stop. My right hand tightens around the Ironwood stick. My left hand pulls my eyebrows toward each other, squeezing out several drops of sweat. Glancing down at the braids around my neck, I glimpse my nose glisten. *Not good. Can't have skin shine.* I reach down, grab loose dirt, rub it on my face, neck, and ears, then on my arms and legs.

I move forward, glancing left and right. I notice my breathing. It is steady. This is good. My mind suddenly spins: *I don't get it. They leave me a trail at first—the white markers—then nothing. Why?*

Then I hear it. My right foot is in mid-air, but I stop. I balance my body upon the balls of my left foot and slowly lower my right. Then I lower my entire body, slow inch by slow inch, until I am in a squat. I make myself solid, virtually permanent. Chewing gum flattened along a city street in mid-July moves more than I do.

It was far off, or so it seemed. *Don't fuck up! The jungle kills sound! Everything seems farther away than it really is.* It was a voice, a man's voice, and all it said was "Chin!"

Twenty feet ahead of me grows a denser patch of ferns. *It's better than this grassy shit.* I slowly periscope. I look all the way around, 360°. I look up and down. I still don't see anybody, so I lower myself onto my belly. Not until this moment have I ever wished I were a snake. I move one elbow forward, then push with that side's knee; then move the other elbow forward, then push with the other side's knee. In this way I squiggle, slowly, all the while probing the ground ahead with my Ironwood stick. *Last thing Meesha needs right now is for me to get decapitated by a leg hold trap.*

I reach the ferns and insert myself, crawling immediately to the middle of the patch. There, I find a large, flat rock beneath the fern canopy. Carpeting the rock is thick, furry moss. I plant my forearms on the moss. Cool rainwater seeps from the saturated cover beneath my arms and down the rock's sides. I barely notice. My pelvis perched on soft ground, my arms propped upon a cushioned slab of solid lava, I raise my head just enough to see over the vegetation. I have become one of the ferns. I am green like them. I sway like them. I make shadows like them.

The voice cuts the jungle air again: "Ya gotta use your head! The one on your shoulders! Ya unnerstan'!", followed by a *click!* I know that *click!* It is the *click!* of a metallic lighter shutting, the cap swiveling on its hinge and clamping, aluminum vs. aluminum, against the lighter's butane-filled body.

*Good. They're smoking. Had the giant been smoking? Is that where that familiar smell had come from?* My mind's eye opens, while my head's eyes stand sentry. That morning's actions replay in my brain. *No, he hadn't. At least he didn't have anything on him that indicated so. And I don't remember smelling any smoke when I was near him.*

*Okay, but there's somebody out there now! Possibly SEVERAL people! And one smokes.*

"Sorry boss. I guess—I guess we, ahh, got a little excited." The tense voice approaches me on the path to my right. It speaks from the Northeast, the direction in which I am heading. Although soft and low-key, it articulates words distinctly. I have no problem hearing or understanding. "Just seem like a dream come true, y'know? Won't—won't happen again."

*"Dream come true"? What are they talking about?*

"Well, it better not! I'll cut another asshole outta the next bastard who fucks up! Can't be screwin' up the operation with this kinda shit! Can't take chances! It's unprofessional and it ain't my way! I won't have it! I expect better from you guys! Especially Screamer, wherever the fuck he IS!"

*A different voice. Heavier. Gruffer. A smoker's rasp. A leader's demeanor. Strict. Reprimanding. What happened? What was "unprofessional"?*

The closest object along the path within my vision is a tunnel of tall trees. Oak-like, grayish-green leaves coif their bare and brawny, cocoa-brown trunks. Observing this, I realize with alarm how close I actually am to the tunnel—to the path! *Damn, I wasn't wrong! Everything in the jungle IS closer than it initially seems. I gotta stay alert!*

It is a naturally formed tunnel, not vegetation hollowed by man's heavy foot. And because this tunnel exists, these men initially decided to travel through it—the path of least resistance.

Suddenly, dirt-brown, ash-gray, fern-green, and other shades of the jungle emerge from the tunnel swirled within a T-shirt. The shirt is small, slightly filled, and spawns thin arms that barely swing with its forward motion. Though tanned the hue of a coconut shell, these arms pale beside the head of hair below which they hang. Thick and slightly wavy, the combed mass glimmers, reflecting equatorial sun.

I watch intently. My nerves are on High Alert. Meesha could be anywhere. I can't afford to blink.

I notice that the man's T-shirt doesn't droop. Rather, it tucks neatly into khaki shorts identical in design, though much smaller in size, to those the giant had been wearing. From these shorts, thin, muscular legs, as darkly tanned as the arms above, carry the spindly man swiftly on black-booted feet, which obviously know the jungle well. The quick and nimble way the slight man moves reminds me of a spider.

This spider does not smoke. This spider walks point. I strain my eyes. This is not a face I will forget.

The features appear Oriental, but only in part. *There's probably a bit of Filipino*, I think, *as well as several variations of Caucasian in him.* The eyes seem narrower than Occidental, but not as heavy lidded as those I typically associate with pure Chinese.

My eyes drop a little: like the hair on his head, the hair above his top lip is full and thick. It ends in twirled points that dip below the corners of his mouth. It doesn't descend as deeply as the giant's had, but rather reminds me of the stereotypical Mexican Bandit.

As if to complement his moustache, the flinty man's cheekbones jut abnormally high and pointy. In fact, if I had to pick one word to describe this guy, it would be *sharp*. Not *sharp* as in *suave, diplomatic,* and *debonair,* but sharp as in *razor blade*. These cheekbones dent his facial skin the way a cardboard box corner pokes ornamental paper in which it is wrapped. They establish outrageous peaks to which the lean contour of his remaining countenance conforms. And this contour, not unlike my mind's version of Lucifer's ferocious mug, pulls undue focus toward the eyes. Even from the distance at which I perch upon mossy rock, I can conclude that these are the most vicious eyes I have ever seen. Like a rabid Doberman's, they seem juiced with lethal voltage. I get the feeling I could be electrocuted were this guy to simply stare at me for too long. I have never spoken to the man,

don't know his history, have never even seen him before. But I
don't doubt that Chin—as I heard him called by the cigarette-
smoking walnut-blonde following him—would lower one hate-
blocking-lid, for one hate-emanating-moment, before slicing my
jugular with a single swipe of the metal, wafer-thin hair removing
implement that best characterizes his demeanor.

Yet, despite Chin's slim-steeled, throat cutting edge, it is the
butt smoking, pallid Re'enevian trailing him who alarms me. Half
as dark as Chin with his sun-streaked pony-tail bobbing upon
his back, Blondie—as my brain's color-conscious-classifier dons
him—displays no explicit characteristics that would solicit fear.
He wears the same type of shorts as Chin along with a solid green
T-shirt and brown hiking boots. But unlike Chin who, with his
attack dog eyes and sharp-boned cheeks, looks like he could stare
down a crocodile and scare the skin off a Cobra, Blondie appears
almost amiable. With a wide, prominent forehead, eyebrows as
thick as his moustache and Re'enevian features chiseled and
softened by the obvious intrusion of Caucasian blood, Blondie
could be thirty, Blondie could be fifty. Yet amicable as Blondie
may appear, I can tell right away that he isn't the kind of guy you
mockingly call "half-breed". Like a Mafia hit man, Blondie emits
the cocky, self-assured aura of what my brain instantly labels:
Bad Motherfucker. With muscular, surfer-like agelessness, brown
hair sun-burnt several lighter shades, ears dangling Re'enevian
jewelry as coral white as the teeth that flare his sinister smile,
Blondie is the archetypal good looking, bad guy who will cut
your throat as nonchalantly as he sparks up a butt. It seems like a
contradiction to me but, youthful face notwithstanding, something
about Blondie seems hard, almost scary. I'm not sure what it is. As
I watch him walk with that confident strut and insolent smirk, I
sense the aura: a radiated warning to the world that you shouldn't
screw with him. He isn't impressively big, so it can't be his size. It
might simply be the cocky way he dangles his cigarette from his

lips. Or it might be his hatless, high-cheeked, squinting disregard for the tropical sun. Or it could be the undeniable authority in his coarse, raw-throated commands. I'm not really sure. But the longer I watch him, the more I think it's his eyes.

They're so bright, I can see their gleam from here. Hazel like a killer cat's, they suck in every sight with intensity. Yet, despite their colorific flare, they seem to contrast Blondie's sun-drenched mane with coldness. They are the kind of eyes that can see thoughts, penetrate facades, and dissect motives; the kind of eyes that deliver pain with contact, that hurt to look into; the kind of eyes that make people sweat, talk, and stutter. They are not overly large eyes, hints of oriental ancestry tugging at their corners, but in no way does lack of size impede their impact; which, I believe, is substantially responsible for the aura I perceive.

Chin is passing me now, looking ahead. He walks with a steady, careful, though purposeful gait. Chin isn't the kind of guy who would blindly step into a pile of dog shit. Chin studies where he's going.

Blondie is 45° to my right. He doesn't appear to be as cautious as Chin, though my gut tells me that is more from ability and confidence gained through experience, than from carelessness or nonchalance. I doubt very much that Blondie ever has to clean canine poop from his boots either.

Right now, though, neither Chin nor Blondie appear unduly vigilant. Neither is periscoping the terrain as I would be, and have been. They are just walking to a predetermined destination. That, I can see. It is obvious. So the chances of them detecting me are slight. Nonetheless, I stay way down, absolutely still. *Thank God I put on camouflage. Good timing. But what about Meesha? What do these two know about Meesha and her whereabouts? Should I follow them? Did I somehow miss Meesh? Overlook her? Not see her?*

Suddenly, Blondie smiles. The corners of his mouth flare as his full, burgundy lips stretch and suck inwards, balancing his cigarette between two equal points of pressure. At the same time, he reaches his right arm across his chest, lifts his green short sleeve, and scratches his upper left arm. This movement triggers a loud *click!* in my head, then the bottom of my stomach drops out. *Why did he smile? Is it the sun?* I study his face. His eyes are slits while his roasted-almond skin furrows from socket to temple. As he sustains the expression, I glimpse the straight-toothed gleam of his regally wicked and wily grin. *Yeah,* I conclude, *it is the sun.* But that is not what alarmed me. I wouldn't be alarmed by a man smiling, whether from humor or from light.

Before smiling, despite his long, full ponytail, Blondie had still looked amiable, sort of avuncular, the kind of brother you'd like one of your parents to have: a bachelor who would take you to ball games and four-wheeling in his Jeep; who would tell you dirty jokes and give you a beer, or two, at his house before you're of age. But when he smiled: Man, how sinister! How diabolically sinister! Even though it was only a reaction to the sun...Damn! Sadism spit from his pores. This guy could laugh while raping a nun. But, still, that isn't what alarmed me. Personified evil I have seen before. That wouldn't necessarily alarm me.

What alarmed me is the ink in his skin, the design beneath the short, shirt sleeve. High on his left arm, just below his deltoid, visible when he lifts the cotton fabric, is an emblem I know. Having Force Recon for a brother and a career jarhead for a father, how could I not know it? With all the books and magazines lying around all the time, I was bound to see the insignia blaring from one document or another. But I didn't expect to see it on the arm of some guy walking in the jungle, on an island in the Pacific, while searching for my abducted, injured wife. More accurate still: I *wish* I didn't see it on the arm of some guy walking in the jungle....

But I do see it. It's as clear as day. To the unknowing, it wouldn't be as distinctive and, thus, intimidating. But to me, right now, it's a stab in the stomach.

Unlike the giant's, this one is older. But then again, Blondie is older than the giant. *So they probably got these things at about the same age in their respective lives.* For some reason, that bothers me. *Why does that bother me?*

Despite its age, the gold in Blondie's arm still glitters: three gold lightning bolts flashing across a gold, upturned dagger. The lightning bolts hang parallel and equidistant from each other, each descending about 30° from its sharply pointed left end to its sharply pointed right end. Thrusting from below, the deadly dagger bisects each bolt. This insignia has always invoked in me the image of Thor, the Norse God of Thunder and Lightning, pointing his sword toward heaven during an electrically violent squall. And upon Blondie's arm, this insignia still gleams against the deep ocean blue arrowhead that symbolizes the craft and stealth of the Native American, our country's first warrior. This stuff I never forgot. How could I forget? It was always in the magazines. The upturned dagger symbolizing unconventional warfare. The lightning bolts representing sizzling speed and overpowering strength within the three mediums of infiltration: land, air, and sea. *Beautiful stuff*, I have always thought. Stuff I have always liked to look at—until now.

This isn't good. Searching for my wife who is injured, possibly dying—God forbid!—I'm in the jungle, a fucking office worker who can barely tell the difference between a deciduous and an evergreen; who has no calluses on his hands or trained skills for surviving, never mind killing; who has impaled one rogue farmer with—of all things!—a walking stick and, therefore, faces the inevitable wrath of his villainous comrades; and who, only then, has the privilege to learn that such men include a Special Forces commando, a Green Beret who looks like he has spent much of his life in this exact type of terrain—some, possibly, in combat. No, this is not good. This is like unknowingly picking a street fight with a black belt; like trying to steal guns from what appears a warehouse, but clandestinely serves as State Police barracks; like attempting an inner city bank robbery, but getting the address wrong and walking into FBI headquarters with a gun in your jacket and pantyhose over your head. Could I possibly fuck up more?

*But I'm still undetected. At least I have that. If there's anything I have to do, it's to remain elusive, to find Meesha and not get caught. I CAN'T get caught. Better yet, I can't be SEEN. I must maintain the element of surprise. That'll be my equalizer. With surprise on my side, I'll succeed: I'll find Meesha and get her the fuck outta here!* Despite my optimism, however, my stomach still feels as if I've swallowed a bowling ball.

Blondie now passes me. I don't move. I don't even blink. I'm so much like stone I'm surprised my eyeballs don't make scraping sounds as they rotate in their sockets.

Now, they're fully to my rear. *Won't be long before they're near the giant. He's gonna be reeking soon. A slab of raw beef that size beneath the jungle sun? Ain't gonna smell like cookie dough! Guy like Blondie might sense it and investigate.*

*Blondie? What is it about Blondie?* Something about him confuses me. *Why would a Green Beret—Is he former or active? Gotta be former—get into something like this? Special Forces is so elite, so noble. Why throw such training aw-? But, of course! Who better to run a covert operation! To patrol the mountains and valleys with satanic-like stealth? My God! Are these the guys running the drug operations! No wonder they're so hard to bust! Damn, I'd hate to be a DEA agent. How the hell do you fight a guy like that in his own element? S'gotta be fuck'n hairy! Like me trying to track Hunter down when he was alive and fight him with guerrilla tactics in the woods of Maine, New Hampshire or Western Mass. Yeah, right! Good luck, Luke!*

Then it dawns on me. For a long, numbing moment, my mind's mouth remains speechless though my brain continues to think. When my mind regains sensation, it takes back the mike.

*Okay, so this is the same thing except, instead of Hunter, I've got Blondie. Now what?*

*What do you mean "now what?" What are you saying?: That when the lights came on, your blind date was uglier than puke? That the new guy on the job has a Harvard MBA, twice your experience, and is competing for your position? That your chute is on, the plane's on fire, but you're afraid of heights? Well, fuck it! Just go! Find her! Where did they hide her? Look everywhere! WHY did they hide her? Doesn't matter! Just find her!*

Then, something else: *Screamer?* Something bothers me about that name. *Screamer? What is it?*

I ponder a while, listening intently for any sounds Chin or Blondie might make. Then it hits me: *Of course! The eagle! Damn! I knew something bugged me about that fuck'n tattoo. Damn it! That's EXACTLY what this is: What set up the trap! What tried to keep us out of these fern fields! What took Meesha! That's what I'm up against! Okay, so one's a former Beret and the other was Airborne—101ˢᵗ—Screaming Eagles. Then what's Chin? He's about the same age as the Giant. Is he a former commando, too? Could be. Probably is. Damn, I'm in the fuck'n jungle fighting renegade warriors who have kidnapped my injured wife! Damn! Shit! Fuck! Damn! What am I gonna do! What CAN I do! Run out of the jungle and report 'em to the authorities? WHAT authorities! Haven't seen a fucking cop since I've been on this island! And even if I found one, what'll that get me?—other than the death penalty for killing the giant. No way a cop on this island is gonna feel compassion for a spear carrying tourist who kills an unarmed Re'enevian—one of his own. Plus, finding a cop won't help me find Meesha—not in time to save her anyhow, and THAT'S all that matters! Take me forever to find someone, get 'em down here, find her, then give her medical treatment. No fucking way! Gotta do this NOW! On my OWN! And another thing!: Once Blondie and Chin find that giant, they're gonna come after you, you know that! They're gonna try and track you down, you realize that, don't cha! They're not gonna just let you run out of here. You'll spend as much time trying to crawl past'em as you would simply finding Meesh and caring for her. But you HAVE to get her outta here! So you need to do it BEFORE they start looking for you! So FUCK Blondie! The HELL with him! Find Meesha NOW! Find her SOON! Get going! Get moving!*

*Okay, so I'm back to square one: I just gotta find Meesha. That's IT. That's all that matters. Just gotta go with my gut—use what I know—and hope and pray for the fucking best. So c'mon! Move it! Go!*

# Chapter 16

I bolt. I screw. I pick up speed. There is no better time for me to move, to advance farther into their territory, to search for Meesha. One dead, another two behind me—one obviously the leader—now is the time to go. I go.

I walk like a duck, my ass on my calves. I move as fast as I surreptitiously can. *Who else is out here! Where would they be!* I fear noise. Every so often, the mud beneath me slurps as I pull my foot from its sucking clutch. I prepare for this. I ease my foot out of the mud whenever I feel suction holding back my heel.

I go twenty steps, forty steps, sixty, eighty, a hundred. Irregularly shaped fields of introduced ferns suddenly appear on both sides of me. *These look like the same fern fields I passed earlier.* But I know that can't be. The curving cliff is behind me. These are new fields, other fields. This agricultural operation is growing before my eyes.

Sweat begins to poke through the baked mud caked upon my skin. Tiny banks of crusty dirt form borders along each percolating stream.

The terrain is the same no matter how far in I waddle: the same ferns—introduced and not—grass, vines, nettles, moss, rock tripe, lichen, and trees I've seen all along.

The second field of introduced "sweet ferns" suddenly ends. I realize this when I see high grass just beyond the long, irregularly shaped tracts slant at angles incongruous to the ferns. This offsetting slant defines a barely perceptible line that crosses before me. *But not that any cop flying over would notice! These guys have done a helluva job camouflaging. But what else would you expect from former commandos? They've been trained to hide tanks—personnel carriers—entire bases! How hard could it be for them to obscure some measly plants?*

I keep going, keep searching—*Meesha! Please! Where ARE you! Oh God! HELP ME!*—but I stop the waddling. *I'm far enough away now. Don't need to bend so low.* I go back to my hunched over, half-squatting strut and start braiding again. *Mud* and *ferns* pass through my mind. *Fuck camouflage! Not critical now! Don't have time!*

I'm booking now, slicing through the humidity, searching everywhere. It's a good pace. I come upon a third, faintly lined path cutting the dense brush in front of me and, again, introduced ferns pop from the indigenous flora on my far flanks. *When does this shit end?*

I move on, faster yet. The day is still bright and hot, though my fern-framed shadow relentlessly spins counter-clockwise. For a while now, the yellow blanket covering the vegetation surrounding me has been changing to a richer, darker hue, as if melted butter were pouring and spreading over it. Soon, the circular, melting wad will fully descend behind the upper jungle canopy behind me.

Before long, I'm practically running. The slightest attempt to maintain stealth is all that keeps me from a full speed sprint. This attempt is a harness. It feels strange, makes me awkward. I sort of run-leap with an upper-body-contracted, accelerated-goosestep. I scan left and right, scouring every square foot. *Meesha's GOTTA be around here!* The Ironwood stick swings with my right arm as I plow through brush. I can no longer braid. I maintain the harness of control, but given one reason to let go and I would in a hummingbird's heartbeat. I'm ready to tear up this jungle, to turn over every stone. I'm on fire! I don't know if it's the heat, or the stress, or my fear of losing Meesha, or I'm simply losing my MIND, but something apocalyptic is happening to me. *Is this what it's like in combat? Is this what guys feel when they know they might die?* I don't know what it is, but it's powerful. *Manic!* I feel I could run through the Great Wall of China, swim to the Azores, kick the ass of every redneck in Texas. And the feeling just expedites my pace.

I roll beneath trees, around logs, through ferns and high grass all along the introduced parcels that undulate on my flanks. *It doesn't end! This field is the longest yet by far! Did I miss a crisscrossing path?* I don't think so. *Well, ya gotta keep an eye out!*

So I do. And then it happens: I discover where the farmers take shelter. And I meet Canine.

I am now jogging through the brush, my breath dry and heavy. My heart is a warped tire at freeway speed, my shadow still a running fern bush at my feet. Maniacally, I check for Meesha within every jungle crevice that I can. *Where the fuck IS she!* Scanning the field of introduced weeds to my right, I think: *This one sure is LONG!* When I suddenly notice that my view to the right will be momentarily blocked by a clump of extra dense brush, I glance left to make sure that that field does not end. When convinced that it does not, I start turning my head back to the right and that's when the canines rush toward me.

They burst from the right. They dart out from beneath the clump of brush, a massive tangle of vines with dark green, heart-shaped leaves. The leaves are large and opaque. Nothing can be seen beyond them. Nothing can be seen below them. The sun cannot penetrate them. I should have known better.

The canines spring straight for me. For a brief, almost immeasurable moment, I think of Dracula; but I have no time to think. As if a pistol target sprung with surprise from the jungle carpet, the canines explode upwards, directly at me, blocking my path. They are abnormally long and jut from a mouth as cavernous as the alcove from which they emerge. They are also very white, the white of enamel reared on well water, devoid of tarnishing fluoride. The lips are thick and wet, and I feel as though my head could be bitten off in a single, guillotining chomp. But what saves me are the eyes or, more precisely, what emanates from them. Dark brown and almond shaped, they burst consternation at my presence. I instantly discern: *heard me running, ran out of the brush, but was expecting someone else.*

With the element of surprise mine, I don't hesitate. Never breaking stride, I thrust the Ironwood spear beneath the canines, toward the abdomen. It is not as clean, nor as powerful, an insertion as that which killed the giant. The spear first hits a rib, ricochets off, then stops somewhere in the belly. I hear a deep, agonizing "ughhh!", the siren of fierce stomach pain and breathlessness, different only by degree from what a baseball bat would pull from a Solar Plexus. The large head drops before me draping straight, shoulder length hair as black and shiny as charred firewood. Simultaneously, soaked hands drip liquid scarlet as they grasp and squeeze the spear's girth while pressed flush against ruptured torso flesh. He is trying to pull the spear out. I won't let him. I push it farther in. Red waves leap from the wound to the galloping cadence of a frantic heart. I have never seen this before. I snap a shot and compartmentalize the sight. I will review it later, when I am less occupied. Then, with reflexive action—preceded by no thought, completely instinctive, purely automatic—I spring my right knee into his face. The large head flies up to expose youth, a flat nose and broad countenance, stout neck and pained, murderous eyes. Just a few hours earlier, I would have felt compassion. Now, I feel myself thrusting my Ironwood stick with all my might, sending the squat warrior onto his back. I pull the bamboo blade from my sleeve. The edge is not sharp enough for me to simply cut his throat. So I grasp the knife's improvised handle with my right hand, the blade's edge upwards, and stab the left side of his neck, just below his ear. A stream of warm red squirts my inner forearm as the blade bores beneath the trachea. Then I pull the bamboo toward me, severing Canine's existence with a single stroke.

His crimson hands drop from the spear as I pull it from his corpse. Waves no longer leap from the wound. Sanguineous lines demarcate strips along the stick where the linear wrapping of his fingers—thin appendages gripping wood in futile desperation—displaced blood. I am suddenly aware of the volume. *I musta hit the aorta. I didn't need to rip out his throat. Fuck it.*

Two down, two left—to the best of my knowledge. *Don't fuck up! There could be more!* Killing, I notice, isn't really that harsh. I don't feel the remorse I had always assumed I would. I don't feel any worse than if I had shot a rabid dog. This surprises me. *Have I always been like this? Or is it because of Meesha?* I begin to ponder the question; but as soon as I look up from the corpse, my mind follows my eyes to the clump of brush from which Canine had darted.

What had seemed simply a large tangle of vines is actually a wooded grove. From any position other than facing its narrow entrance, I can see only the dark green, heart-shaped leaves of its opaque outer covering. But within the leaves is a complex shell. Tan-colored trunks, branches, and roots intertwine in a tangle so dense it forms what I see as igloo shaped—a jungle igloo with sinewy, snarled wood substituting for snow. It is too dense for me to climb through; I think a squirrel would have a problem. In addition, the criss-crossing thicket of limbs, branches, and boughs is so entangled that, lined with a layer of outer leaves, it creates a waterproof cavity inhabitable by humans.

I feel my stomach crawl up my throat. *Is she in there!* I don't breathe. I don't blink. *Is this where they put her! It MUST be!* My heart kicks my ribcage as I move to the edge for a better look. I do so quickly. My gut tells me Chin and Blondie are running straight toward me at this very moment.

My eyes suck in the whole shelter with a single sweep: the carpeted floor of tall, brown grass mixed with newer, green grass—the tables, chairs, and cots constructed from wood, bamboo, and other jungle growth—the table bowls woven from long, thin leaves that have turned light-brown over time—the ceiling insulated with jungle-camouflage-patterned tarps to seal against rain—the four sleeping bags hanging from the thicket walls, airing out—and the assortment of freeze-dried meals, canned goods, and bottled water that lay along the ground. BUT NOWHERE DO I SEE MEESHA!

I move in further, look closer, make sure I missed nothing. Then I do it again. Then again. *FUCK'N SHIT!* After my fourth search, my body begins to shake while my vision turns a deep, hateful black. Where I go, I do not know; but when I return, I arrive with a plan.

Still shaking, but now seeing—my rage popping a porthole—I grab a bottle of water. I don't have the time or desire for food. *Not until I get Meesha outta here!* But I *need* water—that is, I'll take it if I can acquire it quickly. The bottle is tall, narrow, and tubular. I shove it into my shorts' pocket. It sticks halfway out. *I will drink some,* I think, *and save the rest for Meesha.* Then I glance back at the body and follow my brain.

I grab Canine and begin to drag him, but soon I stop. Although short, he is heavy. *TOO heavy.* I look back at the spot where he had lain. Blood demarcates the corpse's former contour the way homicide detectives outline a victim's silhouette with chalk. In spots, the blood has saturated the dirt to form thick, viscous burgundy.

*But I need SOMETHING for the draw!*

I pull the bamboo knife from my sleeve. A drop of red slips off its tip. *This has gotten dull. I'll sharpen it when—and if—I can.* With my left hand, I grab a clump of black from the rear of Canine's head. Slick with sweat and blood, the hair slides within my perspiring palm, so I briskly twist it a couple of revolutions. The hair becomes rope. I wrap the rope around my hand. My grip is now good. I don't hesitate. My left knee rises. I balance on my right leg. I snap my left leg out. It is a karate kick with poor form. My foot connects with the corpse's neck, but I hear nothing, so I kick again. I hear nothing again, so I kick a third time, and this time the *crack!* ensues. It is a good break, a clean break. I can tell by the way the head suddenly detaches, becomes loose, independent of the body in my clutch. The neck bone severed, the head dangles in mid-air simply by skin. I slice the skin with several strokes of my bamboo blade and Canine's head plops upon the ground.

*Am I going crazy? I must be going crazy. I've GOTTA be going crazy.* I can't believe I'm doing these things, thinking like this. But as the head hits the ground, the word *fumble!* pops into mine. Then, no slower than were I on some white-lined field, I reach down, pick up the bloody ball, tuck it beneath my right arm and run.

*What happens to the mind,* I wonder while running and searching, *when the only world it knows begins to wobble? Does it, too, wobble a bit?* But I have no time to think.

I move on, past the enclosed shelter, farther North, deeper into the camouflaged plantation. I move fast, taking the established path, no longer caring about which trail I follow. Time is now the critical factor. Although there were only four sleeping bags hanging in the hut, that does not mean there are—or were—only four farmers out here. If there are more, they'll be better able to see me on this path, despite its intentionally winding curves, than were I making my own in tall vegetation. But I have to make time. I need to gain time. I must put distance behind me and between us. I have to take the chance. It's the only one I've got left. I can't search anymore. I've found their camp. She isn't there. I don't know where else to look. In addition, time is running out. How long can Meesha possibly last? Her leg's mutilated! I gotta find her soon!

If I am hungry, tired, or thirsty, my senses don't tell me. They tell me to keep moving, to move fast. I follow my senses.

I continue through the jungle, along the trampled path, past field upon field of fern mixed ingeniously—patches and parcels of introduced mixed with patches and parcels of indigenous. I glance left and right, up and down, over and over. How many sections are there? I have no idea. I no longer count. I no longer care. However, there is one thing I do know: *This ain't no operation. This is an enterprise.*

Head in hand, I slosh on for what seems like an hour. I look up. The gas light no longer rides a rail over my head. It is now a golden pendant radiating to my rear.

*Far enough*, I think. *This'll give me the time I need. Have I run too far? No,* I decide. *They have to come. They've got no choice. I've seen too much. I've done too much. In their minds, I've committed the unthinkable. No, they have to come. They simply have no choice.*

I jump from the middle of the path to my right. After sailing about three feet, I land in tall grass and indigenous fern. Immediately, I go back to my evasive tactics: sweeping for traps while hovering, strutting, then covering. I make no sound; I leave no tracks. Back bent and eyes beaming, I head South, the direction completely opposite of which I had been running.

After about fifty yards, I hurdle the path. I jump completely over it. I prefer to travel in the main growing section, between the two parallel paths running through the introduced fern fields. Traveling outside of either path would make it harder to find Meesha—it is easier to search a territory from its median than from its flanks—as well as detect a party on the opposite path. It would also take me out of the zone in which I plan to operate.

Now in the main growing section, the wide middle, the zone, I check my tracks. I brush them with the Ironwood stick, making my imprint on the land negligible.

I move, I strut, I search, I scour.

I stop at some indigenous ferns and replenish my camouflage. Finding a rock, I sharpen my knife and stick. I muffle the scraping with leaves. Then I quickly pick some fresh fiddleheads and down them with a couple gulps from the bottle I stole. *Tastes good. But gotta leave some for Meesh!*

I push on: a blood smeared, blood pumping vessel of stealth. A human head in one hand, a spear in the other, I search for the right spot. *I'll know it when I see it.* I saw several earlier, when I didn't need one. Now, however, I need one, and need it soon.

When I have tracked back about a quarter mile from the spot at which I jumped across the path, I pass four clustered trees. They are not conjoined like a clumped species, but simply a bunch growing close together. *This is it,* I think. I go to work.

I scan the earth around me, hyper-vigilant in all my senses. I'm so primed, I feel I could hear carbon decay and see amoebae split; yet, Meesha never leaves my mind: *Oh God, please take care of her until I find her! And even AFTER I find her!*

As I scan, I notice the vegetation around me turning buttery. *It's that time of day again. I hafta work fast.* I need to get as much done as I can while the sun still shines. I don't know how much I'll be able to accomplish in the dark.

Through the green, a few yards farther in, pokes a moss-padded appendage. I rush over. I grab the appendage and pull. It turns out to be the end of a large branch. As I pull, the whole branch—about twelve feet long—rises, as does the forest floor around me. The latter clings to many smaller appendages branching out from the main limb.

*This thing fell recently,* I think. *Stuff in the jungle rots fast, but this is still pretty solid. Well, if one fell, there'll probably be another.*

I look around. I am correct. Several feet farther in, another moss-padded appendage protrudes from the jungle green. I pull it out. This one is a bit shorter, maybe ten feet long; but it, too, is solid.

I pull both fallen limbs to the cluster of standing trees. Then I hunt for portable rocks. I find seven. I detect them by their contour, a jagged edge or tip poking through the jungle floor. There is no way I would have found them at night. All are laden with moss, much like the fallen limbs, next to which I lay the rocks.

The stout end of each limb is roughly six inches thick; the narrow end, roughly three. I start at the thicker end of each. Moving upwards, I break six branches from one, five from the other. With the exception of one, these branches are about an inch thick and a foot long. The eleventh and remaining branch, however, is about two inches thick and a yard long. My size selections are deliberate.

I grab the ten smaller branches and the largest of the seven rocks. After tearing moss off the rock, I begin to scrape the narrower end of each branch against the rock's rough surface. I muffle my scraping with vegetation. I scrape each end in full circumference until I have furnished a point. Then I notice that the buttery film on the green around me is turning rancid. *I don't have much time left. I've got to hurry.*

The four clustered trees are thickly covered with reddish-brown moss. Each reaches over the path with a hairy, cinnamon limb, but I am only going to use the first and last. Using the trees on the ends will minimize the chance that any jutting branches will interfere with any mechanical movement. Furthermore, the distance separating the end trees is about that which exists between two men when they walk in a single file. Even if I am wrong about this, my tactics could still work. The tree part is only the first. If that fails, I can still recover with *my* part. Wounds are all I need, and the element of surprise is mine. It's a huge chance based on a lot of assumptions, but it's the best chance I have, for it's the only feasible plan my brain can conceive. The *search* for Meesha is over.

I pull the lumps of vine from my shorts' pockets. I untangle the clumps. I finish braiding what remains undone. The result is numerous pieces of varying lengths. *I hope I have enough. I should.*

I search for a perch. I find a rotting stump. I set the narrow end of the longer, fallen, tree limb upon the stump. I grab three rocks and five scraped-till-pointy branches and begin tying them to the limb's narrow end. The braided vegetation is tough and strong. I am not gentle in making the knots; I draw them tight. I strap the five branches, at their mid-point, perpendicularly to the limb's end. Their sharp ends point downwards, below the limb. Their blunt ends point upwards, above the limb. I alternate the branches between the left and right sides of the limb so that three line the former, two the latter. Then I place the three rocks on top of the limb between the upper, blunt portions of the branches. I secure this configuration of tree limb, rocks, and scraped branches with a long piece of braided vines and as many improvised knots as the braided piece will yield. When I'm done, the tree limb looks like a gargantuan toothbrush with giant toothpicks for bristles. I then replicate my efforts on the shorter limb. When finished, I notice that the rich yellow blanket coating all things has turned that first shade of gray which dampens the day when the sun begins its slide from sight. I quicken my pace.

I grab one of the four remaining rocks. It is just a little larger than my fist, but bears a jagged edge. I slip back to the Northernmost tree in the cluster, the one farthest to my left when I face the path.

Stone in hand, I drop to my knees. There, I find, on the side of the tree facing the path, a knotty growth cloaked in moss. *Looks good,* I think, though I know I can't rely on it alone. So, just below the growth, I begin to saw. The stone cuts well. After every few strokes, I stop, look, and listen. Though the trunk may be solid, its outer edge has accumulated so much organic matter that I am able to cut a two-inch indentation in short time.

I grab the remaining offshoot, the longest and thickest branch I'd ripped from the two fallen tree limbs. This will be my trigger shaft. I insert the trigger shaft into the indentation I just finished cutting in the tree's trunk. Hanging parallel with the ground, the trigger shaft fits into the indented notch snugly. I try moving the shaft up and down. It does not move. The trigger shaft moves only when I pull it away from the indentation in the tree along a plane parallel with the ground. This is good. I am satisfied.

I grab the longer tree limbed toothbrush and a lengthy piece of braided vines. I tie the braid of vines tightly to the limb, just below the toothpicks. I repeat this process with the shorter toothbrush. With the shorter one, though, I use the longest piece of braided vines I can find. Of the two toothbrushes, the shorter will hang much farther from the trigger shaft, three trees to its right.

*How close are Chin and Blondie now? Have they found the headless Canine yet?* I haven't heard anything. *But that doesn't mean shit. Their surprise is gone. That got killed with the giant. These are hard people. They won't be so surprised to find another corpse, headless or not. And, all the while, they're gonna be tracking, cat-like, just like I've been trying to do, only better. Fucking berets! Fucking commandos! And they might be right down the path, just a few yards away, almost here! Ya gotta move your ass!*

I lean the larger toothbrush upright against the hairy limb jutting over the path from the Northernmost tree, the one cut to hold the trigger shaft. The toothbrush's thicker end indents the earth, while its heavier end—with the giant toothpicks—points toward the path from twelve feet above. I throw the braid of vines tied to the toothbrush up and over the hairy limb. Then I tie the braid's loose end to the left side of the trigger shaft.

I grab the shorter toothbrush and hustle three trees to the right. I replicate the procedure I performed for the longer toothbrush, but throw the braid of vines tied to the shorter toothbrush up and over the *three* hairy limbs to its left. Then I tie the braid's loose end to the right side of the trigger shaft.

I reach into the pile on the ground and grab two more pieces of braided vine. I tie one piece to the center of the trigger shaft, then wedge the shaft into the notch cut for it in the tree. I tie the other piece around the tree trunk, strapping the trigger shaft into its notch. I tug on the trigger shaft. It stays in the notch. This is good. I am satisfied.

I grab the longer toothbrush and slowly lower its upper, heavier end so that the toothbrush hangs in mid-air, supported only by the braid of vines tied to the trigger shaft. The bottom end of the toothbrush stands upon the ground. No part of it remains against the tree limb. Then I replicate the task with the shorter toothbrush. I ensure that each toothbrush, aligned by their giant toothpicks, points directly toward the path. Accuracy is everything.

I retreat to the trigger shaft. I grab the loose end of braided vines tied to its middle. Reaching back, I lift Canine's head by its long, blood-slick hair. As I intertwine braided vine with black mane, Canine's eyes, wide open, stare at me. I glare back: *Fuck you, your mother, and the dogs she blows.* When finished tying, I scan and listen. I concentrate on the path. I scour it both ways, trying to glimpse a shimmer, something off-color, the merest of incongruities. I find nothing out of the ordinary.

I lean over the path, calculate the longer toothbrush's intended trajectory, and drop Canine's head directly in line. I don't release the hair-vine extension. The head hits the soft earth with a *thump!* louder than I expected, or would have liked. Then I slowly tug the head toward the path's edge, trying to effect the appearance that the head rolled and wasn't dragged. I pull the head a couple of inches into the tall vegetation below me. I study it. The decapitated cranium lies slightly embedded in wild grass. I lay the long hair behind it, farther in, further hidden, further camouflaged. I carefully tighten the braid of vines connecting the hair to the trigger shaft and tie knots in the braid to take up the slack. Then I retreat, smoothening the trail of my incursion, satisfied that I left the human skull the way it would appear most natural if dropped along a jungle path by a running man.

Back behind the trigger tree, I kneel and breathe deeply. I wrap my arms around the tree's trunk and grab the ends of the horizontal trigger shaft. I attempt to press it upwards, then downwards. It doesn't budge. *Good.* I pull my hands back to the rear of the trunk. I untie the contingency braid of vines that held the trigger shaft in place while I worked. I use my bamboo knife to sever the knots. The shaft doesn't move. *The trigger shaft will stay in place.* I back away slowly. I feel good. I am satisfied. I pick up the water bottle and suck down several squirts of its sweet liquid.

# Chapter 17

My shadow is now barely discernible as the gray shade of day turns black. Yet, the weight of the sultry jungle still labors my lungs and burdens my skin.

I am facing the path, lying to the right of the four clustered trees. Suspended above me, to my left, hangs the shorter toothbrush. I can practically feel its spikes straining to pierce the path a few feet beyond my head. Thick patches of fern and tall grass surround and engulf my supine body. Just beyond my head, ending stretched arms, my hands clutch Ironwood. With my chin indenting dirt and black mud masking my face, I wait motionless except for flitting eyes which seek the enemy. Though pretty sure the unnerving tickle climbing my right leg is an insect, I don't move. I wouldn't care if it were a King Cobra. *I ain't moving for NOTHIN'.* Until, that is, it is time to move.

Breathing gently, evenly, I hear my heart thump as dusk darkens. How quickly, I notice, light dims in the jungle. So rapidly it wanes.

Now the night is black except for open areas like the path, where milky moonlight spills through the upper canopy onto lower foliage. However, such areas are limited; most of the jungle is dense and, therefore, dark. Though just five feet away, I can barely make out detail within the red tassels suspended from bushes along the opposite side of the path.

These bushes are perfect—not only for their beauty, but due to the way they are situated. I couldn't have picked a better spot. The green bulge of their outer edge pours over the path, forcing anyone walking it to favor the side on which I hide. Unless one walks right through these bushes, there exists no way to travel the path without brushing by the vegetation in which I lie. Were it not for the bushes, a person traveling this path would instinctively veer away from the colonnade of trees to my left, due to natural spatial relations: typically, people distance themselves from the bigger objects around them. However, the position of the thick, tangled bushes prevents someone using the path from doing so.

About a half hour passes, though I feel I could have used a calendar to track its passing. *Where are they? Did I run THAT far?* I don't think so. *They should be here by now!*

Points as sharp as the shaved stakes above my head begin to poke at my intestines. I feel like I've swallowed a bunch of toothpicks and they're now stuck at different spots along their digestive path. *So what? Don't move!* I don't. I maintain absolute sound discipline. I sweep all pain, all tactile interference, under the neurological carpet.

I am stone still. Just another rotting log, slowly decomposing, gradually turning into soil, I have become my environment. I am one with the jungle. The ferns bound to my body are interloping chameleons mingling with the hundreds that hide me. *I'm a plant. I no longer inhale oxygen and exhale carbon dioxide; I do the opposite.* Fibrous shreds of fiddlehead dissolve slowly, still lodged in my teeth. Raw jungle dank rises high, seeping deep into my nasal cavity.

Then I hear it; or, rather, I *don't*—*that's* the problem. *Where are they? I should hear them. This is feeding time. The sun is going down.*

Then it dawns on me: *Birds, like other animals, usually know when people are around, even if those people are hiding. But will Blondie and Chin be aware of this? Hope not! Then they'll know I'm nearby. I'll be screwed.*

About five minutes pass during which I sense my eyes adjust. I'm getting my night vision. Objects appear clearer, more distinct. Another five minutes pass. Then another. Then another.

*I don't get it,* I suddenly think. *It can't possibly take them this long to get here. Did they go somewhere else? How could they? They've just found two of their comrades dead! One without a head! OF COURSE they'd come after me! How could they not! But where the fuck are they?*

Then I hear it: the faintest *snap!* This time it *is* something, not the lack thereof. It hails from my right, from the path, from exactly where I expected to hear a sound were one to be made. And although I objectively know its decibel level is minimal, the *snap!* is a gunshot to my ears and a hammer to my heart. Every nerve in me tightens. I can practically feel the electricity jumping synapses and sparking neurons. If I'd been all eyes and ears before, I'm now radar-enabled. A worm couldn't burrow five feet beneath me without my knowing. My breath is frozen, a truncated exhale hanging in midair with the still rigidity of an icicle. I don't even move my eyes. I fear that anything remotely near eye contact might give me away, that a force or energy I can't define could pass between our cognitive states. Then, without even seeing me, my enemy would pick me off. He'd know I was here. As a result, I try to see with my mind and my mind only.

*Where are they? Are they on my side of the path?* I can't tell. *The SNAP! was to the right.* That's all I know.

I wait. I can feel the pores of my mud caked forehead opening with that same tingle I get during my morning run. My scalp, too. It's like each of my hairs is being gently pulled to tighten the skin from which it grows.

PHIIIITTTT!

*What was that? A branch? A leaf? A blade of grass? It brushed against something—or was it someONE? And it's closer! Just to my right! But I can't see anything! How am I supposed to wound—? But that's okay. If you can't see him—them?—they certainly can't see you.*

*Or CAN they? These guys are highly trained! One's a Green Beret! Maybe BOTH! That's Fort Bragg! JFK Special Warfare School! Are you shitting me! Wearing welder glasses and an eye patch while plagued with conjunctivitis and cataracts, he'd still spot you in the darkest corner of Hell if hunting you were his mission!*

*But why the noise? Why so much noise? Doesn't seem right. These guys are trained for stealth. Hunter would never have made so much noise. And it's not like they rushed here. It's been a while.*

Then I see him! It's Chin! I can barely make out black hair. I can frame the wiry silhouette. *Blondie must be right behind!* I'm a rock. I'm a tree. Sweat streams down my face as my pulse plucks my neck. If I could only put my heart on pause. He's right in front of me! I could literally grab his ankle! *Hold still! Let him pass! You've gotta get them from behind. Remember: you're outnumbered. You have to use surprise. The element of surprise is your equalizer.*

I hold tight. My hands are steel clamps—vices clenching Ironwood. Though I can't move a muscle yet, my leg and foot springs coil tightly in my mind. A simple flip of my mental switch and I'm sprung. My wife is injured and missing. I've got to find her. I'm screaming to go!

*Will he see it? What if he doesn't? What will I do? Did I pull it too far into the bushes? Maybe I should have left it in the middle of the path.*

His steps are short, but not the type of bounding I expected. He's walking more like the delinquent country boy trespassing on the farmer's land. *There's no military training here!*

Then he stops. *What's going on? Has he seen me? Why's he stopping? What's he doing?*

"Shit!"

This shocks me. There was barely an attempt to suppress. Either he thinks there's no way I'm here—or he doesn't care. *But he has to care!*

*Why isn't he moving? Why is he just standing there? I wish I could see his eyes. Damn it, I wish I could see his eyes! For all I know, they're*

*LOOKING at me! There's no way to know! Shit, I can barely see his BODY, never mind his EYES! What if he suddenly strikes! What if he suddenly leaps onto me with a Bowie knife! Or comes hands-over-head with a machete! How will I stop him!* A moment passes. My thoughts thicken. My cranium crackles. *I know!* I get ready to roll. *I'll go left.* My legs and torso tense. *I'll hurl myself into the brush. Then I'll immediately lunge, skewering this skinny prick with my stick!*

But he doesn't come; not yet, anyhow. His outline is faint—an ebony apparition. Only if he moves can I track him. Stopped, his silhouette practically dissipates into the night.

He suddenly moves, a flash in the black. No more than a flicker, it's all I can see. *Which way is he going?* While the jungle remains a closed, dark theater, the cinema in my head reacts with million-candle-intensity. Images flash, scenes evolve, thoughts reverberate. Fight-or-flight juice stings my inflamed nerves. I can't get any tighter. My muscles are like bones, my bones like bricks. In reality, I'm still on the ground; in my mind, I'm hovering two feet above. *Is he coming my way or not? I can't roll, then discover he's not moving. That would fuck everything up!* But I'm so close. The slightest breeze would get me started. Nonetheless, I hold.

I'm glad I did. It takes me a long moment, but when I finally detect the direction of his motion, I see that it is not toward me. It is to my left. He moves slowly, forward, a dozen carefully placed steps. To see him, I must now turn my head. I do so cautiously; try to, imperceptibly. He is near the other end of the tree column. *Beneath the FIRST ONE?* I can't tell from this angle and distance—too much darkness and foliage between us.

He stops again—walking, that is. He doesn't stop moving. As soon as his feet come to a rest, his back bends. His torso flips downwards, forward, his body breaking at the hips. From where I lay, I simply see buttocks and legs with a body above bending beyond. *Is he going for it!* As he continues down, I pump up. I am already as coiled as a body can be; only now, I prepare for a lunge without a roll.

"Ssssshhhhhiiiit!" courses through the air as Chin grabs the long and tangled scalp growth. But I don't hear the entire word. Half of the stretched "shi", along with the ending "t", are truncated by a cacophony of vegetative *swish!* and timber strain. But this lasts only a moment before the toothbrush farthest to my left connects. To me in the darkness, it is no more than noise, movement, and mass displacement; but my mind knows what is happening. Because it remembered the trap from one of my father's manuals and set it up conceptually before my body did physically, my mind can see it executing: the head tugged; the horizontal, trigger shaft dislodging; the rock-weighted, shaven sticks suddenly dropping; the whole toothbrush arcing toward earth with swift, unfettered recklessness. It occurs like this, chopping axe-like into the path, inches to my left as well as several feet beyond. And while I'm wondering whether I'd built in enough accuracy, I hear a pulpy *schliitt!*, like a knife plunging into ripe melon, followed by a terrifying howl: "Aaaaarrgggh!" cuts through the heavy, jungle air as unimpeded as hunting arrows through cheesecake, neurologically piercing me. *Now!* my mind responds, for I know the element of surprise is still with me and must remain my ally; or, more accurately, I its.

I thrust with my legs, my arms, my stomach. I do a squat, a push up, a sit up, all together, all at once. I'm on my feet. I'm running. The Ironwood stick rides my right hand; the guiding hand of Hell leads my left. I don't know who I am; that guy left my body long ago. I'm an imposter, the current inhabitant of a killing machine on legs; and the legs are moving, as are the arms, which carry a spear. The legs stride by the toothbrush-shaped shaft lying in front of me, just to my left. *Why did I bother with two? It would have been so much easier setting up one.* But, of course, I know why. And that fact lacerates my mental state with the sharp shards of lethal reality. *Where is HE?* I quickly glance right to see nothing but black path. *Is he trailing by a long distance, waiting for the chance to decapitate me, the way I did Canine?* I have no idea and, therefore, no reason to discontinue my motion. I plug one foot in front of the other in rapid succession. So far, I've gone forward, to get on the path. Now, I turn left, pulling a hard, barely curved, ninety degrees. It is just steps after the hard turn that I see Chin. And I like what I see.

The toothbrush didn't whisk his head off, or plunge through his heart, spilling Oriental blood all over the green jungle path. That would have defeated my purpose. It simply sunk into his lean, muscular back. *That explains the pulpy "schliitt!" sound.* And now he writhes before me, still on his feet with spikes along his spine, a twelve foot shaft for a tail and another man's head in his hands. He is in too much pain to even realize I'm running toward him. However, being the Good Samaritan into which this jungle has turned me, I plan to help Chin out of his misery—for a price, of course.

But the moment I reach Chin, I realize that I've erred. *Shit! All the way through! I've* erred badly. *Damn it! And I was worried about ACCURACY!* From his chest and stomach protrude several spikes. Oily red pours from their exit holes.

I rush up to his face, grab his throat, shake him. His black mane bounces, lips stretch outwards, broad nostrils flare. "Where's my wife! Where've you put her! Tell me where she is and I'll get you out!"

He glares up at me, dark eyes smoldering. He maintains his grimace, says nothing, knows he's done. I know it too. I really fucked up.

"Where's my wife!" I hear myself scream. I sound desperate. "Tell me or you're gonna die!"

He sneers, eye teeth exposed, the twirled ends of his bandito moustache twitching. *Damn, did I fuck up!* He's bleeding fast. The red oil's puddling around his black boots. Doesn't matter. Pathetic as I sound, I have to try.

"Tell me where my wife is and I'll save ya! I'll pull the sticks outta you!"

His mouth opens. Blood and saliva bubble over his lips, then drool down his chin. He staggers, toothbrush in back, looks at me, coughs. The ejaculation splatters my face. I wipe my left eye. Rage percolates in me, molten lava from my emotional caldron. I could rip out this man's heart and eat it while he watched, but I need him alive. *Oh God, how could I have fucked up so bad! I didn't mean to KI—!*

But the puddle grows. Red oil pumps on pulse from his face, squirting out his mouth and nose. He hacks. Then again. He staggers, almost falls. His mad dog eyelids sag. His jaw slackens. And it's all my psyche can stand.

With an upward stroke that is becoming perfect through practice, I plunge the Ironwood stick into the dying bastard's abdomen. The stick pierces him just above his navel; then, to my surprise, plunges through his back. He's even thinner than I'd thought: felt as if there existed only one side of him to penetrate, as if I were poking the stick through a wet cardboard box.

The dying man drops his colleague's head as his own body arches into a human C. After witnessing a long moment of extreme physical tension, abject agony, almost unwatchable struggle, I start to wiggle the stick as well as pull it back and forth like I had with the giant. But it isn't necessary. I am already holding him up. While his bleeding torso slumps upon the spear, I notice the sheathed knife hanging from his belt. *He was in too much pain,* I quickly deduce, *to reach for it with the spikes sticking through him. I'm lucky.* With my right foot, I push him off. I feel no more compassion than were I disengaging a black-striped hot dog from a barbecue fork. What used to be Chin slinks into the oily red puddle spreading across the path.

*Now what?* As far as I know, there is only one more out there. *Where is he? Why wasn't he with Chin? Did he stay behind? Maybe at the giant's grave? Why would he have done that? Or is he with Meesha?* I have no answers. I have only a plan. So I go with it.

I take Chin's sheathed knife and shove it in my shorts' pocket, but leave his body where it lies and Canine's head where it fell. I make no attempt to hide them. They are the best bait I could possibly find and I want them as exposed as possible. I do, however, brush up markings along the path leading to where I had lain in the bush. Then I slice into the bush, smoothening the trail as I progress, toward the tree I had lain beside; then, past the tree, to the rear of the four-tree cluster.

I ponder tactics. Another trap is out of the question. Not only do I lack the time to build it, but I don't think it would work. Something tells me Blondie wouldn't fall for it.

I've got bad feelings about this guy and for reasons other than the obvious: that he's a trained killer with experience in the environment in which I currently am, and for which I have minimal familiarity. I find something unsettling about the man's swagger, his demeanor. The giant was big and Chin looked mean, while Blondie is hardly big and appears almost angelic. But there is just something about the way he walks that squeezes my throat and strangles my entrails. *Forget it! FUCK Blondie! Ya gotta find MEESHA! And SOON!*

*Would a tree work? What if I climbed up one of these trees and stayed perfectly still? When he came around, I could ambush him from above.*

*No,* I decide. *Too high. Too much time to drop. Could get picked off before hand. Too many unknowns. Don't wanna trap myself in a tree.*

Still pondering, I start collecting new vegetation—ferns, grasses, branches, and leaves—for whatever I decide to do. While collecting, I glance at the path every so often and, during one of those looks, it hits me: *Of course! Why did I bother smoothening this out? Shoulda just left it.*

So I grab the vegetation I have collected thus far, as well as the old stuff on my person, and throw it all messily around in front of the mossy, four-tree colonnade. I make sure each piece lands in a spot visible from the path. When done, I grab my Ironwood stick and head back out the way I had come in. But I don't smoothen the trail. In fact I purposely, though quietly, rough up the vegetation as much as I can. On the path, however, I hop daintily over the fallen toothbrush and cleanly cut into the brush on the opposite side. Once on the path, I leave no trail. I smoothen everything. I restore it all, fastidiously, meticulously. I remove every unnatural gap, wrinkle, and twist as if I were operating a plant iron beneath drifting clouds of misty starch.

When finished purging evidence of my presence from the flora, I immediately loop behind the red-tasseled bushes bordering the path and push my way in. Maneuvering through the bushes is not as easy as through a fern patch. I have to wiggle in and throughout the interior tangle. Maintaining stealth and noise discipline is especially difficult. I must operate slowly and deliberately. About a minute passes before I reach the path's edge.

I sit down and pull Chin's knife from my shorts' pocket. *Was this the blade that was used,* I wonder, *to cut the ties securing Meesha's splint?* I start sawing at the lowest point possible along each clump of green with red tassels. I work fast. I have no idea when Blondie might come. *Where is he? Why's he taking so long? Is he still with the giant? Did he stop to bury Canine? Is he with Meesha?* In any case, I know that he'll get here soon. Like a shark drawn to blood, his arrival is inevitable. I hurry.

I excavate clumps of red and green the size of basketballs. I want them big for two reasons: to simulate the actual look of a bush, and to hollow my hideout so that I have more room for maneuvering. The overall displacement will be the same. But with the plants tied to me as opposed to poking me, I will gain flexibility. I will be able to function better.

I fill up the ties around my head, arms, and legs. I use all that I cut, but cut only what I need. I discard nothing. My goal is to be a bush, the best bush that I can be.

When finished with vegetation, I dig deep into the earth. It is black like the night; but no darker, I feel, than what my soul has become. Clumps of moist dirt rise within clamped hands that open into cupped, adjacent palms. I lower my face. Moving my head in circles both clockwise and counter, I re-smother my skin. Then I redo my arms and legs.

Grabbing the Ironwood stick with my right hand, shoving the sheathed knife back into my shorts' pocket, I move up to the edge of the path. I poke through the bush's face, become part of the bush's exterior. For six square feet along the path, I am the bush's outer side.

I gaze at the decapitated head and dead, intact body lying in front of me. My eyes flit back and forth between the supine toothbrushes that lay across the path as if—or, in essence?—demarcating an ambush site. Then I study the corrupted vegetation facing me from across the walkway. The disorder looks good. *It would distract ME,* I think. I reflect for a moment. *I'm fucking ready.*

A few, very silent, very dark, very strange minutes pass. *The calm before the storm? Better yet: the eye of the hurricane?* I wonder if cops conducting a dangerous stakeout feel like I do.

*How long should I wait?*

*As long as necessary.*

*But how do I know he's even gonna come?*

*He has to, and you KNOW it. Eventually, he's gotta find out what happened to Chin. It would be illogical for him not to—if only to get rid of the bodies. Corpses lying near the crop ain't good agriculture. Wouldn't be good for business.*

So I crouch. And I wait. No lying down for this one. I can't just hide beneath or behind the elements. No, for this one I have to *be* the element. I *need* that extra second it takes to rise from the ground. I need to be in the position to kill right from the start.

I glance down. I've done myself up well. My figure is bulging. I imagine it to be oval. Red tassels dangle from every spot not glossy green. *I must look like a fucking Christmas tree.* My arms, so thick with mud, hang barely visible against the nothingness of night. Ditto for my squatting legs. The air has cooled a bit, though this doesn't dawn on me until I realize that sweat no longer ticklishly rolls down the bridge of my nose.

About a half-hour passes. My thighs now ache. *Should I kneel? I won't be as quick in rising. Or will I? Isn't there something to be said about having fresh legs? I crouch like this for an hour and I'll be just as slow as if I were lying on the ground.*

I lower my right knee. The earth is moist and warmer than the air. *The earth takes longer to cool,* I think. *Same thing with the ocean.* This reminds me of sunny summer days, back home, when Meesha and I would go to the beach, Meesha always luscious in a pastel bikini, and the water always warmest in late afternoon although the air had cooled. This then makes me think of early morning sea smoke and the dawn mist floating just above the placid, Canadian lakes Meesha and I have camped beside. *Beautiful stuff.* I stare at the path. *With my beautiful wife.* I continue to stare. Then I feel like crying. Then I feel like screaming with rage.

*How can you think of beauty when a man's severed head is lying five feet in front of you?*

*I'm going insane. I must be. I wouldn't be this callused, this nonchalant.*

*But can you be insane and know it? Isn't that the proverbial Catch-22?*

*Okay, if I'm not insane, what am I? Gruesome death no longer affects me. I can stare at flappy skin caked with dried blood hanging from a decapitated man's shredded neck and think of wispy, white sea smoke and camping in Canada and swimming in the ocean on a hot summer day. That's not insane? If that's not insane, what is?*

*'What IS?' AH'LL tell you 'what is'! Fucking up Meesha like they did is 'what is'! And kidnapping her! While she's seriously injured!*

*THAT'S what's fucking inSANE! And if I don't GIVE a shit about seeing their SEVered heads lying all over their POT popping fields, who CARES? They FUCK'n deserve it! I just gotta find Meesha! That's all that matters! And if I fuck up this Blondie while I'm at it, so much the better!*

But then my mind pictures him. I wonder where he is. And I think: *The guy's ex-Special Forces. Green Berets. A BAD motherfucker. Don't get cocky just because you've killed a few guys. Sure, the giant may have been a Screaming Eagle, but you had the stick. He broke his hand. You got lucky. And these other two: for all you know, they're just goons, locals who wanted to make quick dough, nothing more than native criminals. So what have you done? Made a trap? Yeah, that was good, but so what? You can't use it against Blondie. There's no time. And it probably wouldn't work. Plus, you STILL haven't found Meesha! So don't be cocky.*

What feels like another half-hour passes. Nothing has changed but the temperature. Air and ground are both cooler, but the head still lies before me, brown eyes bulging, staring at a world it can no longer see. *Where's the tongue? What does the tongue do when you cut off a guy's head? Where does it go?* I look at the mouth, but it is barely open. And due to the dark, I can see nothing inside. But I do see the last look on Canine's face. He is yearning, begging for his life, for pain relief, for some mercy. But, of course, I gave him none, and that fact registers through the rigor mortised-grimace he retains posthumously.

My thoughts spring back to Meesha. The iron foot of feeling crushes me under its heel. *What the FUCK!* The pugilist of pathos pounds my aching chest. *How did I get us here! How could I have done this to her!* While I rage, something in me snaps. *How? Why? How could I?* I wrestle with it, but find no way out; it's got me headlocked: *You hung loose!* The world is silent save the chaos in my skull: *That's it, isn't it? That's what happened. The metaphor of modern existence, it snared me! Strung me from its gallows! FUCK! The damn powers that be:*

*they want you to let down your guard, abide by their rhetoric. Everything feels safe, appears okay. But, in reality, it's not. And most suckers swallow it hook, line, and sinker, just like you did. You gulped it faster than the cheapest whore, sucked it down like the Deep Throat of head queens. You wanted to lay back, have it nice, safe, and comfy. You wanted it just like they portray it to be. True, most of your life you haven't bought it, didn't trust 'em; but sometimes you did, and THIS was one of those times. You strolled around this island like a fool, not wanting to see through the façade, but to follow its lead, no matter how artificial it felt. And look where it got you.*

Then I hear the action, metallic and behind me. Whoever has heard a shotgun pumped knows the sound. For a moment that could be measured in months, my stomach spews fire as it prepares to be blown open. But the buckshot never flies. Instead come words, roughened by tobacco: "Drop the stick and knives."

*What can I do?* For a long moment, I think. Then I reluctantly let Ironwood, steel, and bamboo fall to the ground.

"Move into the path. Don't turn around. If ya ain't in the path by three, I shoot. One."

*What should I do! Dive to the ground?*

*Hurry up! You've got two seconds!*

*If I dive into the path without getting shot—if I'm quick enough—I could roll around, get out of his range.*

*Oh? And you don't think he's gonna just track you down again?*

"Two."

*But isn't he just gonna shoot me anyway?*

*Maybe. But you don't know that for sure. What's your best bet for finding Meesha?: Giving up and hoping for the best, right? Buying some time till you can kill him, somehow, or break for it, right?*

I step into the path. I stand there, motionless, if one doesn't consider the glossy green leaves shaking on my arms and legs.

The jungle crinkles to my right. It is the soft, sweeping crackle of a body bending brush. Though no longer subdued, the steps are still muffled, almost unheard. *This guy snuck up on me when I was at my most alert. Damn! And he hasn't told me to clasp my hands behind my head. He knows I don't have a gun and I didn't even know he was there! Shit!*

A black image emerges from my extreme right between red tassels hanging before my face. *Black? Was he wearing black when I saw him walking earlier? No, he was wearing green, wasn't he? A green T-shirt. So if it's him, he changed. If it's him, he changed when the jungle changed. He went black when the jungle went black.* I get the feeling the man holding my existence in the curl of his trigger finger doesn't simply change with the elements, but believes he is one of them.

He moves directly in front of me, ten feet away. To his lower right lie Chin's body and Canine's head. I have to tilt my head to see him, due to the red tassels in my face. It IS him: Blondie. That allays at least one of my concerns: that there may be others of which I'm not aware.

He looks down. He's a little older than I thought—or so it seems, by the wrinkles. Up close, with the rich moonlight, I can see how deeply they branch from his eyes and mouth. *Probably early fifties. Can't really tell for sure, though.* His almond skin seems more weathered, prematurely aged, than that of the full, darker Re'enevians. And he isn't all that gray, though that's also hard to tell. Any gray would mix well with the copper and gold highlighting the sun-bleached brown ponytailed upon his back. *This guy's so good—or thinks you're so bad—that he didn't feel the need to camouflage his skin. Fuck!*

"You did a good job." He smiles as he nods at the dead flesh between us. Nicotine brown tints his native dental luster. An uncommonly wide gap separates his upper middle teeth. At any other time, the gap would make him seem kinder, friendlier, jocular. It does not do so at the moment. "Where'd you get your training?"

"On the job."

I don't know where that came from. I didn't mean to be flippant. It's not easy being flippant staring down the shadowed interior of a shotgun barrel. But, then again, maybe I did. A part of me doesn't care. It's the oddest feeling.

Artificial laughter bisects the man's face, pulling each half into a smear of rubbery creases. I know he intends to kill me. I can see it in the yellow fire with which his hazel eyes burn. I also know he has no choice.

"Where's my wife?"

He ignores me. "Who are you? What'dja come down here for?"

*Real rough. Must be at least three packs a day. Doubt he could keep up with me. If I got away, he'd never catch me. But with Meesh—.*

"I'm just a tourist. Got lost." This invokes another laugh—a laugh that irritates me—downright pisses me off.

"Didn't you see the signs?" His smile vanishes as he speaks. "Plenty of signs out there said not to come down here."

I don't know what to say. What *can* I say? Do I tell a hardened criminal, a guy for whom killing humans was once a living, a specialty, that I never thought this shit would exist down here? That this beautiful island could contain such horror and evil? That I'm a fool, and an idiot, and a moron? That I purposely ignored the signs and led the most wonderful creature I've ever known into Hades? No, I can't say that. So I don't say anything. I just look down.

"Who ya working for?"

"What!" This draws my head right back up—almost *too* fast. It startles him. The red tassels flop up and around. I imagine they look like streamers trailing my head. I think for the shortest moment how foolish I must look, but the severity of the moment truncates the thought.

"I said, 'Who ya working for?'"

"'Working'! I'm on vacation!" My stomach starts to hurt again, spikes jabbing my entrails. A part of me fears I won't be able to run or fight as well with cramps wrenching my gut. *Ah, fuck it!* "I ain't working for anybody!"

"Whataya do for a living?"

*What is this? A damn interview? Should I have brought my resume?* "I'm a systems analyst. I work with computers."

This gets a nod. How less encouraging a nod seems when it rocks toward you down the barrel of a shotgun.

"Where's my wife?" My tone could dent lead.

"Move."

"What?"

He lifts the black cylinder quickly in conjunction with his chin. They both point down the path, back toward the shelter where I killed Canine. *He doesn't care about my hands. Doesn't care if I leave them by my side.*

I begin to walk. I'm unsure of what we're doing, where we're going. I begin to ask him, but he yells, "Keep moving!", before I can twist halfway around. In the periphery, between glossy green and vibrant scarlet, I see deadly black say more with motion than words ever could. For a mere flicker of time, I find it incredible that a mere metallic tube could vanquish my life.

I keep walking. *Where am I going? Where's he taking me?*

Suddenly, the moon ducks behind upper jungle canopy, making the night so dark that I can barely see two yards in front of me. I study the ground as I walk. It sinks slightly beneath each of my steps.

We walk seemingly forever. It's the same path over which I ran with Canine's head. We're just backtracking. *Where's he bringing me?* I don't have a clue. I just walk and walk and, while I'm walking, look for some way to escape. I think about grabbing a boulder and throwing it backwards, then about pulling on a springy branch and letting it fly into his face—something that would distract him enough to let me get away.

*Oh? You think getting a branch flung into his face will prevent him from wasting you? Reverse roles: would a branch flung into YOUR*

*face delay YOU enough from shooting HIM? And what about Meesha?*
*Howaya gonna find Meesha?*

*Alright! So is there ANYTHING I can do before he fills me with*
*buckshot?*

The answer is obvious. I keep walking. I don't see him, but I
hear him no less, and no more, than five feet behind me. Like a
vigilant automobile driver, he deliberately leaves a safe distance
between us. I feel so impotent.

Not a word has been spoken since he told me to move.
My brain, however, hasn't stopped. It continuously looks for
something—something to help me. But there is nothing to be
found. *What the hell is goin' ON!*

But what I am feeling is more ominous than obvious. There is
something here that I just can't put my finger on. It has something
to do with this guy's manner—so matter-of-fact, so deliberate,
so casual. *Is it just his military brand? Or is it something deeper?* I
know Green Berets are extremely well trained, the epitome' of the
professional soldier, but there is something more. There seems an
unspoken knowledge, a sort of hard acceptance to his demeanor.
I can practically feel the aura of a human being intent on hurting
another blowing harsh cold against my exposed, sweating
back. This march he's got me on feels almost ritual. It's like he's
conducted it before and knows exactly what to do—like a cop
walking his tenth arrest of the night to one of the overnight cells
in the basement of his barracks. Though I can't see Blondie, I can
feel the frigid nonchalance of his actions just a few feet behind
me. And the casual rote by which he performs them scares me
more than the cocked twelve gauge he carries.

About ten minutes pass. *How many steps have I taken? How many*
*potential weapons have I passed? And where the fuck are we going?* It
seems to me that we should be practically upon the shelter at
which I decapitated Canine. *Why would he be bringing me there?*
*Does he plan on camping for the night? I don't get it.*

Another ten minute span slips by, but I'm still walking.

"Where are we going?" I finally ask, the movement of my lips unaffecting my legs.

The rolling *flit!* of butane becoming flame rips behind me. "None ya fuck'n biz'ness," echoes back with the hairlip-like elocution that results when a foreign object fuses one side of a man's mouth. Tobacco smoke reaches my nose seconds later.

*Alright, so this is a freaking secret. Wonderful.* Then my brain spasms. I feel strange, a bit manic. *We'll just play "Guess my way through the high-producing hay", or "Just think of jokes while the hemp grower smokes," or "Find my way while the drug farmers play," or "Try not to react, but maintain your sense and tact, despite the lethal fact, there's a shotgun in your back." Whatever.*

Then I see it. It's right up around the bend. We're turning one of the corners this narrow path frequently weaves to minimize its conspicuousness from above, and the enclosed shelter breaks into view below dappled moonlight; but, by itself, I wouldn't know this. I know it only by the headless body that lies in front. It hasn't moved. *Why haven't they moved Canine?*

*When was there time?*

*I thought that's what Blondie was doing all along, the whole time Chin was out looking for me.*

*Guess not.*

Suddenly, narrow hardness out of the dense dark behind me jabs my upper back, just below my right shoulder blade. Actually, more than a jab, this jolt, this thrust with concentrated force, strikes completely out of the blue, not just the black. Not expecting it, I stumble forward several steps. I almost fall. All the Christmas veggies with which I am bound make me feel awkward. They throw off my balance. At the end of my stumble, I begin to—

"Stop! Don't turn! Walk left!"

I listen. I make a hard left. My back throbs. Shotgun barrels don't tickle. I feel like punching this Green Beret bastard in the mouth ten times for what he just did. I feel like ripping out his Adam's apple with my bare hands and watching him bleed to death from his throat. Never before have I considered killing someone with an instrument-free tracheotomy. But something about the jolt keeps me walking.

My walk leads me into brush just short of the enclosed natural shelter. Only after venturing in several steps do I realize that another path exists. *Why didn't I see it when I ran by before, when I did in Canine? Musta been going too fast, simply missed it.* But *now* I see it and, despite the limited light, see that it is pronounced, obviously used often. *Where does it lead? Why is it here? There are no planted fields back here. Where's he bringing me?*

"Stop!"

I do.

"Don't move!"

I don't.

He is somewhere near the entrance to the enclosed shelter. I can't see him, but my senses detect that he, or at least part of him, is inside the shelter. Then I hear a plasticky noise, similar to the sound the cue ball makes when it *clicks!* another on a pool table. But this *click!* is muffled. *Something hit something inside there, against the wall.* I try to deduce from the sound what this *something* is, but I cannot tell. It doesn't matter. Two seconds later, he shows me.

The illuminating, long-necked anti-shadow he casts upon the earth to my left surprises me. It doesn't stun me like an explosion would; it just surprises me. I didn't expect such technology out here. Although, as soon as I think this, I realize how irrational a thought it is, considering the warrior-turned-illegal-drug-farmer is toting a modern firearm.

Now exposed by a slightly quivering oval of translucent white, the trail snakes forward. We walk about a hundred yards. All along, on both sides, the jungle encloses us. Thankfully, the moon's spotty blanket, augmented by shifting shards of battery-powered incandescence, enables me to see a few feet ahead. Without it, I would probably have already walked into hanging branches, or tripped over jutting debris.

At a certain point, I suddenly feel like stopping, though I don't. I don't need another whack to the shoulder. Instead, I keep walking albeit with confusion, not to mention apprehension. Something's wrong. REALLY wrong.

Ahead of me, the upper curve along the projected circle of light faintly reveals unpenetrated jungle. Before it lies the well worn path on which I walk spreading into a circular clearing. *I don't get it. Am I on the road to nowhere? Is this some kind of joke?* If so, I don't find it funny.

As I enter the clearing, a terrible odor attacks my nostrils. It is a horrible stench, far worse than any decomposition I've smelt thus far in the swamp. The closest resemblance my mind can ascribe to it is the putrid reek of raw sewage. *Doesn't make sense,* I think, *we're too far from any development for a sewer.*

Gun or no gun, I can't take it anymore. "Where are we going? Where am I supposed to go?"

To my surprised relief, I get words in lieu of metal.

"Nowhere. You're there."

"What!"

An oblong of battery-powered brilliance swings from the forest before me to cleared ground a few feet to my right. There, the light reveals an unforeseen hole, about four feet in diameter. I look down at the hole, which appears deep, then back up at Blondie. He meets my eyes a second later and smiles. Just below, the shadowed mouth of his shotgun barrel howls at me with mocking silence. Fear germinates in my gut.

"That's where they usually go."

"What!" I think maybe I misheard. I wonder who "they" are.

"Our latrine," he says, nodding his head toward the pit, his features and expression nightmarishly visible in the flashlight's scattered illumination, "that's where we throw our shit. *All* our shit: everything—or body—we don't want."

Now a pang repeatedly pelts my gut the way fear did when I was a kid and facing a fistfight. I don't know what to say; I don't know what to do. I just stand still, watching him, biting my bottom lip, barely aware of the half-day old whiskers pricking my upper, inner one.

He looks at me and laughs. I don't like the laugh. I know he is laughing because I am frowning. He sees my fear, thinks it's funny. Now my anger erupts. My brain calls him an asshole, a bastard. My rage wishes *I* had a gun.

"C'mon, look for yourself." He takes a couple steps toward the pit and inserts his flashlight's glowing extension into the hole. I follow, several steps to his side, look down. I see the origin of the stench. It cakes the wall, covers the ground, festers in puddles. Then something—actually, some things—in the cascading light snag my attention. I see white, a sort of ivory. *No!* I think—I hope. Then I notice other colors. They are darkened with filth, but hues inconsistent with dirt. I see blue and red and green and multiple combinations within, some draping fabric-like along the wall, others lying about the ground, all mixed with the ivory white and feces brown. Then I see fur. This I recognize immediately. It is the carcass of a rotting pig.

My eyes flit back to the colors. I would not have seen them without the light. But even with the light, I would have had a hard time identifying them had he not intimated their owners. Then I see ivory within the colors and his candor turns my whole world darker than the blackest hole in the cosmos. Beside me, slightly jiggling the light, the asshole notices my recognition and laughs: "Ha! Ha! Ha!" It is such a sinister laugh. I hear it with not only my ears, but my heart, stomach, and soul.

"See, you're not alone. You're not the first." He pauses, then laughs again. "You shouldn'ta come down here. None of you should've." When finished, he spins his rolling flint, faintly flickering my ear's inner hairs. As much as I hate cigarettes, I wish he would smoke several at once to overpower the subterranean stench.

I scrutinize the contents of the hole. I see the remains of several people, but none of them recognizable.

"Where's my wife!"

"Ahhh! Ya wife!" he says nodding, without malice, almost matter-of-fact, like an eccentrically aloof doctor delivering a diagnosis. "Lemme tell ya somethin', man: ya done alright. Dat bitch s'got some knockers on her! Damn!" He shakes his head once approvingly, pauses, returns to nodding.

I feel steam rise from my eyeballs. I don't blink. My heart is a hunk of hate rumbling with rage. The thoughts that spring through my skull are bound to keep me out of heaven. Never before have I felt such malevolence. Given the chance, I would torture this man until pain itself killed him. I would show absolutely no remorse.

"Where is she?" I hiss sibilantly through clenched teeth, losing concern about the shotgun pointed toward my chest.

"That's why I brought you here," he says, exhaling, eyes still staring into the pit.

"Whataya mean?" My eyes focus through anger shrunk sockets.

"I tol'ja: 'Our latrine. This pit. It's where we throw our shit. That includes people we don't want."

My eyes shrink further. My abdominal muscles clench. The air I breathe spawns fire in my throat. "What the fuck's that got t'do with m'wife, mistah!"

He looks at me now, continues nodding, the butt hanging from his lips, the shotgun steadied toward my heart. My anger is getting to me. I'm caring less and less about what he does, about consequences. I abruptly, impatiently, raise my hand and rip the camouflage off my head, then from the rest of my body. When I'm done, he talks, eyeing me warily.

"Coupla d'boys got outta han', had some ideas,"—he stops nodding, stares right at me—"which ain't my style, ya unnerstan'. I wasn't too happy 'bout it. But I wasn't there when they took her, so there was nothin' I could do." He pauses again, just stares at me. I can feel fear and venom searing my veins as they course through.

"Fact is: Screamer shoulda lef'cha wife where she was, lef' well enough alone. Then we wouldn't have any problem. You wouldn't be here worrying 'bout her and m'men would still be breathin'. But Screamer couldn't do that. Hadda interfere. Guess y'wife was just too damn sweet. Funny thing about it, though, is that Screamer nevah woulda got none. Can't figger how ya got past him. Ya sure got lucky. Good ole Scream liked to pick intruders apart nice and slow. Wuz pretty good wid his mitts. I think he fancied himself an executioner or sumpthin'. It was a game to the big guy. Gets kinda borin' out here. Some fool comes aroun', Screamer liked to have his fun. Toughest, meanest bastard ah evah saw. Broke ever'one of 'em apart. Ya seen some of 'em in the latrine. But you got away! Don't know how ya did it, man, but while you were doing it, dem other boys was itchin' t'do ya wife. Like ah said, don't approve of it m'self. No sense rapin' a woman when plenty a willin' ones aroun'. But I can see how dey got tempted. Gotta hand it to ya, man, ya sure done alright w'dat one. Nice lookin' woman. *Nice* lookin' woman."

Contemplatively, he pulls a long drag from his cigarette, holds it in, then squints while blowing plumes from each nostril. I watch him with a feeling I can define only as deeper than hate.

"Where is she?" If the edge in my voice were physical, not merely audible, the son-of-a-bitch would be in ribbons.

"Hold on, man. Ah ain't done. Story ain't over." He takes another drag, squints his eyes, exhales nasally. He keeps the flashlight on the pit, never moves his finger from the trigger, never lets the barrel drift away from my chest.

"I was just gettin' back from a look aroun' d'fields when ah see coupla my guys wid a busted up woman. She was naked and beautiful and bleedin'. I thought mebbe I was hallucinatin' or sumthin', mebbe the heat wuz gettin' to m'head. So I run up and one of m'guys—Chin—s'got his pants down and a fuckin' hard-on, ready ta do her. She was sorta passin' in and out, in lots a pain. I said, 'Hey man! What the fuck!' So that's when they tol' me Screamer found her and took her. Pissed me right off. Then they said she wuz widda man and Screamer wuz takin' care of 'im. Man, to me it's one thing when Screamer takes care of intruders, looters, island scum tryin' to steal our shit; but it's another thing when he takes a hurt woman for his pleasure. That ain't m'style. Den to find out she's gotta husban' dat Screamer's gonna take out. What am ah supposed ta do?: waste the bitch when they all done wid her? Nah, I couldn't do that. Goes against m'principles. Ain't good for the operation. Would gimme a bad reputation on Re'enev. We got somethin' goin' on here, man, somethin' good for d'island, somethin' good for d'people. I don' wanna do nothin' ta fuck it up. Know whadda mean?"

I shake my head several times, my eyes crunched with incredulity, before I can force even one word from my mouth: "No. I don't have a fuckin' clue what you mean. Where's my wife?"

"S'what I'm tryin' t'tell ya, man. I took care aya wife."

"What the fuck—whataya mean you 'took care of her'!"

"She's inna hospital."

"Hospital! *What* hospital!"

"Island's only got one, man."

For several seconds, I cannot speak. I just stare at him. He stares at me. The cigarette in his lips is getting short. Ashes break off and fall when it moves. His nose blows smoke drifting upwards away from his face.

"My wife's in the hospital?" I hear my words. I sound like someone else.

"Yeah, man."

"How'd she get there?"

"Friendza mine. Ah called 'em."

I can feel my eyeballs glaring. I'm too intense for cigarette smoke to irritate them. "I don't—I don't get it. What about cops? Whataya gonna do when she tells the police?"

He lowers his head and smirks. Removes the cigarette from his lips, throws it to the ground, then just nods, looking down. He looks back up. "Nothin'."

"*Nothing?*"

He nods again.

"Whataya mean 'nothing'!" I pause, perplexed, my eye sockets dilated, my jaw hanging. "You got an illegal drug farm here! And murders in ya shit pit to boot! They'll fry you, man! You'll get the juice. Lethal injection. They'll poison your ass! Don't you get it! Your breakin' the fuckin' law! And you send my wife to the *hospital*! I appreciate it, but I don't get it! What's your game? What's your act? Don'tcha think cops are gonna come lookin' for ya?"

He smirks deep rubbery creases, pops in another butt, spins his flint, drags, then exhales in lowered-head-contemplation. I'm so confused. I no longer feel that I'm trying to reason with my predator, but trying to show reality to a blind criminal. I don't understand. One of his men tries to kill me, his trap injures my wife, then he hunts me down with a shotgun, yet sends Meesha to a doctor. I don't get it. Where's the logic?

He pulls again, his dark cheeks indenting, then billows white into the black of night.

"You won't get away. You know that?" Again, I don't recognize my voice. It sounds high, strained, even less familiar than what I would hear from a recording of myself.

"What!" shrieks like a laugh from behind the light.

"They'll get you."

"Whataya mean 'they'll get me'? Who the hell could get me?", followed by a couple of chuckles.

"The police. Once they find out about this, you're history."

"Really?"

"Yeah."

He waits, slightly nodding. He wants to make sure I'm through. He wants to hear everything I have to say.

"'The police', huh?" He then removes his right hand from the trigger, pulls the cigarette from his lips, spreads his legs, places his right hand holding lit butt on top of the barrel, retains his left arm underneath for support.

*This guy isn't afraid of shit,* I think. *He doesn't even put his fuckin' finger back on the trigger.*

Then he speaks, smoky-voiced and deliberate.

"Well, let me tell you something, man. You got balls, bigger than any fool who took the dive in our shit hole. So I think you're gonna really like to hear this. When you say 'police', you say law enforcement—authorities. And when you say authorities, you say government. And when you say government—local, that is— I say to you: who the fuck do you think I am? Do you really think the people who *truly* and *inherently* own this island would just let all this land sit idle? Just let it all go to waste? Our ancestors didn't. Why should we? Nah, we got something goin' on here, man. We're gonna get our home back—our independence. That effort takes money—cash—green stuff. I mean, c'mon! Do you really think that, with all the fuckin' choppers buzzin' this joint, I could operate without assistance?" He chuckles with silence, confidence, arrogance.

I can only stare and listen. I am beyond shocked. I look down at the pit. When he stops chuckling, he follows my eyes.

"Worried a bit?" He grins, so sinister. He enjoys my fear, thrives on it; it's gas for his engine. *Fuckin' prick! Says I 'got balls'. Why! For what! Being sneakier than some other guy! Knowing how to make a trap! Winning at hide-n-kill! Big fuck'n deal! Fuck him!* Right there and then I realize without doubt that, were no gun in the way, I could take this man. For some reason that remains obscure, this makes me feel good. It also makes me think of my father.

"Nah, I ain't worried. My wife's in the hospital, you say?" He nods. "Well I got no way t'prove it, but no reason t'doubt you. So if that's true, then everything's all right with me. I don't give a fuck about anything else. At this point, nothing else matters."

He smiles again, so menacingly, his weathered skin stretching and creasing like a used balloon. How I'd love to put a fist through the gap in his teeth.

"So whaddaya think I should do with you then, 'nothing else matters'?"

I try to stay as still as possible, giving no glimpse of my nerves. "That's up to you. You're runnin' this show."

"You're damn right 'I'm runnin' this show', and you killed threeah m'men! I should probably throw y'ass in the pit. White blood's good for d'soil. Makes the plants grow strong."

He smirks again, the bastard. I stare back as stoically as I can. I'm glad the vegetation is off me. I suspect it would be quivering right now.

"Then again, as I said, 'you killed threeah m'men'. Nobody's ever done that before. Not three of 'em—not in one day. Not a bad performance, man. But now you got blood on your hands. The blood of three islanders. Unprovoked, as I saw it. No one had weapons but you. Armed t'the teeth when I found ya. Camouflaged and hiding after killing three innocent hunters is what I saw, and my word's pretty good on 'is island. No jury here is gonna find a white boy innocen' akillin' one of their own, nevah min' three. And, like you mentioned before, we got the death penalty. 'The juice,' I believe you said. Helluva thing if you made it by alluh m'men, then had to get juiced. Downright anti-climatic, I'd say. And for a guy who simply walked off course, accident'ly got his wife hurt, then fought as well as you did: I'd say a bit unjust, if you know whaddah mean. Can't help respectin' a guy like that, comin' from m'backgroun', havin' m'history. Might even be willin' to call things even wid a guy like that—li'l quid pro quo, if you know whaddah mean. Not good for the movement to have bad publicity, 'specially if it can be prevented. Of course, if I didn't fertilize my pit and m'operation got bad publicity anyhow, somethin' that would give me more aggravation than I've already had—somethin' that would hurt the cause—I'd have to pull the evidence, which I've collected, plan on keeping, and will pass to the 'authorities', as you say. You know whaddah mean?"

I nod, biting my bottom lip.

"The way I see things now, the only people who know anything are here. The pretty woman: she was out mosta da time, far as I could see. She ain't gonna remember nothin' admissible in any court o'law. And everybody else is dead, 'cept you and me. You see whaddah mean?"

I nod again.

"And, of course, if it turns out things need to be handled differently, *anybody* can be found. Tracking is a skill, you see. I got lotsa friends in lotsa places with skills, you know whaddah mean?"

I nod once more, my upper ivory still clenched on flesh.

He stares at me a second, puts the butt back between his lips, drags deep, exhales, says, "So I ask you again: whaddaya think I should do with ya?"

He glances at the pit, then back at my face. I expect him to smirk once more, but he doesn't.

"I wanna see my wife."

He nods, keeps the shotgun leveled toward me, points the flashlight at the tall vegetation behind me.

"Move."

I turn toward the rear of the clearing, see nothing but the same wall of unpenetrated green I had faced previously.

"Where?"

"Just go."

Bewildered, I walk toward the tall green. Then, just a few feet before it, thanks to the light, I notice a slight cut in the face of the vegetation. I walk toward the cut. It is a faint path that zigzags throughout the brush. Blondie points his flashlight at the ground ahead of me, tells me where to walk, where to turn. Every twenty feet I have to dodge a trap. If Blondie weren't with me, I'd be crippled. Still, he trains the shotgun on my back. We walk about a half mile. It takes a while; the trail is arduous. We reach a tall cliff, sheer rock, wide as the light will let me see on both sides. I don't say anything. I know, now, that Blondie will show me. He's had this figured out all along. He flashes the light to my far right. Behind some brush hangs a wire ladder with tubular metal rungs.

"Climb."

I do, at least a hundred feet, probably more. He does not. He stays on the ground watching me, shotgun by his side. I wonder why, but I do not ask. I wonder where I'm climbing to, but I do not ask. I'm done asking on this island.

When I reach the top, I pull myself over the edge. Only then, suddenly, several feet beyond me, do I see the light. Actually lights. Dark orange. Then bright white. Blinded, I remain on my knees, but only for seconds. I hear *clicking*, metallic and solid; then footsteps, human and heavy. Suddenly, two arms grab each of mine, not roughly, just firmly. I'm lead to a black vehicle. I recognize the shape: Ford Explorer. I'm placed in the back seat. Separating the front and back seats is a metal gate. On the front dash sits a blue light. Below it hangs a radio with a microphone attached by cord. The radio is on. Red lights flicker from its front panel. Neither of the dark, burly men in front are wearing uniforms.

# Epilogue

The drive out is long, bumpy and dark. All I see is brush. But before we go anywhere, the men in front take my fingerprints. "Jes' in case we evah wanna see ya again," followed by a smile reminiscent of Blondie's. I am touched. Then they hand me a bucket of water, soap, and a towel. *Blondie musta radioed my condition.* When they drop me off in front of Re'enev Hospital, I am fairly presentable.

They're gone before I even reach the sliding glass doors. When the doors open, I face a Re'enevian cop on hospital detail. I lock eyes with him, then turn right.

I inquire at the front desk. A woman makes a phone call. A young, friendly nurse arrives. She tells me Meesha is in a room on her ward and that her surgery went well; that her leg had needed deep cleaning as well as steel reinforcements, but that she is okay, just needs rest. I ask if I can see Meesha and the nurse suddenly stiffens. Her head lowers, pops back up, cheeks flushed.

"Mr. Ferless—your wife—she requested...she doesn't want visitors."

Now I stiffen. *I can't deal with bureaucratic bullshit right now.* I feel my throat tighten.

"C'mahn, I'm her *hus*band. That can't apply—"

"She said, 'No exceptions'".

I blink several times, staring into the nurse's pink, lipless expression, while I try to locate my tongue. My eyes are bulging—as if that will help me to see the situation more clearly—but I'm oblivious to their protrusion.

After what feels a lengthy silence, I say, "When...will I...be able to see her?"

"That, Mr. Ferless, is entirely up to your wife. If, and when, she wishes to see you, we will let you know. But, uh, I wouldn't wait around. Should we need to reach you, we have your number at the hotel. Actually, if anyone contacts you, it'll probably be the police."

"The po*lice*! Why the police!"

"Mr. Ferless, your wife has requested protection, an emergency restraining order."

For several seconds I don't speak, just stare, my eyes still bulging.

"A re*strain*ing order! Wha—Why! For *who*!"

"Uhhh, I'm not quite sure. I had *assumed* for *you*. They're usually issued for a spouse—a significant other."

My face slackens. I try to think, but my mind is frozen.

"Me?" It is a whisper, a strained murmur. I don't recognize my elevated voice.

"Well...I don't know. I don't know everything that happened to your wife, Mr. Ferless—just that she stepped into a trap. But I do know that she's contacted a local attorney."

"An at*tor*ney! What *for*!"

"I don't know—presumably legal advice of some kind. I didn't eavesdrop. I just happened to be checking her monitor when she made the call. When I finished, I left. She seemed very scared, though...excessively scared. I found that curious. Her injuries are bad, but they're not life-threatening. And we stabilized her soon after she arrived. So I assume she experienced something horrible,

something that really terrified her, something...something that
made her feel she needed legal counsel."

The nurse hesitates, her eyes suddenly vacant, her crimson
countenance in contemplation. After several silent moments, she
abruptly breaks her trance.

"I'm sorry, but that is all I know." Then she walks away
through double doors into a beeping, luminous labyrinth
leading to her ward.

I don't move. I don't know what to do. I just stare at the fake
marble floor. Then I realize I'm standing still in the middle of the
hospital concourse, right in front of the registration desk. I feel
disoriented. *I need to sit down*, my mind tells me, *I need to think*.

I stagger to a cushiony sofa in the air-conditioned waiting
room. A somber newscast spills from a television hanging above,
celebrities cast plastic smiles from magazines strewn on a table
by my side, families of patients whisper and cry all around me,
but none of it captures my attention. I simply sit there, not really
seeing, feeling or hearing—just thinking.

Meesha's face monopolizes my mind. I behold her beauty,
her wholesomeness, her consummate, conspicuous essence. The
surrealism of the day has popped me my own dimension, my own
solitary latitude; and I now drift in it, searching for sense, trying
to find reason. I am alone for the moment—though physically
in the middle of it all—and my mind wanders; leaps; at times,
rockets. It strays all over my cognitive cosmos. It is my first chance
to think—at least *try* to think—somewhat calmly, somewhat
rationally in almost twenty-four hours; and my neurons savor the
opportunity, though dread the issues they must confront.

When I am calm enough, it becomes dreadfully clear.
*"Excessively scared" the nurse had said, "Something horrible, something
that really terrified her." REALLY TERRIFIED HER. Yeah, it could
have been the near-rape, but Blondie said she was out most of the time;
she wouldn't remember a thing. And if the kidnapping and near-rape*

*were it, who would she be taking a restraining order against? The whole island?* Biting my bottom lip, I shake my head. *You have to name SOMEbody.*

*No, maybe she DOES remember the near-rape and it DID terrify her, but that would still only be a consequence of her REAL terror. Shit, that's why we came to the island in the FIRST place: to get some REST from the past. But instead I go and REPlicate it. The way I coaxed her into the hike, then lost my way, then left her on the rock: it's impossible she'd see it any other way. It's the way her mind works, her ultimate fear—a psychological wound that I, like a damn fool, keep reopening. And now, well, self-preservation is what Dr. Quint has taught her. She's just doing what she feels she has to do—to surVIVE. Fuck, fuck, fuck ME!*

As I begin to accept the facts, the ache behind my eyes and within my throat suddenly give way and dollops burst from my face. These are to tears what typhoons are to storms. I dip my chin into my chest and cover my eyes with my right hand. I try not to make noise, but I doubt my convulsing goes unheard. My solar plexus bellows in and out with each bereaving breath. I hold my left hand against my stomach, but it does no good. Before long, I quit trying. I just let myself go. Head between legs, my face spews fluid, pain, fear, and fury. I bawl for at least ten minutes straight. I don't care who sees or hears me, as long as they don't come near me. No one does. At the apogee of my agony, I feel as though I have the Dry Heaves, so much ache does the churning of my stomach cause. Then, suddenly, as if my emotions have run out of feeling to fuel them, my crying subsides—stops just like *that.* My stomach, throat, and tear ducts are sore, my face and shirt soaked, my eyes swollen and red, my breathing labored, but I am calm—calm because I am exhausted, but nonetheless calm. Sorrow still stabs at my heart, but it will have to wait till I regain strength before I can fetal-curl into another bawl.

I lean back on the couch, tilt my head, and close my eyes. My mind drifts again. I think about Meesha, our marriage, our past. I think about the incredible day we have just endured, the outlandish ordeal we have just survived, and how no rational person would believe me if I told him about it, prompting me to ponder how "truth is stranger than fiction". I think about Hunter, his world, his life, his death, then about Blondie and how, to my surprise, he actually complimented me on my ability to kill his men. I feel my brow furrowing with this thought and my mind segues to my father. The association psychologically scrapes me. I wonder if my father possesses the same mentality, unconsciously wishing he might not, but knowing damn well that he does. I imagine him complimenting me for having killed someone skillfully, or possessing the ability to make field expedient weapons, and my chest fills with contempt. However, at the same time, I acknowledge that a person—even an "alpha"; *Fuck that shrink!*—can never fully erode the psychological link between his childhood needs and his parent's desires, no matter how antiquated and emotionally buried his needs become, or absurd his parent's requirements ever were. I find this notion both amazing and disturbing, especially when the child's needs are repressed to the lowest level of his subconscious strata, seemingly digging through emotional bedrock to break free. *I can't believe I still have an impulse, no matter how slight, to obtain that man's approval.*

Then my thoughts return to Meesha, and something steam-like and scorching rises within me as I realize that I had a wife who loved me for whom I was, not for what I could be, not for things associated with me. Then I shred my insides with my cerebral skin grater for having lost this beautiful wife, this treasure of a human, this creature from heaven. My emotions suddenly tap an unexpected reserve such that I again become blurry-eyed while I sit on the sofa and pray. With a TV blaring, people babbling, and that benign looking Re'enevian cop standing guard at the entrance, I thank God for rescuing the most wonderful person I have ever known from all the traps into which I so carelessly led her. I ask that He forgive me for all the sins that I have ever committed. And I beg that He help me to never hang loose in any part of my life ever again. Amen.